THE CZAR OF HALFADAY CREEK

James B Hendryx

THE CZAR OF HALFADAY CREEK

JAMES B. HENDRYX

ILLUSTRATIONS BY
PETE KUHLHOFF

POPULAR PUBLICATIONS • 2024

SERIES EXECUTIVE CONSULTANT
Richard Hall

PUBLISHING HISTORY
"Goldie" originally appeared in the July 25, 1934 issue of *Short Stories* (Vol. 148, No. 2).

"Black John Acts as Guide" originally appeared in the May 25, 1934 issue of *Short Stories* (Vol. 147, No. 4).

"Secret Service" originally appeared in the July 25, 1935 issue of *Short Stories* (Vol. 152, No. 2).

"Kidnappers Invade Halfaday" originally appeared in the October 10, 1935 issue of *Short Stories* (Vol. 153, No. 1).

"Black John Buys Some Bonds" originally appeared in the November 10, 1935 issue of *Short Stories* (Vol. 153, No. 3).

"The Forty-niner" originally appeared in the March 10, 1935 issue of *Short Stories* (Vol. 150, No. 5).

"Trouble on Halfaday" originally appeared in the August 25, 1935 issue of *Short Stories* (Vol. 152, No. 4).

"A Letter From Halfaday Creek" originally appeared in the July 25, 1934 issue of *Short Stories* (Vol. 148, No. 2).

THANKS TO
Robert Loomis, Cynthia Whyte, & the Leelanau Historical Society

TABLE OF CONTENTS

GOLDIE

HE WAS AN innocuous little man with soft brown eyes, mild and confiding as a setter dog's, yet with a haunting, hurt look in them that spoke of confidence betrayed. He stood blinking just within the doorway after leaning his paddle against the wall, depositing his pack upon the floor, and carefully closing the door behind him. In a mildly apologetic voice he addressed the two men who stood at the bar:

"Is this Cushing's Fort, on Halfaday?"

"The same," answered the solemn faced man with the drooping yellow mustache, who presided behind the bar, as he shoved aside the leather dice box, and elevated his steel rimmed spectacles from nose to forehead. "Step up, stranger, an' have one on the house. It's quite usual hereabouts." The man advanced to the bar, and lined up beside the only other occupant of the room, a huge black bearded man, who stood with one foot resting on the battered brass rail and regarded him with interest.

"Snowin' eh? She's comin' early this year. It looks like, pardner, you got here on the last water."

The newcomer removed his cap upon which snowflakes were melting into tiny drops of water, and beat it against his knee.

"Yeah, but it don't amount to nothin'. It started about an hour ago. I be'n breakin' ice in the still places the last three mornin's. Water don't leave no trail."

"That's what they say," agreed the big man, shoving the bottle toward the other. "Fill up."

Grasping the bottle eagerly, the man filled his glass and, with a furtive glance toward the door, he raised it. "Here's how," he said, and the three downed their liquor. "Fill 'em up agin," he ordered, tossing a well filled gold sack onto the bar. "Which my name's Smith—John Smith—"

"Not," interrupted the black whiskered man, "on Halfaday, it ain't."

"Wha—what?" stammered the little man, his eyes on the speaker's face.

WHITE TEETH FLASHED in a smile behind the black beard as the big man explained. "Meanin' that sixteen, seventeen other folks arrived at that same solution—me included—before you come. Of course, we ain't none of us got no patent on the alias, but further indulgence in it would lead to monotony an' confusion—at least, ontil some of the present incumbents is thinned out. In the meantime, the name-can there beside you will furnish a name that will answer the purpose jest as well as John Smith, er the one you was born with."

"But—this name-can?" queried the man, with a glance toward the tin molasses can that stood at the end of the bar. "How do you work it?"

"It ain't complex. In fact, when me an' Cush devised it, we geared it to fit mentalities that couldn't think back no further than John Smith fer an alias. You simply stick yer hand in the can an' draw out a name which then becomes yourn ontil circumstances removes you from our midst, as a newspaper would say."

With a grin of understanding the man drew a slip of paper from the can and held it to the light.

"George Cornwallis," he read aloud.

"Yeah," observed the black bearded man, "me an' Cush copied them names out of a hist'ry book. We mixed up the front an' hind ones, so if any of the real parties would show up on Halfaday they couldn't make no trouble. But at that, I s'pose most of 'em's

dead. This here Cornwallis, I rec'lect, was a general that made a famous retreat."

"Him an' I, both," said the newcomer. "Let's licker."

The bottle was passed, and glasses were filled.

"Here's mud in yer eye, George," toasted the black bearded one, "An' by way of introduction, I might add that the party behind the bar there is Lyme Cushing, an' I'm Black John Smith—to all intents an' purposes."

"Glad to know you," said the newcomer, and as he drank, Black John noted that again he shot a furtive glance over his shoulder toward the door.

"Two drinks calls fer a third," he said, refilling his own glass and shoving the bottle along. "An' not to git personal, I might inquire if you was expectin' some one? It's fer yer own good," he hastened to add. "Bein' located only a little ways from the Alasky line, we're in shape to do a stranger a good turn, now an' then."

"My Gosh!" exclaimed the man nervously. "I hope not! No—I ain't hardly expectin' no one—way up here. It ain't like White Horse, er Forty Mile, er Circle, er Eagle, er Fort Yukon, er Dawson, er Mayo—"

"Cripes sakes!" exclaimed Black John, in undisguised admiration. "An' they mentioned this here other Cornwallis's retreat in hist'ry! Where, if one might ask, was the origional sin, if any, committed?"

"In New Bedford, Massachusetts," replied the man lugubriously. "I figgered I could lose myself in the gold rush. But up to now I ain't had no luck."

"The offense must have be'n one of importance," observed Black John.

"An' that ain't the half of it."

"Alasky's American territory," reminded Old Cush. "It would be best to stay on this side."

"Boundary lines don't mean nothin'," replied the man sadly. "It would be the same in Timbuktu, er Chiny."

"Gawd," breathed Black John, in an awed tone. "I robbed an army an' retreated less than five hundred miles, an' feel reasonably safe! Keep yer sin to yerself, fella. We'd never be able to hold it!"

"You, ner no one else," sighed the man, raising his glass. "Here's lookin' at you."

THEY DRANK, and once again the two noted the stranger's furtive backward glance.

"A man can't walk on three legs," observed Old Cush, giving the bottle a push. "Have another on the house."

"Is the hull crick staked?" inquired Cornwallis. "Er could a man locate him a claim?"

"Plenty of room up the crick from here," answered Black John. "She's mostly staked, below. She's spotted, but a man kin most always take out better'n wages."

"Wages would suit me—if I was left alone to enjoy 'em. I heard, down on the river, that Halfaday is a good place to— er—er—"

"It is," interrupted Black John, "provided a man keeps in mind a few simple rules. Not favorin' the police nosin' around up here, we aim to keep the crick moral. Murder, claim-jumpin', larceny in any form, an' skullduggery is punished by hangin', after conviction by miners' meetin'. Other offences is winked at."

"What's skullduggery?"

"Skullduggery," explained Black John, "is any hangable offence that ain't included under murder, claim-jumpin', an' larceny. We ain't got no hard an' fast definition of the term, as a perfesser would say. We leave it to the jury, which it consists of such citizens of the crick as kin be rounded up—except the defendant who, outside of tryin' to lie out of the charges, ain't got no voice in the proceedin's. The way we look at it—a man had either ort to git hung; er he orten't. If he ort; we 'tend to the matter. If he didn't murder no one, er jump no claim, er steal nothin', then we hang him fer a skulldog.

"What a man done before he come to Halfaday, no matter how magnanimous, ain't none of our business. But what he does after he gits here is vicy vercy."

"I think I'm goin' to like it here," opined the man, as the three swallowed their liquor. "I'll go on up the crick a piece, an' when I stake me a likely claim, I'll be back fer supplies."

"You better cut you some logs, an' when you come down, a bunch of us'll go on back with you an' help you roll up a cabin. Winter'll be onto us d'rectly. An' logs has got canvas beat all to hell."

After the man had retrieved his pack and his paddle, and closed the door behind him, Old Cush mopped perfunctorily at the bar with a rag. "Cornwallis is a quiet appearin' man," he observed, "an' he's got kind lookin' eyes."

"His looks," opined Black John, "on-doubtless belies him. They wouldn't have run him out of New Bedford fer havin' kind eyes—ner yet, neither, fer quietness."

"What's New Bedford—a town?"

"Yeah. Back in Massachusetts. It's where they make shoes—er stockin's—er mebbe it's collars."

"He might of robbed a fact'ry," hazarded Cush.

Black John shook his head. "Nope. A man couldn't hardly steal enough shoes, er stockin's, er collars to git chased clean acrost the States, an' all over the Yukon, an' half of Alasky fer. An' besides—what in hell would he do with 'em? No sir—it ain't nothin' less important than murder—an' a damn good one, at that. It jest goes to show that you can't never tell by the size of a frog, how far a stone kin roll. You better jest slip word to the boys that it might be best not to rile him."

II

FOUR DAYS LATER Cornwallis reappeared.

"I've staked me a claim," he announced, "on a bend, about four miles up the crick. There ain't be'n no one inquirin' fer me?"

"Nary soul," reassured Black John. "Halfaday's hard to git to, with the freeze-up comin' ahead of the snow, like it done this year. You've prob'ly throw'd off pursuit—anyways till the snow comes."

"It's a comfortin' thought," said the man. "I'm buyin' a drink."

When the glasses were filled, he laid a slip of paper on the bar. "Here's the list of what I'm needin'. The crick's froze above the rapids, so as long as there ain't enough snow fer sleddin', I'll have to backpack the stuff. It'll take three er four trips."

"Did you git out them logs?" asked Black John.

"Yeah, I got a few cut. I only want a little cabin. It's easier het."

"Don't bother about extry trips fer them supplies. Me an' some of the boys'll be up in the mornin' to help you with the cabin. We'll fetch 'em."

"Drink up, an' have one on the house," invited Old Cush.

They drank, and once again, the two noted the furtive back glance.

"It shore is white of you boys to help out with the shack," said the man, as they refilled the glasses.

"Oh, we're like that on Halfaday," replied Black John. "We all hang together—er stick together, I should say. That word hang has got a kind of a forebodin' sound, somehow. You see, most of us is outlawed fer one thing an' another, an' we've got to kind of co-operate, as the fella says. That's one reason why we've got to keep Halfaday so damn moral—so the police won't come buttin' in on us. When one shows up on the crick, we sort of pass the word along, so them that don't want to meet up with him kin lay low, er cross over into Alasky, as his judgment dictates."

"It's a good system," agreed Cornwallis. "An' anytime I kin be of use to you, jest let me know. Every man's got to make a last stand, sometime. An' I ain't afraid of no police that ever walked. I'll be goin' now. See you tomorrow. An' I'm shore obliged."

"Yer welcome," answered Black John. "An' by the way—a man can't walk on two legs when one of his feet's on the brass rail. I'm buyin' a drink."

WHEN THE man had taken his departure, Old Cush glanced at Black John. "He looks over his shoulder a hell of a lot fer a man that don't fear no police," he opined.

"It might be caution, rather than fear," replied Black John. "He don't look like a man that would brag."

"He don't go heeled," grunted Cush.

"Huh! Jest because he don't go 'round strapped to a couple of six-guns ain't no sign he ain't heeled! I seen a fella onct, which he didn't look no more warlike than a fishin' worm. But one time in a card game, he got riled—an' that afternoon we buried the hombre that dealt off'n the bottom—an' his pardner, too."

"He claimed every man had to make a last stand," said Cush. "An' if he's as bad as you think, I don't want him makin' no last stands in this saloon. S'pose he was to knock off some police-man—Corporal Downey, fer instance. What a hell of a fix we'd be in!"

"Downey wouldn't be huntin' him, chances is—the way the chechakos is pourin' in on 'em down on the river. The Mounted ain't got no time to be doin' chores fer the police of New Bedford, Massachusetts. An' besides—jest because a man makes a last stand ain't no sign there's goin' to be killin'."

"Huh! I seen a chromeo, one time, of Custer's last stand—an', believe me, there was plenty of killin'! I ain't favored the idee of last stands, ever sence."

"Time'll tell," observed Black John sagely. "Of course, we don't want no police knocked off on Halfaday—not even Ameri-can ones. If any shows up, we'll slip Cornwallis the word, so he kin lay low till they go back where they come from. An' mean-while, some of us'll go up tomorrow an' help him with his shack."

III

CUSHING'S FORT, THE log trading post that catered to the needs and the wants of the little community of outlawed men that had sprung up on Halfaday Creek, close against the Alaska-Yukon boundary, was situated on a high bluff at a sharp bend of the creek. The front door opened directly into the spacious bar room, and together with several windows, commanded an unobstructed view of several miles of the creek bottom, which anyone approaching from the Yukon River country must traverse to reach the fort. An old fashioned brass telescope, kept just inside the door in summer, and just outside in winter, to prevent the lenses from frosting, was at all times available for the minute scrutiny of any approaching traveler.

Thus it was that one morning, two weeks after the men had returned from rolling up Cornwallis's cabin, Black John Smith paused before the bar-room door and fixed his gaze upon some tiny black specks that showed against the white floor of the valley. Deliberately, he reached into the section of hollow log that was the receptacle for the telescope, and withdrawing the instrument, rested it against a corner of the building, and focused it upon the moving black specks. For several minutes he continued the scrutiny, then, returning the telescope to its place, opened the door, and approached the bar where Old Cush had already set out a bottle and two glasses.

"Someone," he announced, after clearing his throat and returning the empty glass to the bar, "is coming."

"Who?" asked Cush, as he wiped at a few drops of spilled liquor with his rag.

"Police," replied Black John, pouring himself another drink. "Two of 'em, an' a guide. They must have be'n waitin' fer this first snow."

"A guide!" exclaimed Cush. "What in hell would the police want of a guide? They all know where Halfaday's at."

"American police don't."

"What would American police be doin' on Halfaday?"

Black John grinned. "I'll never know, except by hearsay. They might be lookin' into the matter of an army pay-roll."

"How clost be they? An' how do you know they're police? They wearin' uniforms?"

"Clost enough fer comfort—an' gittin' closter. They'll be here in half an hour—an' I won't. They ain't wearin' no uniforms. I'm basin' my assumption, as a lawyer would say, on the theory that anyone comin' in here fer personal reasons wouldn't need no guide. I didn't; nor neither did the rest of the boys."

"Yer assumptions is kind of far fetched, it seems like to me. You'll feel kind of foolish if it turns out to be a huntin' outfit, er some such."

"Mebbe," admitted Black John. "But I'd a damn sight ruther feel a little foolish whilst remainin' at large; than to feel sorry under restraint. I'll git over it quicker. I'm goin' down to Red John's shack an' hole up. I'll start a couple of the boys out to warn the American wanteds."

THREE-QUARTERS OF an hour later, two men entered the room, and stamping the snow from their feet, approached the bar.

"Are you Mr. Cushing?" asked the larger of the two, as the other eyed the bottles on the back bar.

Old Cush nodded somberly. "If you want to put it that way."

"I'll buy a drink," said the man who had eyed the bottles. "Will you join us?"

"Shore," answered Cush, setting out bottle and glasses.

"Where's the guide?" asked the larger man. "He'd prob'ly like one, too. Here he comes. He's be'n looking after the dogs."

"Siwashes ain't served," announced Old Cush, with a glance toward the guide.

The man objected. "He's only half Indian. He told us that his father was a white man."

"His father could git a drink, then," replied Old Cush.

"But it's pretty cold, an' he's come a long way."

"So's the dogs."

"You can't call a half-breed an Indian," insisted the man. "He's half white."

"Separate him, an' I'll serve the white half," advised Cush. "We're law abidin' on Halfaday."

The two exchanged glances, and as they filled their glasses, the smaller man's eyes roved the bar as though searching for something. "Haven't you got some water?" he asked.

"Water?"

"Yes. Water—for a chaser."

"A which?"

"A chaser. A wash. Something to follow the whiskey down."

"We gen'ally foller it with another whiskey," said Cush. "But if you want water you kin have it. Wait till I find a bucket, an' I'll fetch some from the crick. The only water I've got here is to rinse glasses in."

"Oh, never mind. I guess we can stand it, if you can. Quite a place you've got here."

"Yeah."

"Do you have much trade?"

"Some."

"Nice crick—Halfaday," opined the other, when they had swallowed their liquor.

"In what way?" asked the somber-eyed Cush, as he shoved the bottle toward them. "Have one on the house."

"Why—er—nice wide valley—and—well, it looks like a good place to find gold."

"Prospectors?"

"No," answered the larger man. "The fact is, Mr. Cushing, we're policemen—detectives."

"Business good?" asked Cush.

The man smiled. "Well, not particularly. We're on the trail of a man that pulled a big bank job in Massachusetts. Are there any newcomers on the crick?"

"I couldn't say."

"Well, if one showed up, you'd know it, wouldn't you?"

"I might. An' then agin, I mightn't," replied the noncommittal Cush. He was hoping that Black John hadn't neglected to send the warning up and down the creek. These were evidently the men Cornwallis expected to be on his trail. He had mentioned fleeing from Massachusetts. Old Cush rather liked the little man with the kindly eyes.

"Oh, come, now," persisted the detective. "You know that if anyone—"

THE DOOR opened, interrupting the sentence, and a man stepped into the room. He was a small man, with mild brown eyes. A rifle barrel snuggled in the crook of his left elbow, and as he advanced toward the bar, he shook the mitten from his right hand, and allowed his thumb to gently caress the hammer of the gun.

Behind the bar, Old Cush's muscles tensed as he noted that the two policemen were eyeing the intruder narrowly. As Cornwallis took a position near the end of the bar, facing the two, the proprietor greeted him with a furtive wink. He wondered whether he was about to witness that last stand Cornwallis had mentioned. At least, he could warn him.

"Cornwallis," he said, "the house is settin' 'em up. I want you should meet these two gents from the States. They claim they're detectives, an' they're huntin' someone fer robbin' a bank back in Massachusetts." He turned to the others, without pausing. "Gents, this here is George Cornwallis. He's be'n a residenter of Halfaday fer quite a long time." And with a stifled sigh of relief, he noted that no hint of recognition showed in the faces of the officers, as they acknowledged the introduction with nods.

The larger of the two spoke. "You haven't either of you run across a man by the name of O'Dowd, have you? Of course, he's probably—"

"O'Dowd," interrupted Old Cush, as a slight scraping sound drew his glance toward the log wall over the back bar, where the muzzle of a rifle was swiftly disappearing from view just beneath a shelf that held a stuffed white owl. "Would you be meanin' Ezra O'Dowd?"

The effect of the name was electrical. The two sleuths faced him with eager eyes.

"Sure!"

"Yes—that's him!"

"Where is he?"

A man stepped through the doorway leading into the store room, and Black John Smith joined the group at the bar. "Did I hear," he asked, "the name of Ezry O'Dowd?"

"Yes. Do you know where he is?"

"I shore do."

"We're United States officers, and we want him for murder and bank robbery in Boston."

"Yer welcome to him. But I'd like to explain that we ain't to blame fer the shape he's in."

"What do you mean?"

"Meanin' that he's bunged up considerable. His fingers an' thumbs is off. But they're all there. He's got 'em in his shirt pocket—the one on the right."

"What the hell are you talking about?"

"Why, Ezry O'Dowd's fingers. He got murdered, an' Corporal Downey, he wanted to take his prints, to make sure it was Ezry. He was froze, so we took him apart to make it handier to git the prints."

"Who in thunder is Corporal Downey?"

"What! Ain't you be'n to Dawson?"

"No. We were headed for Dawson, but at White Horse we got a tip that our man was up here—his accomplice, too."

"Yeah," answered Black John. "They was. Ezry's here yet—in body; but not in sperit. His pardner, which we know'd him as Ulysses S. Lee, is down in the Dawson jail, along with the bird that murdered Ezry. So's about forty-nine thousan' out of the fifty thousan' dollars they lifted off'n that Boston bank. You was askin' about Corporal Downey. Well, he's the young fella that slipped up here an' done you fellas' chore fer you. The Mounted's like that. We work hand in glove with 'em, up here on Halfaday."

AFTER THE officers had departed, Old Cush turned to Black John. "What in hell was you doin' in the store room with a rifle bar'l shoved through the peek slot? I thought you went over to Red John's. An' I thought you was goin' to send the warnin' up an' down the crick! I damn near throw'd a fit when Cornwallis, here, walked right in on them two, jest after they'd got through tellin' me they was police from Massachusetts."

Black John grinned, and eyed Cornwallis, who still stood fingering his rifle. "I got some askin' to do, too. How about it, George? Didn't no one warn you that American police had showed up on the crick?"

"Why, sure! A fella come hurryin' up an' slipped me the word, an' I grabbed my gun an' come down here as fast as I could leg it. I thought you was needin' help, bein' as you'd spoke about that army job."

"Cripes sake!" cried Black John. "The warnin' was so's you could hide!"

"I won't hide from no police," said Cornwallis. "I ain't afraid of 'em."

Old Cush set out bottle and glasses. "This un's on the house," he said. "But I don't know, yet, why you was in the store room, John?"

"Why—I slipped over to Red John's an' sent him an' One Armed John out to warn the boys. Bye-'n'-bye I peeks out the winder an' seen George, here, slippin' into the saloon with his rifle. I figured that somehow the boys had missed warnin' him. So I snuck over an' come in the back way, an' shoved my rifle through the peek hole. You all know I don't favor no violence on Halfaday—but us outlawed men has got to stick together."

IV

THE LONG WINTER passed. The sun appeared in short, but ever lengthening arcs, above the valley rim, and the snow softened at midday.

"Where," asked Black John, as he stepped one morning into Cushing's bar room, "is the book?"

"There's two," replied Cush, setting out bottle and glasses, "The Bible, an' the singin' one. My wife was religious."

"Wimmin's liable to be," commented Black John. "Them an' preachers. But I mean the hist'ry book which Short John left behind when we hung him, that time. It's regardin' the name-can. There's one showed up on Halfaday!"

"One what?" inquired Cush, wrinkling his forehead into furrows.

"One woman, of course! We was jest talkin' about 'em, wasn't we?"

"A woman!"

"Yeah, a woman—of all the damn things to be showin' up! An' bein' such, there ain't no provision in the name-can to pervide her with an alias, in case she couldn't think of none, off hand. Anyways, she won't be claimin' her name is John Smith, like everyone else does!"

"Mebbe, bein' a woman that-a-way she wouldn't need no alias," ventured Cush.

"What the hell would she be doin' on Halfaday, then?" demanded Black John.

"I couldn't say."

"We was gittin' along fine till this had to happen to us," bewailed Black John, pouring another drink.

"Mebbe she won't stay," hazarded Old Cush, hopefully, refilling his own glass, and entering two drinks against Black John's account in the well thumbed book. "It might be she's what you might say, a transient."

"Transient—hell! She's moved into Olson's old cabin down the crick. It's a jinx cabin, anyhow. Out of the five that's lived in it since Olson built it, two was shot, an' the Derelic' got married, and two was hung. But you can't hang a woman!"

"Not as such," agreed Cush, "onless there was aggravatin' circumstances. I wonder why in hell she come to Halfaday?"

"Why does anyone come?" grinned Black John. "But at that, I'd ruther it had be'n most anything but a woman! They shore raise hell wherever they're at!"

"They're sharper than a serpent's tooth, an' they stingeth like a adder, the Good Book says. I read out of it now an' then when I git the bar chores done. There's some good sayin's in parts of it."

"I wouldn't wonder," admitted Black John, "but we couldn't use them Bible names fer the name-can. They didn't have no hind names—er is it the front ones that's lackin'? It don't make no difference—we couldn't none of us say most of 'em, if we got 'em wrote down. At that, I don't rec'lect no wimmin's name in the hist'ry book, outside of Marthy Washington, an' Betsy Ross, an' Molly Stark."

"There was Barber Frisky," suggested Cush. "She's in the hist'ry, somewheres. I rec'lect hearin' a piece spoke about her an' Stonewall Jackson."

"Barber Frisky!" exclaimed Black John. "He would be a man. There ain't no wimmin barbers."

"The hell an' there ain't!" cried Old Cush. "One shaved me, onct. In Chicago it was, an' she talked me into gittin' a shampoo, an' a massage, an' hair dye, an' tonic, till it cost me better'n four dollars, an' I come out of there smellin' like a drug store had tipped over an' spilt all the bottles."

"Even if we could find the book," said Black John, "how are we goin' to work it? If we mix up them three, four wimmin's names an' put 'em in there, how do we know she'd git one of 'em? Chances is, she'd draw out a man's name; an' the next man that come along would git a woman's."

"The only way I see," said Old Cush sagely, "is to have a separate can fer the men an' wimmin'. That would save trouble, all around."

"Percautions agin trouble is futile, if there's a woman mixed up in it," replied Black John forebodingly. "We better jest let things ride, an' hope fer the bad luck to fall on other shoulders than ourn."

"There must of be'n wimmin' in yer past, John," hazarded Cush.

"Plenty. Any one of which, if she'd show up, could start in an' raise partic'lar, hand-painted hell! How about you?"

Old Cush shook his head. "Nope. Too fer back to bother about. My conscience is clear, er at most only slightly befogged. Who told you about this here woman?"

"One Armed John. He seen her from acrost the crick."

"Seems like One Armed John is the first one to find out about whatever happens along the crick."

"He gits around more. Bein' crippled like he is, he can't do no good minin', so he hunts most of the time, an' sells the meat to the boys."

"What fer lookin' was she?"

"One Armed didn't know. He didn't stop to look her over good. As soon as determined her sect, he come bustin' hell-bent up the crick to tell me."

"Of course," speculated Old Cush, "if she's good lookin', an' would mind her own business, things might go along all right."

"Good lookin' ones never does," growled Black John. "An' the better lookin' they are, the more hell they kin raise with a crick."

THE DOOR opened, and Cornwallis crossed to the bar.

"What ails you two?" he grinned. "You look as solemn as a couple of buzzards. There ain't nothin' should ort to make a man feel glum on a fine bright day like this."

In silence, Old Cush set out another glass and shoved the bottle toward the smiling man. "Bad luck has hit Halfaday," he said.

"What d'you mean—bad luck?" asked Cornwallis, raising the glass to his lips.

"The worst that could be," replied Black John. "A woman has showed up on the crick."

Cornwallis choked suddenly. Liquor spilled into his beard, and slopped from his glass to run down his wrist and disappear beneath his sleeve.

"A woman!" he gasped, coughing the burning liquid from his throat. "What kind of a woman?"

Both Old Cush and Black John stared in astonishment as the little man, with trembling fingers, refilled his glass, and downed its contents at a gulp. "Where's she at?" he continued, question after question hurling itself from between his lips. "What does she look like? Is she big; er little? Light; er dark? What's her name?"

"Hold on!" cried Black John, checking the torrent of queries. "We don't know nothin' except what One Armed John seen in one look, from acrost the crick. She's got pants an' a parka, an' she was throwin' her stuff into Olson's old cabin, about six miles down."

"It's her! It's her!" moaned Cornwallis, reaching again for the bottle. "I've got a premonition! I might of know'd my luck was runnin' too good."

"It's who?" persisted Black John. "What the hell are you talkin' about?"

"It's—it's—Goldie! My wife! She's ketched up with me, at last."

Black John heaved a sigh of vast relief. "Is that all!" he cried. "Well, that's fine! Narrowin' the trouble down to one man, that-a-way, shore dispels the gloom."

"It shore does," seconded Old Cush. "Here, Cornwallis—have another one on the house!"

"What d'you mean—dispels the gloom?" faltered Cornwallis. "By God, if you fellas was married to her, it wouldn't dispel no gloom to have her show up on a crick! She's run me clean acrost the States, an' all over the Yukon, an' half of Alasky—an' now she's ketched up with me!"

BLACK JOHN grinned broadly. "Cheer up, George," he encouraged. "Nothin' should ort to make a man feel glum on a fine bright day like this! So it's a woman yer on the run from? Do you mean to say that you ain't in no trouble with no police?"

"Hell—no! I wisht to God I was! I'd ruther have forty police chasin' me, than her!"

"Have one on me," invited Black John. "You've shore took a load off'n my mind. When me an' Cush heard about this here woman showin' up on the crick, we foreseen plenty of trouble ahead fer all of us—with the boys up an' down the crick plottin' an' counter-plottin' agin one another, till a man couldn't trust no one. They might even begin tippin' one another off to the police—an' hell would have be'n to pay, all around. Fill up, Cush! An' we'll drink one to Cornwallis. He's the savior of Halfaday! Like the boy that stuck his thumb in the dike, an' saved Switzerland from the big washout. It's a case of hist'ry repeatin' itself!"

"Yeah," murmured Cornwallis disconsolately, "but does hist'ry tell what become of the boy?"

"Damn if I remember," said Black John. "An' this long after, it don't make no difference. The main thing is, Switzerland still sticks up there, high an' dry."

"It was Holland," corrected Old Cush loftily. "An' it was the boy's finger—not his thumb. William Tell saved Switzerland."

"It's immaterial," said Black John. "The p'int is that our woes has rolled off'n our shoulders onto Cornwallis, an' that's a grand thing. It localizes the menace, you might say. Narrows it down to where it kin be met. An' it's our dooty to meet it, Cush. One good turn deserves another, as the sayin' goes, an' I hereby pledge the combined an' total resources of the whole damn crick in George's behalf."

The little man shook his head. "It won't do no good," he said dolefully. "You don't know Goldie. She's shore got a will of her own."

"Where there's a will, there's a way to bust it," comforted Black John. "S'pose you go ahead an' tell us about this here Goldie, an' then we'll figger on a way to out-guess her."

"Well—it's like this. Fer years I prospected in the Birch Crick, an' Forty Mile country, an' about three years ago, the flapjacks got me. I got to ailin' in my stummick, an' I went down to Seattle to git doctored up. In the hotel a fella give me a paper which he'd got through with. 'Hearts Beats,' the name of it was, an' it was printed fer to bring lonesome folks together, which their intentions was honorable. You could write in an' they'd send you the name of a woman which she was huntin' around fer a man to marry, er vicy vercy. An' if you got married, you give 'em a fee. Well, I was kind of lonesome down there amongst all them strangers, so I wrote in, an' they sent me Goldie's name, an' we got to writin' back an' forth, an' she sent me a picture. So I went an' got one took, an' sent it to her. She wrote me how she was the widder of a sea captain which he was dead, an' she'd bought a hotel in New Bedford, Massachusetts, an' was makin' big money off'n sailormen. An' I told her how I was a gold miner up around Forty Mile.

"Well, the long an' short of it was, I went East an' seen how the hotel was a good property, an' full-up with boarders most every day. An' I figgered how a man might do a damn sight worst than marry in on it. Of course, the widder, she didn't come quite up to specifications as to looks, the photographt she'd sent me havin' be'n took a long while back—an' was of someone else to boot. But I was tired of livin' in the bush, an' sloshin' around in wet gravel all summer, an' freezin' to death all winter, so I was willin' to give her considerable rope in the matter of looks. 'Specially with her so nice an' friendly as she was—givin' me the best room in the hotel free, an' what not.

"It looked to me like the job of settin' back an' runnin' the hotel, an' takin' half the profits, had minin' beat all to hell—so I suggests that we git hitched. Well, she was smart, er she thought she was, an' she wanted to know all about my mines, up north. I had a lot of papers, like a fella will—claim grants, an' transfers, an' water-rights, an' so on, an' I showed 'em to her. They wasn't worth a damn; the propositions havin' be'n abandoned. But they looked important.

"So, she suggests that, as a matter of mutual love an' affection between us, she'd deed me a half interest in the hotel, an' I'd deed her a half interest in them claims an' water-rights.

"It was a go with me. I was right there on the ground, where I could see the hotel, an' that it was a goin' proposition. An' I figgered that as long as I could keep her out of the Yukon, she'd never know about them claims.

" 'It's a trade,' I says.

" 'Call me Goldie,' she says.

"So, we went to a lawyer an' had the papers draw'd up, an' then we got hitched."

THE LITTLE man paused and poured himself another drink. "That same day," he continued, "I got moved out of that good room down to her room in the back of the house, an' it didn't take me no time to find out I hadn't married no desk job, runnin' the hotel. I wasn't even the bartender. I was chore boy, janitor, bell hop, porter, dishwater, an' potato peeler, an' I didn't even rate eatin' in the dinin' room. I got what I could snatch out of the kitchen.

"The hotel done a good business, bein' mostly filled up with sailormen, an' I didn't kick none—figgerin' that, what with the bar, an' all, we was makin' good money, an' at the end of the month my share would amount to quite a roll. Goldie done a cash business, an' she banked it in her sock.

"She was capable, all right—big, an' yaller haired, an' raw boned, an' she bossed them sailormen an' stevedores around like they was afraid of her. They was, too. I'd hear 'em talkin', now an' then, in the bar, when they didn't know I was around. She was the widder of a sea captain, all right—a big Dane that traded along the Labrador coast, an' acrost' into Greenland, an' she sailed with him. But he was four, five husban's back, there bein' some intervenin' ones that she hadn't told me about. They was all men of property, too—accordin' to the whisperin's. An' they all died under such circumstances that made them sailormen an' stevedores to kind of wink, an' wag their heads, an' to kind of slant me glances that seemed like they was sort of waitin' fer somethin' to happen.

"The hair along the back of my head would git to pricklin' when I'd think about it, but I figgered on keepin' my eyes open, an' hangin' on till I seen what the job was payin'.

"Well, the first of the month come, an' passed, an' Goldie never cut me in on no money, nor neither mentioned any. So one night, after we'd went to bed, I asks her about my half."

" 'Your half? Your half of what?'

" 'Why, of the money,' I says. 'Of the profits of the hotel.'

"She laughed out loud there in the dark, an' believe me, it wasn't no silver tinkle. An' then she cut loose a string of cussin', which if she learnt it off'n her first husband, he could not of be'n nothin' less important than a pirate. 'Listen, darlin',' she says—speakin' the word darlin' like you'd tell it to a dog that had

raided the grub cache. 'Git this,' she says. 'There ain't no profits! An' what's more, you got to dig up fifty-five thousan' dollars
by the tenth of the month, in hard cash, er gold. The mortgage
on this dump comes due then—that's forty thousan', an' there's
fifteen thousan' back taxes.'

" 'That's all right, sweetheart,' I says. 'Jest as quick as the bank
opens in the mornin', I'll 'tend to it.' Figgerin', you see, that with
fifty-five thousan' in sight in the mornin', she wouldn't do nothin'
drastic that night—like if I riled her. I couldn't help but think of
that gang of dead hus'ban's as applied to my own case.

"Well, bankin' time come at last, an' after I'd finished up with
the dishes, an' mopped up the office, I put on my good clothes
an' went up town. I went to the court house an' verified her statement about the mortgage an' the back taxes—they was there,
all right, to an extent where her equity in that hotel was a damn
sight more of a liability than an asset.

"I had a thousan' dollar bill that I'd slipped in under the insole
of my shoe fer emergencies, an' deemin' this to be one, I slipped
it out, in an alley, an' sneaked to the deppo, an' ketched me a train
fer Boston. That same evenin', I was on another train fer Seattle.
An' the day after I got there, I ketched a boat fer Skagway, an'
come on inside."

Once again, the man paused, filled his glass, and gulped his
liquor.

"If you think that's the end of the story, it's 'cause you don't
know Goldie. That's better'n two years ago, an' she's be'n on my
trail ever sence. You see, before she got here she thought them
claim papers an' water rights covered goin' propositions, an' she
figgered on gittin' in on 'em. Chances is, she knows better now.
It wouldn't take a woman like Goldie long to find out—but
instead of quittin', she kep' a-comin'. Somehow, I've always be'n
lucky enough to hear about her, an' git a-goin' before she ketched
up to me. The way it looks, it's me personal she's after now—an'
she's had time enough to git good an' damn mad. I keep thinkin',
somehow, about that row of dead husban's. I thought I was safe,

up here on Halfaday. I shore thought I'd throw'd her off, at last. But—it ain't no use. I'll have to move on."

AS THE man turned disconsolately from the bar, Black John laid a detaining hand on his shoulder.

"Hold on," he reminded. "Wasn't it you that spoke of makin' a last stand on Halfaday?"

"Yeah—but that was before Goldie got so clost."

"Lesten—there ain't nothin' beyond Halfaday but mountains an' such. You couldn't git nowheres without dogs. You'd git bushed."

"It would be a pleasant death, at that. Wait till you see Goldie."

"Look at here, Cornwallis—git holt of yerself! An' let this be a lesson to you not to have nothin' to do with wimmin. If they can't gyp you one way, they will another. Her hornswogglin' you into marryin' her constitutes a swindle, *per se,* an' as such would be hangable on Halfaday under the skullduggery provision. But the act wasn't perpetrated on Halfaday, so we'll have to think of some other way out. You done me a good turn, that time you come down here when you thought the American police was closin' in on me—an' now I'm goin' to square the book. Go back to yer cabin an' lay low till you hear from me. Leave me an' Cush handle Goldie."

A gleam of hope flashed in the mild brown eyes, as the little man glanced from one to the other. The gleam faded, and he shook his head sadly.

"I can't do it, boys. You've be'n kind to me. Yer friends of mine. It's askin' too much. Nope—I'll be on my way. So long."

As he turned once again toward the door, Black John reached out, grasped him by the arm, and spun him around in his tracks.

"Listen, you!" he said gruffly. "Go to yer cabin, an' stay there! Like you said—we're friends of yourn. An' there ain't man, beast, god, devil, nor woman that me an' Cush can't stop in their tracks! Things has got dull on Halfaday. This here eppy-sode will be a diversion, as the fella says, to break the monotony."

"Yer welcome to yer diversion," said Cornwallis dryly. "You've had fair warnin'. I'll do like you say. But believe me, I'll have a stampedin' pack handy, an' keep one eye on the back-trail."

The man crossed the room and opened the door. The next moment it slammed violently shut, and he whirled, white faced, toward the two at the bar.

"The back door!" he cried. "Where's the back door? Quick! There's someone on the crick, right there at the foot of the bank—an' it's her!"

"Did she see you?" asked Black John.

"Hell—no! I seen her first! She'll be in here in a minute! What'll I do?"

"Slip into the store room," advised Black John. "Never mind the back door— you couldn't find the tunnel, nohow. Jest slip along that wall behind the bar till you come to the peek slot, which is clost up under the owl shelft, yonder. Then you kin peek through an' see if it's really her."

<h1 style="text-align:center">V</h1>

HARDLY HAD THE terrified man faded from the room than two dull thuds sounded from the direction of the door.

"Knockin' the snow off'n her snowshoes" said Black John. "Git that third glass off'n the bar! She'll be in here d'rectly."

Scarcely were the words out of his mouth than the door was flung violently open, and a tall, parka-clad figure entered and strode toward the bar. Below the parka skirt showed caribou breeches and mukluks.

"My Gosh!" cried Black John in well-feigned surprise, as the figure threw back the hood to disclose an untidy mop of yellow hair. "It's a lady!"

A pair of pale green eyes regarded him with a fish-like stare, and wide, thin lips twisted into a sneer.

"Smart as hell, ain't you? How'd you guess it?"

Behind the bar Old Cush shifted uneasily. "I'm buyin' a drink, mam," he said. "Have one on the house."

"Make mine rum," ordered the woman, "an' see that it's pipin' hot!"

Old Cush ran a finger beneath the collar band of his flannel shirt, as though the garment had suddenly become uncomfortable.

"I ain't got no rum," he apologized, "but if you ain't in no hurry, I kin b'ile you up a mess of whiskey."

"Git at it then," snapped the woman, "an' in the meanwhile I'll take one neat."

Filling her glass, she tossed off the raw liquor, rasped the dregs from her throat, and spat viciously in the direction of Black John's mukluks.

Old Cush disappeared through the door leading to his living quarters, to return a moment later with a tin pan, into which he slopped a liberal portion of whiskey, and carried it to the stove.

The woman turned to Black John. "This is Cushing's Fort, on Halfaday Crick, ain't it?"

"Yes, mom. This is the place."

"Are you Cushing?"

"No, mom. That's him. My name's Smith."

The woman eyed Old Cush, who had resumed his place behind the bar. "Huh," she snorted. "I thought he was the bartender. So yer name's Smith, eh? An' I s'pose everyone else's name up here is Smith, too, ain't it?"

"No mom. There's a scatterin' of others."

"They say yer a hard outfit up here—outlaws, an' all that line of bull. But you don't look hard to me! I came up here to find my man; an' I'll find him, too—outlaws, er no outlaws!"

"Yes, mom. I wouldn't wonder an' you did. Who is the party? An' what was you wantin' of him? Mebbe we could be of help to you. We always like to accommodate a lady, on Halfaday."

"Never you mind what I want of him! I'll 'tend to that part! He's my husband, an' his name's Hubert Morningstar. D'you know where he's at?"

"No, mom. We ain't saw Hubert. How come he got mislaid?"

"Don't lie to me! I'm goin' to look over every damn man on this crick, if it takes a year! It won't do him no good to try to hide out in the brush. He might's well step out an' face the music first as last—er else keep right on a-goin'. I've run him out of fifty camps already—the dirty bum! An' I'll run him out of fifty more if I have to. But I'll git him!"

"Yes, mom. You must want him bad."

"I'll say I do! He's a dirty, low-down, ornery swindler—that's what he is! An' a deceiver an' deserter of women, to boot!"

"Well, well!" sympathized Black John. "Such acts is reprehensible, to say the least. If you could give us a few facts in the case, mebbe we could help you. Hubert might of slipped in on us under an alias. We've got an inklin' that a few others has. What did Hubert look like? An' when was he s'posed to have come amongst us?"

"This winter—er maybe late in the fall. He's a little shrimp, with a smooth tongue in his head."

"Tongues is hard to identify."

"He's got sort of mild, soft eyes—like a sheep's. But he's a dirty, schemin' loafer—fer all his eyes!"

"Sort of a sheep in skunk's clothin', as the Good Book says, eh?"

"He's a no 'count, lousy, parachute—goin' around marryin' women, an' livin' off'n 'em!"

"Yer case seems like a sad one," observed Black John. "How come you married him, in the first place?"

THE WOMAN turned on Old Cush, who had been a silent listener. "Where's that hot whiskey?" she demanded. "You'd stand there like a spare anchor an' let it all b'ile away while a body froze to death waitin' fer it! Shake a leg, an' fetch it over here. What kind of a way do you call that to run a saloon? What you need around here is a good capable woman to look after things! Are you married?"

"No, mam. That is—yes, I was," stammered Cush, and seizing the bar rag, he hastened to the stove, retrieved the pan, and carrying it to the bar, filled the woman's empty glass.

"Fill 'em all up," she ordered. "A shot of good hot grog under yer belt'll do you both good. If it was good old New England rum instead of this damn rot-gut, it would be better. But there ain't no rum in this whole God-forsaken country!"

"If it's jest the same to you, mom," said Black John, "we'll take ourn cold—out of the bottle. We ain't use' to drinkin' b'ilt whiskey—nor yet to pourin' it out of a pan."

"Suit yerselves. It'll leave all the more fer me."

She downed the hot whiskey, and as Old Cush refilled her glass, her eyes roved about the room. "Does this place pay?" she asked abruptly, focusing her fishy gaze upon him.

Black John caught the look of sudden terror that flashed into Old Cush's eyes, as he stammered a reply. "No—no—mam! It don't pay! Ain't never paid! Ain't long, now, till I'll have to close down."

The heavy black beard concealed a certain twitching at the corners of Black John's lips, as he interrupted. "You see, mom," he explained gravely, "Cush has got so many minin' interests to look after that pays real important money, that he ain't got time to give proper attention to the post here. I've often told him that if he could git holt of some woman that onderstood the saloon an' hotel business, this place would be a gold mine of itself. Of course, Cush, he don't run no hotel, now—but there's some rooms upstairs that could be fixed up, an' it wouldn't cost much to put on an addition. A good hotel on Halfaday ort to pay big money—providin' Cush could find the right woman to marry.

28

"But we're kind of driftin' away from our subject, as a preacher would say. You was about to tell us how come you married this here Hubert."

THE WHISKEY was taking effect, and the woman drew a red bandana from the hip pocket of her caribou hide trousers, and dabbed at her eyes. Behind the bar, Old Cush's eyes shot daggers at Black John.

"Like you said," sniffled the woman, "my case is a sad one, an' should be a warnin' to pore, trustin' women not to marry up with slick tongued strangers. I was happy till he come along with his lies about his gold mines, up north. I was jest a pore little New England girl, tryin' to git along—an' an orphant, to boot. I was runnin' a quiet little boardin' house down by the sea, in a quaint old New England town. Like I said, I was happy an' contented, an' peaceful, with my cats, an' my books, an' lookin' after the comfort of my boarders. I was makin' a modest livin', but I'd had to give a big mortgage on the place when I bought it. An' what with the interest, an' taxes, an' all, debts was pilin' up on me. It was then I got acquainted with Hubert. I give him the best room in the house, free—'cause I loved him. It was a case of love at first sight, I guess— like the books tell about. An' he told me about his mines, an' showed me a whole thick packet of deeds, an' water-right papers that he carried around with him. An' so, when he asked me to marry him, I give in, hopin' that maybe I could take life a little easier. We deeded one another a half interest in what each one had; he transferrin' over to me half his mines an' water-rights—an' me deedin' him a half-interest in my little boardin' house.

"Only one month went by till I found out, all to a sudden, that it wasn't me he wanted at all—it was money! Yes sir—jest nothin' but money! It nearly broke my pore heart when one night— right out of a clear sky, you might say—he up an' demanded his share of the boardin' house profits. Well, I hid my grief as best I could—like a woman will—an' I explained to him how there wasn't no profits outside of our bare living, which I had gladly shared with him. An' then I tells him about the mortgage, an' the taxes, an' asks him fer a few dollars to make the payments, an' keep the roof over our heads."

The woman paused, swallowed a hot whiskey, dabbed at her eyes with the red bandana, and proceeded in a voice trembling with emotion. "Yes, sir, jest a few pitiful dollars out of all them gold mines that I had a half interest in, to keep the roof over our heads. An' what do you think he done?"

"Why—shelled out the money, of course," bellowed Black John, heartily. "Jest like any right thinkin' man would do fer his wife! Wouldn't they, Cush?"

Old Cush made a choking sound in his throat, and the woman continued. "That's what you'd think he'd do. But he didn't! Not him! He lied to me—that's what he done! Yes, sir—layin' right there beside me in bed, he lied! He says, 'All right, sweetheart,' he says, 'jest as soon as the bank opens in the mornin', I'll git the money.'"

THE WOMAN paused, refilled her empty glass, and gulped down the luke warm whiskey. When she proceeded, her voice broke, blubberingly. "He dressed up next mornin' an' went out, tellin' me he was goin' to the bank—an'—an'—that's the last I ever seen of him!"

She broke off to sob loudly into her bandana, her shoulders heaving so that the mop of yellow hair flopped up and down on her back-thrown parka hood. "Yes, sir, he run out on me—jest like that! He done me dirt! Kin you beat it? Kin you even tie it? I'm askin' you?"

"Our hearts bleeds fer you, mom," comforted Black John. "An' you say you ain't never ketched up with him?"

"No. I figgered he'd come back up north, where his mines was, so when they sold the roof over my head, an' kicked me out alone in the world, I took what few dollars I'd managed to save out of the wreck of my happiness, an' took out after my husband. I was goin' to forgive him, an' live happy with him up here in the mines. I had the half of them papers he'd turned over to me, an' I hit fer Forty Mile. When I got there I found out he'd lit out jest ahead of me! An' I found out somethin' else, too!" she cried, her green eyes suddenly taking on a murderous gleam, as her voice rising to a scream of fury, as the fist that held the crumpled bandana banged on the bar. "I found out that not a damn one of them claim papers an' water-rights is worth the powder to blow 'em to hell! That dirty, lousy, low-down, good fer nothin' swindler had not only deserted me, right in the middle of, what you might say, our honeymoon—but he'd gypped me, to boot! But he won't git away with it! I'll foller him to his dyin' day! To his dyin' day, do you hear—an' that will be the first day I ketch up to him!" Her voice broke in a screaming falsetto. She fumbled in a pocket, and slammed a photograph down onto the bar. "There's the dirty little swindlin' deceiver of women! An' don't stand there an' try to tell me he ain't showed up on Halfaday! I know different!"

Black John picked up the photograph and studied it. Finally he shook his head. "It don't favor no one I kin think of," he said. "But a man might change. This one's shaved. Here on Halfaday, we mostly run to beards—except Cush, here, which he favors a mustache. But there ain't no one huntin' him—not even no woman."

As the woman focused her gaze on Old Cush, the angry gleam faded from her eyes. "You look like a nice man," she said. "A man that would treat a lady right, onct you'd married her. I know all about the hotel business, an' about runnin' a saloon, too. I had a nice quiet little bar in my boardin' house. I ain't the one to hold a grudge again all men; jest because one of 'em done me dirt. Between the two of us, we could make this dump pay."

"What—what d'you mean—between the two of us?" gasped Old Cush, in sudden panic, his somber eyes widening, as he mopped furiously at the bar with his rag.

"Why—if we was to git married—you an' me, we could—"

"Shore, Cush," urged Black John, grinning broadly. "That's an idee! Here's what you might say, opportunity knockin' right at yer door! Why—you an' Goldie, here—"

The woman whirled on him like a flash. "How'd you know my name? You've be'n talkin' to Hubert! He's be'n tellin' you lies! He—"

SENSING HIS blunder, Black John regained his poise, and held up a silencing hand. "Hold on, mom. You got me wrong. I ain't talked to no Hubert. Nor, neither, I ain't seen none. It's yer hair, mom—shinin' out like a big lump of pure gold. Why, mom—a lady with such a perfusion of beautiful yaller curls like you've got, a man couldn't call her nothin' else but Goldie! I hope you won't take no offence, mom. I shore didn't mean none."

After a searching scrutiny into Black John's guileless blue eyes, the woman's gaze dropped, and she simpered tipsily: "That's all right. I thought, first, you might of be'n talkin' to him. You see—Goldie—that's what they call me back home. My dear old dad, he named me that in the first place. His little Goldie, he use' to call me—an' the name stuck."

"It couldn't help but stick," said Black John. "It fits you like a glove. Don't it, Cush? You know, you always claimed you favored yaller hair."

"Oh—do you?" cried the woman, reaching for the hand that wielded the bar rag, just as Cush jerked it away. "Everything's all set then. We'll git married, an' make this old dump pay!"

"Shore," echoed Black John. "It ort to pay big."

"You shet up, an' keep out of this!" cried Cush, and turned to the woman. "An' what do you mean—git married? Yer married a'ready!"

"Never mind, Cushie, dear," murmured the woman, leaning over the bar and regarding Old Cush with a loose-lipped leer. "When I ketch up with Hubert, there won't nothin' stand in our way. It looks like fate."

"I'll say it does!" cried Cush, as Black John roared aloud to drown the sound of a hurried movement from beyond the partition, in the direction of the peek hole.

"Cushie, dear!" roared the big man, in a paroxysm of mirth, "Don't git excited, Cushie, dear! Keep yer shirt on!"

"Git to hell out of here—the two of you!" yelled Cush. "I'm closin' up. I got to go shoot me a moose!"

"An' I'm goin' back down the crick, an' start huntin' fer Hubert," said the woman. "But, first, I want twenty pounds of salt pork, an' five pounds of sugar, an' a pound of tea."

Crowding the supplies into her pack sack, the woman shouldered it and departed, pausing in the doorway to wave a mittened hand at Cush. "Take care of yer self," she called. "I'll be seein' you! An' when I git my job done, if you still insist on it, we'll git married."

When the door had closed behind her, Black John reached for the bottle, and poured himself a liberal drink. "This un's on the house, Cushie, dear," he grinned.

"You go to hell!" cried Old Cush. "You've got me in a nice jam now—what with eggin' her on, like you done! You'd ort to be shot! My God—what a woman! Cornwallis didn't tell us the half of it!"

"Haw, haw, haw," roared Black John. " 'Cushie, dear!' You'd ort to have seen yer face, when she pulled that one! I wouldn't have missed it fer nothin'."

"You've got a hell of an idee of a joke," growled Cush. "But it ain't no joke fer me—nor Cornwallis, neither. A woman like that's as dangerous as a cocked gun! What the hell are we goin' to do about it?"

"Speakin' of cocked guns," cut in Black John, "gives me an idee. I've got a hunch we kin pull off another drayma—"

"Not by a damn sight!" cried Cush. "No more draymas! Not with me in it! One's enough! You damn near scairt me to death the last time!"

"Shut up, an' hand me that rifle—the old 45-90 there in the corner. That's it. So long. I'll be seein' you later."

"But—Cripes, John—you—you hadn't ort to shoot her! We'll figger a way out, somehow."

Rifle in hand, Black John paused in the doorway. "It's all right, Cush. I got you into it—an' I'll git you out. What's one woman, more er less, between friends? I'll be back in a little while. It won't take long."

A FEW minutes after the man had gone, a timid head thrust into the room through the store room doorway. "P-s-s-s-t! Cush!" sounded a sibilant whisper. "Has she gone?"

"Yeah—she's gone, all right," answered Cush. "Come on up, Cornwallis, an' have one on the house. You shore raised hell when you tolled a woman like that onto Halfaday! I'd ruther it had be'n the police!"

"You an' me—both," agreed the little man. "I didn't think she could foller me. I thought I was shet of her, at last."

"Well—you ain't," said Cush somberly. "An' now that damn Black John has gone an' got me mixed up in it, too. His idees of humor is shore warped."

"Yeah, I heard him when I was lookin' through the peek slot. I stayed there till the time she says how when she'd ketched up with me, there wouldn't be no more reason why she couldn't marry you. Then I got to hell out of there an' crawled in under that pile of moose hides. How'd I know she mightn't take a notion to come in there?"

Both started at the sound of a shot that roared loudly up from a short distance down the valley.

"What's that?" asked Cornwallis, starting nervously.

"That," answered Old Cush, solemnly, "would be Black John. He's fixin' to stage him a drayma."

"A drayma! What kind of a drayma?"

"I couldn't say," answered Cush. "It sounds like it might be a tragedy. But at that—John hadn't ort to of shot a woman."

"Shot her!" cried Cornwallis. "Good God, Cush! You don't mean he's shot Goldie?"

I couldn't say. Black John would go a long ways fer a friend. It would save you an' me a hell of a lot of trouble if he had. Anyhow, what John done; he's done. Stick around a bit. He'll be back, d'rectly."

A few minutes later, the door opened, and Black John stepped into the room, crossed to the bar, and handed Cush the rifle.

"Put it back where you got it," he ordered tersely, and assumed his usual position before the bar. Then his eyes fell upon Cornwallis. "Git back in the store room!" he cried. "She'll be back here in a minute—madder'n hell! An' if I was you, I wouldn't want she should find me!"

"You—you didn't shoot her then?"

"Hell—no! Of course, I didn't shoot her! But, I shore shot hell out of her salt pork. I'm settin' the stage fer a drayma."

VII

TRUE TO BLACK John's prediction, the door burst violently open a few minutes later, and the woman catapulted into the room, her pale green eyes a-glitter.

"Back agin, mom?" greeted Black John placidly. "Me an' Cush was jest speakin' of you, an' the raw deal you'd got from yer man. We was jest about to take a drink. Won't you jine us?"

"I've be'n shot at!" screamed the woman. "Down the crick—it was! Not a quarter of a mile from here!"

"Shot at!" cried Black John, his eyes widening in well-feigned surprise. "Was you hit?"

"No—but it was a damn clost call! The bullet hit my pack an' knocked me clean off my feet! I thought I was killed. It's a wonder you didn't hear the shot. It roared like a cannon."

"You was closter'n what we was, mom," reminded Black John. "What with the door shut, an' all. But at that, it seems to me I did hear somethin' that sounded like a shot. I didn't pay no heed to it, though—what with the boys huntin' moose, up an' down the crick. Hold still, mom, an' we'll take a look at yer pack." As he spoke, he lifted the pack sack from the woman's shoulders and, setting it upon the bar, proceeded to examine it minutely. "Yes, mom," he announced, peering into it. "It missed yer tea, an' yer sugar, an' went right plumb through the middle of yer salt pork. But there ain't no harm done—barrin' a couple of small holes in the sack."

"No harm done! An' if that bullet had gone a foot further ahead, I'd be layin' dead out there on the snow."

"Yeah," admitted Black John. "The case calls fer an investigation. We aim to keep Halfaday moral. Think what it would have meant to us if some son of a gun had murdered you right in cold blood, as you might say. Like as not the police would have come in, an' it would have be'n a nuisance, all around."

"Meant to you!" cried the woman angrily. "What the hell do you suppose I care what it would have meant to you? Look what it would have meant to me!"

"Yeah," agreed Black John. "There's that angle, too. S'pose you jest stay here a while an' keep Cush company, an' I'll slip down an' investigate the shootin'. Whoever fired that shot must have left his tracks in the snow. You say it was about a quarter of a mile down the crick? An' which side of the crick did the shot come from?"

"Yes, about a quarter of a mile. I had jest rounded that big bend where the crick swings in clost to the woods, an' whoever fired the shot, laid fer me in the timber on the right hand side, goin' down."

"Good," approved Black John. "I'll slip down there an' find out what come off. Like I said, whoever done it must have left tracks—an' I know every snowshoe track on the crick. Jest rest easy, lady, an' leave it to me. I'll git to the bottom of this myst'ry—

don't you worry. We don't stand fer no crime on Halfaday. An' bushwhackin' is one of the lowest forms of skullduggery. You an' Cush kin kind of lay yer plans fer the future, whilst I slip around through the brush an' find out who done the shootin'."

Grinning broadly as he caught the murderous glare in the somber eyes of Old Cush, Black John disappeared, to return a half-hour later, a look of extreme gravity upon his face.

"Well," demanded the woman, who had seated herself at a card table, while Old Cush stood behind the bar in grim and stony silence, "what did you find out?"

"Plenty," answered Black John, leaning an elbow upon the bar and striking an attitude. "I gathered enough evidence to hang the skulldug higher than Gilroy's kite."

"You mean, you know who done it? Who shot at me?"

"Not only that, mom—but I know why he done it."

"Who was it?"

"Before I go ahead I'd like to ask you if you know anything about rifles—the kinds, an' calibers?"

"No. I've got a rifle—bought it when I come into the country 'cause they told me I'd need it to git meat with. But I never seen anything to shoot, an' probably couldn't hit it if I did. I buy my meat."

"I'll explain then," said Black John, producing an empty brass shell from his pocket. "Here's the shell that the bullet was fired from that went through your pack. It laid there in the snow, right where the damn cuss throw'd it out of his gun."

"What good is the shell? What I want is the man that fired it!"

"I'm comin' to that," replied Black John. "Now this here is a 45-90 shell—an' there's only one 45-90 on the crick." He paused, suppressing a grin at the swift glance of apprehension that Old Cush flashed toward the rifle in the corner behind the bar. "Yes, mom," he continued, "an' what's more, this rifle belongs to the very man whose snowshoe tracks was there in the snow, right where he stood when he fired the shot!"

THE TENSE silence that followed the announcement was broken by the woman. "An', you know who it is?"

"I shore do. He lives on up the crick a few miles, an' that's right where his tracks headed fer. When his shot knocked you down, he ondoubtless thought he'd finished you, so he throw'd out the empty shell, an' lit out fer his shack."

"But—why would he want to kill me?"

"The motive's plain to anyone that savvies such things. This here party's a—a philanthropist, which that's the scientifi- cal name fer a woman hater. He's often told me how he hates women, an' how it's always a chore fer him to refrain from killin' one, on sight. It's quite a bad habit, as a general rule—but it didn't bother none on Halfaday, on account of there not bein' no wimmin to kill. Of course, when you showed up it was different, an' I s'pose he jest natchelly yielded to his desire—him havin' lived under, what you might say, a repression fer so long."

"Why—the damn lunatic!" cried the woman. "What's his name?"

"His name," announced Black John, as both Old Cush and the woman waited in breathless silence, "is George Cornwallis."

"What's that noise?" asked the woman, glancing toward the peek slot.

"Rats," answered Black John. "There's a lot of 'em in the store room."

"But what'll I do? He'll probably shoot at me again!"

"No, mom. He won't. You jest go on back to yer cabin, an' rest easy. He thinks he got you, an' he's gone on up the crick. Tomor- row mornin' we'll go up an' fetch him down here, an' at three o'clock in the afternoon, we'll call a miners' meetin', an' try him, an' hang him to that there rafter right over where yer settin'. Yer cordially invited to attend the same, besides bein' needed as a material witness in the case."

"But," queried the woman, "how you goin' to hang him when he didn't kill no one?"

"Bushwhackin'," explained Black John, "is skullduggery, *per se,* an' as such, is hangable on Halfaday, whether the *quid pro nunc* was accomplished or not. You'd better git goin', now, mom, er you won't make yer cabin before dark. Remember, three o'clock sharp, tomorrow afternoon."

A few moments after the door had closed behind her, a white-faced, trembling form appeared in the store room doorway. "What—what in hell are you framin' me fer? Good God, man—hang me tomorrow afternoon!"

Black John grinned broadly. "Come on up, George, an' have a drink. Like I told you—I'm settin' the stage fer a drayma. An' I've got you cast fer one of the leadin' parts."

"Yeah—it sounded like it."

"Shore," agreed Old Cush. "John claims it's quite an honor to have a leadin' part. I had it, onct. An' believe me—there wasn't a dull moment in the hull show!"

Cornwallis filled the glass Old Cush set before him, and turned his, mild brown eyes accusingly upon Black John. "Why did you tell her where my shack is? There ain't nothin' left fer me now—but to move on."

"Move on—hell!" exclaimed Black John. "If you'd pull out on us now, you'd sp'ile the whole show! You've got to stick around!"

"Yeah—stick around an' git hung—like you told Goldie!"

"I'm comin' to that," replied Black John.

"*You're* comin' to it! What do you think about me?"

"That's so," seconded Cush, gnawing at his plug of tobacco. "An' me, too! I'm warnin' you, John—I won't have nothin' to do with yer damn drayma! I won't take even a *little* part!"

"Listen!" exclaimed Black John disgustedly. "You fellas holdin' back like that is liable to ruin the drayma—after I've went to work an' got it all thought out! It's like this—George here he's the villain of the piece. Goldie's the heroyne. An' Cush is the hero—which the heroyne flees to the arms of, after the villain gits hung."

"Not by a damn sight!" cried Old Cush. "If that damn huzzy flees at me, I'll knock her cold with a bung starter!"

"An' I ain't goin' to git hung, neither!" vociferated Cornwallis.

"Hell—it ain't nothin' but a fake hangin'! We'll pass the rope around yer chest, under yer shoulders, an' run it out under yer coat collar. We'll pass another loop of rope around yer neck, so it will look like a *bony fido* hangin', an' run the other rope through it. But yer weight's supposed to be on the chest rope."

"Yeah—but at that, it's liable to choke like hell, pullin' again' that neck loop," objected Cornwallis.

"Well, if you was to git a little black in the face it would look more like a real hangin'. Anyhow, you don't need to worry. You'll be onconscious."

"Onconscious!"

"Shore—so you'll look damn good an' dead, hangin' there, when Goldie comes in. I've got it all doped out—timin' an' every-thin', jest like clock works. I told Goldie to be here by three. She'll prob'ly make it by two-thirty, so's not to miss nothin'. We'll set the clock, an' all our watches, an hour ahead, an' then we'll rig up like I said, an' you'll be layin' there on the floor, under the rafter, ready fer the boys to haul you up when the lookout reports that Goldie's gittin' clost. When she comes in, we'll tell her she's late, an' prove it by the clock an' our watches. She'll recognize you, hangin' there, as her long lost Hubert, an' she'll realize that at last her quest is ended, as a poet would say."

"Yeah," grunted Old Cush, "an' I s'pose that's my cue—I'm the new quest!"

"But," persisted Cornwallis, "you claimed I'd be unconscious! How you goin' to work that?"

"It's easy," replied Black John. "In the safe, yonder, reposes a little bottle of knock-out drops. Me an' Cush has 'em in case we've got to knock out someone's achin' tooth, er like when someone gits too obstreperous fer the good of the crick. We jest slip a few drops in his licker, an' he wakes up sober an' peaceable.

You'll simply go to sleep, painless an' peaceful— an' when you wake up yer troubles will all be over, as a preacher would say."

"Yeah—I've heard 'em say it—at funerals," interjected Cush. "But how about me? As I see the plot, my troubles begins where his'n leaves off!"

"That's it!" cried Black John enthusiastically. "Now yer enterin' into the sperit of the thing! When she sees how she's lost Hubert here—she turns to you fer solace, as a book would say."

"Yeah—an' she'll git a bung starter! I tell you, you kin leave me out of it! I won't have no truck with that turrible woman! An' how do you figger this drayma's comin' out? As fer as we've got Cornwallis is hung, an' I'm gittin' fleed at by that damn woman. An' I don't mind tellin' you, that would be a hell of a place to quit."

"Like this," explained Black John. "George, here, by the simple little ruse of gittin' hung, is shet of Goldie fer ever. His troubles is over—we could even cut him down an' bury him, jest to make the play good—in case Goldie persisted in stickin' around."

"That's all right, as fer as Cornwallis's troubles goes," admitted Cush. "But how about mine—in case she sticks around?"

"I ain't figgered that fer ahead yet, Cush—an' we don't have to. 'On with the show,' is my motto—an' let the chips fall where they may. It'll work out all right—take it from me. Things always do. It's a cinch she can't marry you. It ain't legal. It's bigotry— because George, here, he won't really be dead, if nothin' goes wrong. We kin keep him fer an ace in the hole—an' if worse comes to worst, we kin spring him on her."

"Like hell you will!" cried Cornwallis. "If I git hung; I stay hung—as fer as she's concerned!"

"Well, there's that angle, too," admitted Black John. "I'll tell you what we might do—an' by Cripes that's an idee! We could go ahead with the weddin'—"

"Not by—"

"Hold on! Hold on, Cush! Wait till I finish! We could go on with the weddin', an' when it was over, we'd have a clear case of bigotry on her, an' could hang her fer skullduggery. She'd ort to be hung, all right—but I wouldn't favor hangin' a lady with nothin' on her."

"It wouldn't look right, at that," agreed Cush dryly. "But we could hold no weddin'. There ain't no preacher."

"That's an angle. But we might git around it. My pa was one. An' I use' to pump the organ in church. I might marry you. I'll take a chanct."

"Yeah—but I won't!" cried Cush. "S'pose it should turn out to be legal, somehow, an' then the jury would turn Goldie loose instead of hangin' her. Where in hell would I be at, then?"

"Oh, all right! All right!" exclaimed Black John impatiently. "But fer Cripes sakes, quit yer objectin', an' let's all pull together on this! We'll go ahead an' hang George, an' then you jest reach right out an' take the bull by the horns, an' put it acrost to her, emphatic an' final—that you won't marry her under no circumstances whatever. Then there won't be nothin' else she kin do, but turn around an' go back where she come from."

"That would be fine—if it works," opined Cornwallis, a ray of hope for a moment dispelling the doubt in his mild eyes.

"Yeah," agreed Cush sourly, "if it works. But I take notice that John ain't got his own self down fer none of the leadin' parts."

"Hell's bells!" cried Black John. "Someone's got to manage it! An' that reminds me—I'll slip out an' notify some of the boys to be shore an' stop in tonight. We got to practice that hangin' act. I wouldn't like fer nothin' to go wrong."

"You an' me—both," breathed Cornwallis, with fervor.

"Don't you worry," reassured Black John. "This here's a simple scene, an' the boys had ort to git it perfect in one rehearsal. All we need to practice is the hangin'. I'll guarantee the knockout drops'll work. I'm goin' now. I'll be seein' you tonight. An' fer Cripes sakes, buck up, an' enter into the sperit of this here drayma! You'd ort to have some consideration fer a fella that's doin' all he kin think of to do fer you."

VIII

AT APPROXIMATELY TWO o'clock the following afternoon, the lookout opened the door of Cushing's saloon and called to the dozen or more men that lined the bar.

"Someone's comin' up the crick. It's three er four mile down, yet. But it looks like a man."

Striding to the door, Black John took the telescope from the man's hand, and trained it upon the moving object that showed far down the creek.

"It's her!" he announced, handing back the instrument. "She looks like a man, an' talks like one—but no man as ornery as what she is would of be'n let live to git that old. All set, now, boys! We want this here to come off without no hitch. You all know yer parts. There ain't no hurry. She won't git here fer pretty near an hour. Red John'll keep us posted. An' when she gits right to the bottom of the bank, we'll haul George up, an' make the rope fast. Hang him high, boys. Pull him clean up out of her reach. You can't never tell what a woman will do. She might start in workin' on him with a knife. Er she might start blubberin', an' makin' over him, like she hadn't never loved no one but him in her life."

"We can't haul him high' enough so she couldn't reach him with a knife," opined a man, eyeing the rafter.

"She couldn't only reach his legs," retorted Black John. "She couldn't cut him fatal. Anyhow, if she draws a knife, one of you boys grab her arm." His eyes strayed from the rafter to Cornwallis, who stood dejectedly with one foot on the brass rail. A coil of rope lay beside him on the bar. One end of this rope, after passing through a loop of rope about the man's neck, disappeared beneath the collar of his heavy coat. "What's the handkercheef doin' in under that loop?" demanded Black John. "Who in hell ever heard of hangin' a man with a handkerchief under the loop?"

"The rope scratches me," complained Cornwallis. "I shore wisht this was over with."

"It won't be long now," reassured Black John. "Hell—you ain't got no kick comin'! You'll be onconscious in jest a few minutes. The brunt of this here falls on us."

"Better git out them knockout drops, Cush!"

Old Cush stepped to the safe, and handed Black John a small vial. "Better not give 'em to him, yet," he cautioned. "He might come out of it too quick. If he'd start to wigglin' around up there when he was s'posed to be dead, it would look like hell."

"That's right," admitted Black John, removing the cork and sniffing at the contents of the vial. "Say, Cush—how much is a dose. I fergit."

Old Cush tugged thoughtfully at his long yellow mustache. "It ain't the same every time. Five, six drops in a glass of licker most gen'ally works. But I rec'lect that when we punched out that tooth fer that big Siwash, that time, we give him double."

"Did it kill him? I disremember that case."

"No, as I rec'lect it, he come to—in time."

"I guess we better slip George twelve, fifteen drops, to make shore."

Cush frowned. "It would be too bad if it killed him. He ain't as big as that Siwash."

"A white man kin stand more'n a Siwash, any day in the week. It ain't apt to kill him. We'll take a chanct on about fifteen drops to make shore he'll stay quiet. Like you say, if he'd start kickin', an' spinnin' around on that rope, an' makin' sounds, whilst Goldie was in here, it would make us look kind of foolish."

"Yeah," cut in Cornwallis, "but how about me? S'pose that dose is too big?"

"You wouldn't never know it," soothed Black John. "Hell—it would be our mistake, not yourn! Quit kickin'! What do you want to do—s'pile the show, at the last minute?"

The door opened, and Red John thrust his head into the room. "You got about fifteen minutes more," he announced. "She's comin' fast."

"All right!" answered Black John. "Come on in, jest before she starts climbin' the bank, an' give us a hand on the rope!" He turned upon the others who waited expectantly. "Set the clock an hour ahead, Cush! An' the rest of you change yer watches! Here, George, throw this into you—an' good-bye! We'll be seein' you—if things goes right!

"Here, you fellas—throw the rope over that rafter! An' you George—you git over in under it. You'll be passin' along in a minute er too, an' it'll save draggin' you!"

"Someone jerk that handkerchief out from in under that loop, an' ease him down onto the floor—his knees is beginnin' to sag!"

"Here comes Red John! All set—George is plumb out! Heave away! Up high with him! Whoa! Ease off a hair! You'd drug him tight agin the rafter! We don't want to pull his head off! Make him fast now, an' line up to the bar an' be kind of lookin' sad at the corpse—like men that had done their dooty!"

The men assumed their places at the bar, with faces dolefully upturned toward the form that dangled at the end of the rope.

"Looks nat'ral," approved One Armed John. "Like a man after he's quit kickin'."

"Yeah," agreed another, in a loud whisper, "but he'd ort to be a leetle blacker in the face."

"She won't know the difference," whispered another. "Most wimmin' ain't never took in a hangin'."

"Shut up!" rasped Black John in an undertone. Even as he spoke the door was thrown open, and the woman stood blinking in the doorway. Her green eyes, sweeping the room, came to rest on the limp figure that depended from the rafter.

"Come in, mom," invited Black John, in a funereal voice. "It's too bad yer late, but—"

"Late!" interrupted the woman, drawing a thick silver watch from her pocket. "You said three o'clock, an' it's only a quarter to three, now!"

"A quarter to four, mom," corrected Black John, pointing gravely to the clock on the wall.

"That damn clock's wrong! This watch belonged to my fourth husband, an' it don't lose a minute a year! You kin see fer yerself—it's jest thirteen minutes to three!" Advancing, she thrust the watch under the big man's nose.

"That's right mom," he agreed, "accordin' to your time." Consulting his own watch, he showed her its face, and called for corroberation.

Other watches appeared, each of which checked with the clock.

WITH A growl of rage, the woman hurled her big silver watch against the log wall. "Carry a watch five year, an' the first time you depend on it, it goes back on you!" she cried "Well—it won't do it agin!"

"That's right, mom," agreed Black John. "It's too bad you missed the trial. It didn't take long. An' there wasn't nothin' spectacular. George hung easy, an' everything come off nice as you please. The evidence was so plain agin him that we convicted him without needin' your testimony. Justice has be'n done. There he hangs—George Cornwallis, the man which bushwhacked you on the crick!"

The green eyes turned upward, and the next moment they widened until they seemed to protrude from their sockets.

"Cornwallis!" she screamed, in a voice shrill and vibrant with fury. "Cornwallis—my foot! That's Hubert! Hubert Morningstar! My husband! So, it was him that shot at me—the dirty, low-lived lyin', thievin', murderin' son of a sea cook! He tried to murder me, an' I hope I'll see him in hell!"

"You ondoubtless will, mom—if he goes there," replied Black John. "The house is now buyin' a drink, as is customary after a successful hangin'. We'd be pleased to have you j'ine us."

Instead of complying, the woman made for the open end of the bar.

"Don't you set out that bottle!" she commanded, fixing her green eyes on the astounded proprietor. "From now on, things'll be run different around this dump! If these lazy loafers wants a drink, they kin pay fer it!"

"What d'you mean?" gasped Cush, as the woman started behind the bar.

For answer, she whirled and pointed to the form that dangled limply from the end of the rope. "That's what I mean! There's nothin' in the way of our gittin' married, now! An' believe me, we'll start in to make this joint pay!"

The whiskey bottle dropped from Old Cush's hand and crashed to the floor as he reached swiftly beneath the bar. The next moment, the woman recoiled from the muzzle of a .45 revolver.

"You git to hell out of here!" cried Cush, his pale blue eyes flashing. "Git out that door as quick as fate'll let you! An' begin pickin' 'em up, an' layin' 'em down fast, an' wide apart, till you git clean down to the Yukon! I won't miss, like that other damn fool did! I know the police'll come in an' hang me fer it—but you won't know nothin' about it! Git now—before I pull this trigger! My finger's a-twitchin', already!"

Wide-eyed, the woman retreated, step by step, before the deadly menace of the glittering eyes beyond the gun muzzle. In the doorway she paused, and her voice rose in a scream of baffled rage.

"I'll go!" she screeched. "I'll go hellbent down to Dawson an' send the police up here! They'll hang the hull kit an' kaboodle of you fer murderin' my man! He was a good man, too! The best, an' the kindest husband a woman ever had! An' you murdered him in cold blood! You murdered him fer nothin'! I'll swear no one ever took a shot at me—down the crick nor nowhere's else! Laugh that one off—you damn hyenas!"

When the door slammed behind her, Black John turned to the bar with a grin. "Set out the bottle, Cushie dear, an' we'll all have a drink. I told you everything would come out all right— if you left it to me. Drink up, boys—an' then we'll let George down an' fetch him to—if we kin. He'll be wantin' one, too. An' besides, we'll need him to swear he ain't dead—in case Corporal Downey comes along."

"Yeah," grunted Old Cush, as he returned the six-gun to its place beneath the bar, "an' as fer as I'm concerned, we kin git along without no more draymas!"

BLACK JOHN ACTS
AS GUIDE

I

ON A SAND spit, on the left bank of the Yukon, just below the mouth of White River, Black John Smith nested his teapot closer against the flame of his little fire, and eyed the poling boat that was slowly approaching from downriver. The dusk of an early autumn evening was settling, and the man frowned slightly, with a swift glance at the pack sack that rested against the overturned canoe close beside him, as he lifted the frying pan from the coals and dumped its contents onto a tin plate. "Chechakos, by the way they handle that boat," he grumbled. "They'll prob'ly camp along side me, an' I'll have to listen to their damn talk. A chechako will talk almost as much as a woman— an' they'll say even less."

True to his prediction, the boat beached a few feet below him and its four occupants stepped ashore, drew the boat as high as possible, and proceeded to unload their duffel. While three of them busied themselves in making camp, the fourth strolled over to Black John's fire. "Campin' here?" he asked, with a glance at the blankets spread beside the canoe.

"No. At present, I'm playin' a game of pool with a couple of friends in Dawson."

The man grinned. "Just by way of openin' the conversation," he said.

"It opened foolish," opined Black John, as he skillfully conveyed a knife load of food from his plate to his mouth.

"My name's Simpson," the man stated.

Black John thoroughly masticated the food as the other waited expectantly. "Well, I s'pose someone has got to be named Simpson," he observed at length. "An' it might as well be you."

"The two larger men with me are my brothers. I'm the oldest."

"H-u-m. It's a wonder they'd of had any more. But some folks is thoughtless."

"What?"

"I say, I s'pose their name is Simpson, too."

"Why—sure. That's Fred an' Tom. Bill is my name. An' the other one, the small man—his name's Deters. We're goin' outside."

"That's good."

"Yup. We're gettin' to hell out of this damned country. We made our pile, and I wouldn't put in another winter here for all the gold in the Yukon. I didn't get your name."

"That ain't surprisin'," replied Black John, engulfing a draught of black tea, "So you done well, eh?"

"You bet. We come in last fall an' struck it lucky with a claim on Dominion. The boys was willin' to stay another winter; but I says 'to hell with it.' 'We'll sell out,' I says, 'while the sell-in's good, an' take our dust an' go back to Frisco an' open up a saloon.' With the three of us in pardners we'd ought to do well. What Frisco needs is a good classy dump."

"Yeah. Every town had ort to have at least one. Ain't Deters in on it, too?"

"No, he jest throw'd in with us on the way out. He's goin' outside, too, an' we figgered that the more of us there was, the safer we'd be, seein' that we're packin' out quite a heft of dust. There's been quite a few hold-ups along the river. But since they hung O'Brien mebbe there won't be so many. You can't tell, though. You goin' outside? We might all five throw in together. I see you've got a good rifle there."

"No, I'm headin' up the White."

"Up the White, eh? If we know'd the country we'd go out by the Dalton trail. They claim there's only one police post to pass, that way. But follerin' up the Yukon there's White Horse, an' Tagish, an' the Summit, an' God knows how many more."

"Dodgin' the police, eh?" grinned Black John. "If I was so damn 'fraid of gittin' held up, the more police posts I could pass, the better I'd like it."

"That part of it's all right," replied the man, "but—well, the fact is—we ain't dodgin' the police fer nothin' ornery—no crime, nor nothin' like that. It's on account of the dust. We ain't paid royalty on only half of what we're takin' out with us. They got us fer the royalty when we cleaned up our dump—but they ain't got us fer the dust we got fer the claim. What the hell's the use in payin' the Government fifteen per cent, if you don't have to? We're packin' out twenty-four hundred ounces, between the three of us. That's thirty-eight thousan', four hundred dollars—an' worth more in the States. We've got royalty receipts coverin' twelve hundred ounces. We figgered that while one of us was checkin' through the police, the other two could slip the rest of the dust past 'em. If we only had to pass one post it would be easier."

"THAT'S SO," agreed Black John. "Is Deters packin' out some dust, too?"

"No. He claimed that gold was too heavy to pack, so he changed all his dust fer bills. When he changed 'em, Curly notified the police, like he's got to, an' they come down an' collected the royalty. What I claim—a man's a fool that'll pay royalty when he don't have to."

"Honesty is the best policy," repeated Black John in a tone of solemn conviction.

"It's a damn fool policy, if you ask me," sneered the man. "Why should I pay the Government fifteen per cent of my dust?"

"Well, a man had ort to be law-abidin,' or his conscience might git to botherin' him. An' besides, if he was to git caught smugglin' gold out of the country, the police could seize all, or any part of it, fer penalty."

"They'd have to ketch him first."

"Well—that's a thought, too," admitted Black John. "That there police post on the Dalton Trail had ort to be easy to evade. The trail runs right between the buildin's, an' like you said, whilst one of you was to check through with the dust he kin show receipts fer, the other two could slip the rest around through the hills. The post ain't so far from the line."

"Do you know the country?"

"Oh, shore. My claim's on a crick that runs into the White, quite a ways up."

"What would you take to guide us?" asked the man suddenly. "It wouldn't be worth much—seein' you're headin' up the White, anyway."

"Such arrangement wouldn't involve no extry work, to speak of," admitted Black John. "But it would raise hell with my solitude. I'm a pore man, however, an' I can't afford to turn down no reasonable offer."

"How would half an ounce a day strike you?"

"Not very hard. Nope. I figger that if a man's solitude ain't worth an ounce a day, it ain't worth a damn."

"Well—an ounce, then. You're hired."

"You to do all yer own packin' an' cookin'," reminded Black John. "I ain't partin' with no added labor."

"In case of a hold-up, I suppose you'd be willin' to do your share in standin' off the robbers?"

"Only to a prudent extent. If robbers was to git the drop on us, you'll find me as willin' as the next one to stick my hands up in the air. I ain't what you'd call a rash man in defendin' other folks' dust."

The other laughed. "At least yer honest in admittin' it."

"Well, I hold that a man had ort to be as honest as the occasion demands—so his conscience won't bother him."

"If yer through eatin', come on over an' meet the boys. Let's see, yer name is—er—?"

"Smith," replied Black John. "It's a name that, onct you git the hang of it, is fairly easy to remember."

II

LOW WATER NECESSITATED much track lining of the poling boat over shallows and rapids in the ascent of the White. Deters, being a small man of light build, was of little use on the track-line, so Black John took him in the canoe, leaving to the huskier Simpsons the task of navigating the poling boat.

"It's their dust that makes it so heavy," said Deters one day, as they watched the three toiling at the track-line, thigh deep in the icy water. "If they wasn't too stingy to pay the royalty, they could of went out on the steamboat, like I was goin' to. But they know'd I could shoot good, an' they persuaded me to go out with 'em in the polin' boat, claimin' it would be cheaper. It's cheaper, all right—providin' we don't git held up. If we do, they'll lose all their dust, unless we could stand the robbers off. Has there been many hold-ups on White River?"

"Not that I've heard of," replied Black John. "But that's no sign there won't be. Ain't you got no dust of yer own?"

"No, I paid the royalty on mine, an' traded it fer bills. I claim a man had ort to pay royalty—if that's the law."

"Shore he had," agreed Black John. "It's onderhanded an' skullduggish to beat the Government out of royalties. It would almost serve 'em right if they was to lose their dust."

"Yeah—in a way, it would. But a man would hate to see anyone get away with a robbery."

"Oh—shore."

"So, I suppose it would be up to us to fight like hell to help 'em save their dust."

"Yeah. An' besides, you'd be savin' yer bills at the same time."

The other grinned. "I don't think the robbers would bother me none—no more'n they would you. We've got on old clothes, an' we don't look prosperous like them Simpsons. Besides, they wouldn't find my bills. I sewed 'em in the linin' of my coat. I'm goin' back to Loway an' buy me a farm. I'd rather milk a cow than crank a windlass, any day. Wouldn't you?"

"I never give the matter no thought," replied Black John. "It seems like there'd be other forms of recreation that would beat either one."

"I sure like the smell of a barn, don't you?"

"Well—what, few I've smelt didn't delight me none. But I s'pose folks's taste differs in the matter of perfumery, the same as anything else. A good whiff of a saloon would suit me better. The odor is, what you might say, more frivolous."

"Men waste a lot of time in saloons," opined Deters. "If all that wasted time was devoted to some useful occupation like milkin' cows—"

"Hell," grinned Black John, "we'd all be drownded, an' nothin' but the highest mountains would be stickin' out of the milk!"

THE ASCENT of the river was slow and tedious, and with the passing of the days Black John grew to like the earnest little man who worked steadily and uncomplainingly at the paddle, while the three Simpsons grumbled and cursed, and in camp boasted blatantly about what they would do in the event of a hold-up.

And then one evening the much discussed hold-up occurred. The five had camped early at the head of a long rapid and were eating their supper beside a little fire that had been built on a gravel bar at a sharp bend of the river, when two men stepped suddenly from the bush, and covered them with rifles.

"Put 'em up, an' keep 'em up!" growled one. "An' anyone that tries any monkey work will git blow'd to hell."

As ten hands shot skyward, the other of the two stepped to the canoe and poling boat that had been drawn up side by side upon the gravel a few feet distant, and, gathering up the rifles, tossed them into a deep pool formed by the bend of the river.

"You kin take 'em down now," said the first robber, still keeping them covered, "but don't make no move toward them packs." He indicated the packsacks that lay close by on the gravel where the men had left them after removing their cooking and eating utensils.

Keeping his rifle close at hand, the second man turned his attention to the packs; those of the three Simpsons, being closer, came in for first scrutiny, and their contents, netting some eight hundred ounces apiece, put the two bandits in high good humor.

"You done fine!" praised the outlaw with the rifle, as his eyes rested for a moment on the little heap of moosehide sacks. "If the other two done as good, we'll have to kidnap one of 'em to help us with the packin'."

"Here's one that ain't got nothin'," exclaimed the other kicking a pack in disgust. "Whose pack is this? Stand up till I see if yer packin' yours on you!"

Deters rose to his feet, and the man frisked his pockets, tossing a packknife, a plug of tobacco, and various other small items contemptuously upon the ground.

Black John, who was awaiting his turn, laughed sneeringly as the man turned to him. "Think yer damn smart, don't you?" he said, lifting his own pack from the ground beside him and tossing it forward. "Search this pack, if you want a couple of old shirts an' a pair of breeches! You kin see it ain't got no helf of dust in it. But I have got a little stake on me. It's in bills, in my wallet. Wait—I'll show you. Thrusting his hand into the front of his shirt, he withdrew an old leather wallet, and opening it, drew out a sheaf of crumpled banknotes. "Three hundred dollars—an' I need every damn cent of it to winter through on. I ain't hittin' fer the outside. I wish to God I was—but I ain't made no strike yet. Hell—if I had any dust, I wouldn't be guidin' this outfit fer no ounce a day, would I? Not by a damn sight, I wouldn't! Tell you what I'll do, boys—I'll dicker. Let me keep my little stake. Go through my pack there if you want to—if you think I'm lyin'—but let me keep my three hundred to winter through on, an' I'll tell you where you've overlooked ten thousan'. The little man there that you jest searched; he ain't goin' outside broke— by a damn sight. He's smart enough to cache his stuff, instead of leavin' it lay around in his pack. An' he's smart enough to cache it where you won't never find it, neither. Here's my three hundred. Take it er leave it. But if you do take it, you'll be kissin' ten thousan' goodby, you kin bet on that!"

The bandit hesitated, and glanced inquiringly at his partner, who still had the party covered by his rifle.

"Sure—deal with him!" urged the rifleman, who seemed to be the leader. "Hell, we can't lose! If we don't git the ten thousan', we git the three hundred anyway! All right—spit it out, old timer. It's a deal! Show us the ten thousan' an' you keep what you've got."

BLACK JOHN pointed to Deters who was staring at him incredulously, his face showing pasty white in the twilight. "He's got ten thousan' in big bills sewed up in his coat," he said. "Jest rip out the linin' an' you'll find 'em."

As the coat was jerked roughly from his back the little man turned on Black John in a fury. "You big yellow skunk! You dirty, low-lived mut! I'll git you fer this, if I have to stay in the country all the rest of my life!"

"An' we'll help you!" cried the elder Simpson. "The damn coward—squealin' on a man to save his own lousy three hundred! Jest wait till these guys go, an' you'll git yourn!"

As the other was busy retrieving bills from the lining of Deters's coat, the man with the rifle grinned at Black John.

"Sounds like they mean business, pardner. Yes sir—I wouldn't like to be standin' in your shoes when we leave here. You've got 'em all riled up. But you claim yer a guide. Mebbe we could use you ourselves. Do you know where Halfaday Crick is?"

"Shore, I know where it's at. But I don't want to have nothin' to do with Halfaday. The talk is that they're all outlaws up there. They might git my three hundred—after I done my damndest to save it!"

The bandit laughed. "Don't worry about yer three hundred. We'll see you through with it. Fact is, we want to lay low fer a while, an' we heard how on Halfaday there ain't no questions asked—an' how it lays right up agin the Alasky line, so if the police shows up, all a man's got to do is step acrost an' tell 'em to go to hell."

"That's right," admitted Black John. "There's a place called Cushing's Fort where these here outlaws hangs out. I know a couple of fellas that was there an' they claim it ain't only a little ways from the line an' the Mounted can't go acrost after anyone unless they've got papers from the American Gover'ment in Washington."

"Will you guide us there?"

"Well," replied Black John with evident reluctance, "if you'll promise to not let none of them damn outlaws rob me of my three hundred, I might. But you'll have to pay me an ounce a day—jest like these men has been doin'. Only I don't collect nothin' off'n them—you havin' took all their dust."

"All right," grinned the bandit. "We'll pay you an ounce a day. How about it, in case we wanted to clear out of the country? Could we go out by way of Alasky? That way, we wouldn't have to pass no Mounted Police posts."

"Oh, shore. Lots of 'em has gone out of the country by way of Halfaday. Jest step acrost the line—an' all Alasky's yourn. The Mounted can't foller, an' there ain't a U.S. Marshal within three hundred mile of Cushing's Fort—an' the ones that's even that near is so damn fat an' lazy they couldn't ketch a porkypine."

"The place sounds good," agreed the other bandit, removing the last of the bills, and tossing the coat onto the ground. "They claim it's run by a fella named Black John."

"Yeah—that's what the talk is. Him an' a fella name of Old Cush."

"This Black John must be makin' a good thing out of it, some way er other—er he wouldn't be there. I wonder what his line is?"

"I couldn't say."

"They claim he runs things damn highhanded up there."

"Well, he might, at that."

"But, it don't make no difference how much power a man's got, er how good a thing he's got—if a couple of smarter men come along they kin git it away from him."

"Ain't that the truth! Look at Napoleon."

"Who?"

"Oh, some fella I was readin' about that run hog-wild over in Yurrup fer a while. But they got him."

"Sure, they'd git him. A man's got to come to the end of his rope some day."

"Quite a few of 'em has, on Halfaday."

THE MAN with the rifle turned to the victims, as the other transferred the gold sacks to a couple of packs. "Pile in yer polin' boat an' drop back downriver," he commanded. "You kin take yer stuff with you an' run the rapids before dark. The boat's lighter, now you've got shet of all that heavy dust. You'll git back to Dawson in a week er so, an' you kin tell the damn Mounted to look fer us on Halfaday. Mebbe we'll be waitin' fer 'em there—an' mebbe we'll be half ways acrost Alasky. So long. An' don't take no wooden nickels."

"Turn that damn guide over to us fer fifteen minutes," implored the little man, "an' by God, he'll never double-cross anyone else!"

The bandit grinned. "Sorry—but we need him ourselves. Git goin' now. We don't want none of you divin' fer them rifles till we git a damn good start."

III

OLD CUSH, THE somber-faced proprietor of Cushing's Fort, the trading post and saloon that ministered to the wants of the little community of outlawed men that had sprung up on Halfaday Creek close against the Alaska-Yukon border, returned from the storeroom where he had just filled four variously labeled liquor bottles from the same whisky barrel, and arranged the bottles on the back bar. Laboriously noting the transaction in his stock book, he called to a comely Indian girl who was returning the broom to its place, after sweeping the floor:

"Give me a hand with this slop tub, an' we'll dump it. It don't rinse good, no more. The glasses comes out cloudy. Then you fetch some fresh water from the crick. A man don't like fer to drink out of a sticky glass."

With the tub refilled and in its place beneath the bar, the Indian girl retired to the kitchen, and Old Cush glanced at the clock, whose hands indicated mid-forenoon. Reaching for a bottle and glass, he poured himself a drink.

"It's about time Black John was showin' up," he muttered. "I sort of miss the damn badger. I kind of looked fer him yisterday. Allowin' fer a three-days' drunk in Dawson, he could of made it by then."

Sloshing his empty glass in the fresh rinse water, he returned it to the back bar, and sauntering to the door, fixed his eyes on three moving black specks that showed far down the creek. Reaching for the brass telescope that was always in readiness near the door, he studied the specks minutely. "Speakin' of the devil, as the sayin' goes," he muttered, "an' up he pops. But who's them two with him? They ain't none of the boys from Halfaday. Prob'ly left the canoe down the crick on account of low water. I'm shore glad he's back. I wouldn't like fer nothin' to happen to him."

RETURNING THE telescope to its place, Cush retreated to the bar where he busied himself with small chores until two pack-laden strangers entered the room, closely followed by Black John, who was pointing toward the two, and shaking his head vigorously behind their backs.

Before Cush could utter a word of greeting, the voice of Black John boomed out. "This here's Halfaday Crick, ain't it? An' this is Cushing's Fort?"

Taking his cue, Old Cush nodded without hint of recognition. "Yeah. This is the place."

"What did I tell you—I know'd I was right!" boasted Black John, as the two men paused before the bar and swung the packs from their backs. "Yes sir—what I claim, if a man knows the country he kin find a place—even if he ain't never been there before." He turned to the proprietor. "Be you this here Black John Smith they tell about?"

"Naw," answered Cush. "I ain't him. He ain't so good lookin'. Anyway, he went down to Dawson a couple of weeks er so ago." He set out a bottle and glasses. "The house is buyin' a drink," he said.

Swinging his own well-worn packsack to the floor at his feet, Black John leaned an elbow on the bar and surveyed the room with interest. "Nice place you've got here," he opined. "They say it ain't far from the line."

"Right close."

"That makes it handy. But what would this here Black John be goin' clean down to Dawson fer—what with all a man would want to drink an' everythin', right here?"

"He took down a batch of dust, fer to git it changed into bills. He'd ought to be showin' up any day now."

"Drink up, an' have one on me," invited one of the strangers. "How much dust did he take?"

"It was quite a canoe load. Run a little better'n six thousan' ounces. He'll be fetchin' back right around a hundred thousan' in bills. This here damn safe of mine don't only hold so much—an' every now an' then it gits all clogged up with dust, what with the boys all fetchin' it in to bank it. So every onct in so often, we take a batch of it down an' trade it fer bills, which they don't take up so much room."

Neither Cush nor Black John missed the swift glance that passed between the two strangers, as one of them casually asked, "Does he make the trip alone?"

"Oh, shore! He jest loads the stuff into his canoe an' drops on down; then he paddles back up agin with the bills."

Again a swift glance passed between the two strangers as the other bought a drink. When the glasses were empty, one of them spoke. "Well, so long. I guess we'll be goin'."

As they stooped to recover their pack sacks, Black John thumped the bar with his fist. "Hold on! Ain't you fergot somethin'?"

"What?" asked one of the men.

"Why, my pay fer guidin' you! An ounce a day, it was—fer seven days. Seven ounces it figgers. There's a set of scales on the bar. Weigh it out."

The two laughed. "Yeah, that's so," admitted one. "An' there's somethin' else we fergot, too—that three hundred in bills that you've got in yer wallet." He turned to Cush with a knowing wink. "We've heard all about this place," he said, "an' we know we're amongst friends. Watch us trim a sucker. The haul won't be big—but it'll buy a few drinks." The man turned on Black John with a scowl. "Shuck out that three hundred—an' be damn quick about it!" he snarled.

"Oh, my pore money!" whined Black John, as his hand tremblingly sought the front of his shirt. "You claimed you wouldn't let no one bother it! Please, mister—ain't you got no heart?"

"Quit yer snivvlin', an' shuck out that money before I smear you all over the place!" The bandit extended his hand for the wallet. "Put it right there—an' hurry up!"

FROM HIS place behind the bar Old Cush looked somberly on as Black John's hand was slowly withdrawn from beneath his shirt. The next instant the two before the bar stiffened with surprise, and the extended hand dropped to the man's side, as both stared wide-eyed into the muzzle of a forty-five six-gun.

"Step back from them rifles!" ordered the man behind the gun, in a cold, flinty voice. "Back away! Er I'll fill yer guts so full of lead they could use you fer boat anchors! An' put them hands up—an' keep 'em there!" He called to Cush, "Come on around here an' frisk 'em. An' be sure you don't overlook ten thousan' in bills that they've got in their pockets. They stole it off'n a pore little cuss that was headin' back to Loway with it to buy him a farm so he could set around milkin' a cow while he smelt the barn. They've got twenty-four hundred ounces of dust in them packs, too—but it was stole off'n three damn scoundrels which it wouldn't sadden me none if they lost it."

When Cush had removed the bills from the pockets of the men, and satisfied himself that they had no side arms, Black John gave further orders. "Tie their hands behind their backs, Cush, an' we'll drop 'em in the hole till we kin git a quorum together an' hang 'em."

"Hang us!" cried one of the men. "We ain't done nothin' you kin hang us fer!"

"Nothin' to hang you fer! Why, you dirty two-timin' skunks! Jest the fact that yer livin' is evidence enough to hang you on! But to be specific, as a lawyer would say—yer charged with, an' practically convicted of, the robbery of four men on White River, an' also the attempted robbery of me, right here in this room, which amounts to the crime of skullduggery, an' is hangable on Halfaday. We don't tolerate no crime whatever on the crick an' its subtendin' rivers, mountains an' gulches."

"Who—who the hell are you, anyhow?" gasped one of the men.

"Smith, is the name—Black John, to be more exact. The hundred thousan' in bills Cush was tellin' you about is layin' there in my pack sack. I'm the lad you told me could be got—when a couple of smarter fellas come along! Yer prob'ly right, at that. I know damn well you was right when you prophesied that every man must come to the end of his rope. When Cush finishes tyin' up yer hands we'll take you out in the store room an' show you the coil of it that you've come to the end of."

"Let us go," begged the other. "We admit we didn't do you right! Turn us loose, an' we'll promise to hit fer Alasky an' never show our faces no more in the Yukon. We'll give you all the dust in them packs—an' them bills, too!"

Black John grinned. "Yer ontrustworthy. We couldn't rely on yer promise. An' besides, I don't deem yer title to the dust an' bills is sound enough fer to transfer by deed of gift. There's a palpable flaw in it, as a lawyer would say—an' besides, the property you mentioned is practically ourn, already."

Aided by Old Cush, he shoved the bound men toward the storeroom where the trap door admitting to a dark little cell beneath the floor was raised. "Give 'em a shove, if they won't use the ladder, Cush," urged Black John, "an' we'll divide the stuff up between us, an' then call the boys."

IV

BACK IN THE barroom Old Cush eyed the two heavy packs that the bandits had deposited on the floor.

"Twenty-four hundred ounces in 'em," observed Black John, "feloniously acquired, along with them bills, off'n four checha-kos down on White River. We'll take it in the storeroom an' divide it between us. The transaction should show a profit of thirty-eight thousan', two hundred in dust—an' ten thousan' in paper money—a matter of twenty-four thousan', two hundred apiece—which is pore enough pay fer the jeopardy we've been placed in by them two damn crooks." As he talked, Black John opened his own pack sack and proceeded to count out some big bills: "Nine thousan'—nine thousan', five hundred—ten thousan'—ten thousan', five hundred— eleven thousan'," he counted aloud, and, making the bills into a packet, he handed it to Cush, who was regarding him with a puzzled expression. "Stick this here in the cash drawer," he ordered.

"But—hell, John, them robbers didn't git that money! It belongs to the boys! Part of it's yourn. An' I've got some in there, too!"

"Yeah—but you ain't got as much as you had, an' neither has none of us. It's like this—when the hold-up come off I seen where I stood to lose that hundred thousan' that belongs to the boys. So, whilst that damn robber was goin' through them pack sacks, I done some fast thinkin'. One of these here chechakos had changed his dust into bills an' had sewed 'em in the linin' of his coat—which fact he had confided in me. Of course, the damn crook didn't have no trouble findin' the dust in the pack sacks; but he didn't find the little man's ten thousan' in bills. They'd passed him up, an' was startin' in to work on me, when I dickered with 'em. I tossed my pack toward 'em, so they could see it wasn't heavy with dust, an' I showed 'em three hundred I had in my wallet, claimin' I needed it to winter through on. Then I told 'em that if they'd leave me keep what I had, I'd tell 'em where they'd overlooked ten thousan' dollars. They dickered, an' I told 'em where it was at, an' they yanked off the little man's coat, an' found the bills." Black John paused and grinned broadly. "It made the chechakos mad as hell, them thinkin' I'd sold out to save my three hundred. They even threatened me with bodily harm, so when the robbers hired me to guide 'em to Halfaday, I was glad to take 'em up. I figgered that onct we got 'em here, we wouldn't have no great trouble in outguessin' 'em—an' it turned out I was right."

"Yeah," agreed Old Cush dryly. "It looks that way. But what about that 'leven thousan' you took out of yer pack sack? How does that figger in?"

"Why—don't you see? I wouldn't play no dirty trick like that on a man, without reimbursin' him, would I? The robbers got the little man's money on account of me tellin' 'em where it was at—an' the boys has got to make the amount good! Hell—it was to save their money I done it!"

"Yeah, but I've got his money right here in my pocket, why not jest give him back his own bills?"

"Not by a damn sight! That's where the doctrine of *pro ratie* comes in! Everyone that had money in that pack has got to kick in with a per cent fer savin' it. Me an' you divides up the orignal ten thou san', along with the dust, as our wages fer ketchin' the damn thieves. You've got to consider the equity of the thing, Cush. We're each entitled to half of that ten thousan'. You helped with the capture, an' it was due to my astuteness that the boys didn't lose the whole hundred thousan'. An' besides, I wouldn't think that quick fer less'n five thousan' dollars, at no time!"

"Well—considerin' it from that angle, I guess yer right, John," admitted Cush. "But s'pose them chechakos shows up with the police?"

"We'll simply tell 'em that the robbers passed on. That's the euphonious way of expressin' death—but the chechakos an' the police will take it that we meant they passed on into Alasky."

"What's euphonious?" grumbled Cush.

"It means polite. Hell—you can't go blurtin' out everything by its common name in general conversation, er you'd soon git frowned on as a boor. A man's s'posed to use a certain amount of tack in his use of words."

"Mebbe," suggested Cush, "we'd ought to git the hangin' over with, an' do the dividin' afterward. If them chechakos was to run onto a patrol before they got clean back to Dawson, they might be showin' up quicker'n we expect."

"That's a thought. But we'll carry them packs into the store-room, so's not to arouse no ondue cupidity amongst the boys at the meetin'. We'll hang the damn thieves fer their attempted robbery of me, right here in the saloon. That way, we won't need to mention the gold an' them bills they took off'n the chechakos. That would only be an aggravatin' circumstance, anyhow. We can only hang 'em onct."

"But," objected Cush, "if we don't say nothin' about them bills bein stole, how are we goin' to account fer the ones you took out of yer pack sack to pay that chechako back?"

"Looks like yer kind of borrowin' a bridge to cross before you git to it," retorted Black John. "No one but me an' you knows how much dust I took down, or how many bills I fetched back. Come on, we'll git these packs out of sight, an' I'll go drum up a quorum."

AT THE doorway, Black John paused and reached hurriedly for the telescope. "Damn if it didn't happen jest like you said!" he exclaimed. "Them chechakos must of run onto a policeman, right soon after they was turned loose. They're three, four mile down the crick yet—but it's Corporal Downey that's with 'em!"

"Hum," said Old Cush. "We ain't got time to hang 'em unless you an' me done the job ourselves."

"Yeah—an' that wouldn't be ethical. Even a damn thief has got a right to be hung by a duly app'inted miners' meetin', an' not jest permiscuous."

"Shore—but what'll we do? We might leave em in the hole, an' explain that they'd passed on, like you said. An' then hang 'em after Downey an' the chechakos had went back."

Black John shook his head. "Nope, they ain't gagged, an' even if they was, they might slip the gags an' git to yellin'. We've always worked hand in glove with Downey, an' I wouldn't like to put nothin' over on him." He paused, and after a moment of deep thought, hastily returned the telescope to its place. "Come on, Cush," he said. " 'Half a loaf is better'n no bread,' as the sayin' goes. We'll hurry up an' divide that dust before they git here—an' put half of it back in the pack sacks, an' fetch 'em back an' cache 'em behind the bar."

"But cripes, John—them fellas knows how much they had in their packs! How in hell do you expect to git away with half of it?"

"Don't stand there an' auger! It'll cut deep into our profit, but it's all I kin think of."

THREE QUARTERS of an hour later the four chechakos, accompanied by Corporal Downey stepped into the saloon to find Black John and Old Cush shaking dice for the drinks.

"Where's them two robbers you guided up here?" demanded the elder Simpson truculently. "An' where's our dust?"

Black John ignored him. "Hello, Downey! Damn if we ain't glad to see you! You popped up jest in time to take a hangin' off'n our hands. Step right up an' have a drink. You others is in on it, too. I jest stuck one on the house."

"It was me won that game," reminded Cush. "You never beat them three sixes!"

"Always quibblin' over technicalities," replied Black John wearily. "Have it your own way. I won't auger with you. Belly up, boys."

"Where's our dust?" reiterated Simpson.

"An' my bills?" seconded Deters. "Of all the damn dirty, low-lived tricks I ever heard tell of, that one you pulled beats 'em all! Squealed where my ten thousan' was to save yer own lousy three hundred!"

"It would seem a trifle small minded, offhand," grinned Black John. "But the fact is, me an' Cush apprehended them two rascals, an' we figgered on hangin' 'em fer the crime as soon as we got a quorum together. Corporal Downey here will take 'em off our hands, so there don't seem to be no reason to delay returnin' yer property." He called to Old Cush. "Hand the man over that package of bills."

Reaching into the drawer, Cush withdrew a packet of bills which he tossed onto the bar in front of the little man who eagerly pounced on them, and proceeded swiftly to count them.

Running them rapidly through, he paused, and counted them again more slowly. Once again he counted them, fingering each bill carefully. Then he looked up with a puzzled expression.

"What's the matter?" demanded Black John. "Ain't the count right?"

"Well—no," replied the little man, regarding the bills with puckered brow. "I only had ten thousan', an' I've made it eleven thousan' three different times."

"Oh, that's all right," grinned Black John. "The other thousan' is interest"

"Interest!"

"Shore—ten per cent, it figgers. I don't aim to borrow no money without I pay interest."

"Borrow—I don't understand!"

BLACK JOHN'S grin widened.

"That's easy," he explained, and reaching down, began to toss packages of bills onto the bar from the pack sack at his feet. "You see, I was comin' back from Dawson, where I'd traded dust fer these bills. I had right around a hundred thousan' in my pack sack, an' I didn't want fer them robbers to git it. So I dickered with 'em, offerin' to tell 'em where they'd overlooked ten thousan', if they'd leave me go—puttin' it acrost to 'em that that three hundred in my wallet was all I had. They fell fer it, an' I told 'em about your bills, figgerin' if they made a git-away, I could repay you out of the hundred thousan', an' still be around ninety thousan' to the good. But as luck would have it, they didn't make no git-away. In fact, they was so damn depraved that they ondertook to double-cross me an' rob me of my three hundred, besides refusin' to pay me the seven ounces I earned by guidin' 'em."

"I see," grinned the little man. "But you don't need to pay me no interest."

"Keep it," said Black John. "We aim to do the square thing when a man does us a favor."

"You say you've got these two robbers?" asked Downey.

"Yer damn right! We tied 'em up an' throw'd 'em in the hole, preparatory to hangin' 'em."

"I guess you wouldn't have gone so far wrong in hangin' 'em, at that," remarked the officer. "I was hot on their trail for a murder and robbery at Five Fingers. That's why these men found me so quick."

"Where's our dust?" persisted Simpson.

"I s'pose," replied Black John, "its in their packsacks. We all seen 'em put it there—down on the White. They ain't trusted me with none of it, an' them sacks sounded tol'able heavy when they thumped 'em on the floor. We set 'em back behind the bar, in case anyone come along whilst we was shovin' the thieves down the hole."

Recovering the packsacks, the men tore into them, and hastily counted the little sacks of gold. "Hey!" cried the elder Simpson angrily. "There ain't more'n half our dust here!"

"Meanin'," asked Black John, fixing the speaker with a hard, level stare, "that you accuse me, or Cush here, of tamperin' with them sacks?"

"I don't know who tampered with 'em," retorted the man. "But half of that dust is gone. It's a cinch you had plenty of chance!"

BLACK JOHN turned to Downey. "Now—what do you know about that! Here, me an' Cush saves their damn dust fer 'em—an' they up an' accuse us of stealin' half of it." He whirled thunderously upon Simpson. "Why, damn you, if we was goin' to steal it, why in hell wouldn't we steal it all?"

"Maybe the robbers cached part of it on the trail," suggested one of the Simpsons.

"It won't hurt to ask 'em," said Downey. "It's possible they might talk." Stepping into the storeroom, he raised the trap door in the floor and called into the dark interior, "Hey, you—this is the Law. How much dust did you lift off those men down on White River?"

"Not a damn ounce!" came the prompt reply. "You don't think we're fools enough to talk, do you?"

"There was twenty-four hundred ounces—that's what there was!" bellowed Simpson. "An' there ain't more'n twelve hundred here!"

Black John turned to Corporal Downey with a pained expression. "Common honesty prompts me to state that I don't deem it probable that them robbers cached no dust on the trail, er I'd of seen 'em do it. Such bein' the case, look at the position this man's accusation puts me an' Cush in! Like we was a pair of thieves, er somethin'! I'll bet Deters here wouldn't claim I was a thief!"

"Not by a damn sight! You sure used me white!"

"As a matter of fact," continued Black John, ignoring the interruption, "these here three Simpsons look to me like men that would lie without no compunctions. Such bein' the case, a simple plan occurs to me whereby me an' Cush kin vindicate our good name. If these men had a certain amount of dust, they're bound to have royalty receipts to show fer it. Ain't that right, Downey?"

"Of course!" agreed the officer. "It's a wonder I wouldn't have thought of that, myself."

"Well, no man kin be expected to think of everything," grinned Black John complacently, as a choking sound issued from the throat of the elder Simpson whose face flamed red with rage.

Corporal Downey turned on the man. "You men have got the receipts, I suppose? Let's have a look at 'em, an' we can check this dust up in no time."

"We've got the receipts all right," blustered the man. "But the fact is we—er—we—a—"

"Let's see the receipts," demanded Downey, regarding the man curiously.

Reluctantly the men produced the receipts, and Corporal Downey totalled them. "These here receipts calls fer twelve hundred ounces," he announced coldly. "I guess you've got all the dust you started with. Men like you really ought to be kicked out of the country! Tryin' to git Black John in trouble—after him gittin' back yer dust fer you! I'm sorry yer receipts is right—I'd sure enjoy takin' a bunch like you back to Dawson an' makin' you serve a good long stretch fer smugglin' out dust, besides seizin' a good stiff share of it fer penalty! My advice to you three is to get to hell off Halfaday, while I'm still on the crick. Black John here ain't no angel—an' he might take it into his head to retaliate fer the wrong you tried to do him!"

"Oh, I'm willin' to let bygones be bygones," said Black John, grinning into the irate faces of the Simpsons, "but at that, it would be better if you took Downey's advice."

TRANSFERRING THE dust to their own packs, the three strode wrathfully from the room. When they had gone, Downey turned to the others. "Well, I'll be takin' my prisoners an' hittin' back fer Dawson. I'm sure obliged to you fer ketchin' 'em. I was afraid they'd make the Line before I could overtake 'em. That was a dirty murder they pulled at Five Fingers."

"Oh, don't mention it, Downey," replied Black John heartily. "You know damn well that whenever we kin, we like to play along with you—up here on Halfaday."

"Guess I'll hit back fer the Yukon with the corporal, an' go outside on the steamboat," said Deters, extending his hand. "So long. I'm sure obliged fer that interest money."

"Oh, that's all right," said Black John. "Mebbe it'll buy you an extry cow er two to milk, er a barn to smell of."

"That sure was quick thinkin' on your part—to dicker with them robbers the way you done."

"Yeah—quick thinkin' sometimes pays a man."

Deters grinned, and when Corporal Downey wasn't looking, he favored Black John with a knowing wink. "I'm glad I paid royalty on my dust when I had it changed into bills," he said.

"Oh, shore! Honesty pays in the long run," replied Black John sententiously. "Don't it, Downey?"

"Yer damn right it does," agreed the youthful officer, with conviction. "If a man don't believe it, all he'd have to do would be to think about what's goin' to happen to these two birds I'm takin' back with me."

When the two found themselves alone in the saloon after the departure of the others, Black John turned to the somber faced proprietor. "Onder the circumstances, Cush," he said, "it looks to me like it was up to you to buy a drink. An', by God!" he added. "I jest happened to think—I never collected my wages as a guide!"

SECRET SERVICE

OLD CUSH FOLDED the newspaper he had been reading, placed it on the back bar, and reached for the leather dice box, as Black John Smith entered the doorway and crossed to the bar.

"Three treys," he announced, as he examined the dice he rolled from the box. "Guess them's good enough to leave in one."

Black John gathered the dice and cast them. "Three sixes," he announced, with a grin, "Don't never send a boy to do a man's job. That's a horse on you, an' here's the second horse. Jest git you an eyeful of them fives—five of 'em in one throw."

Cush glanced at the five fives that Black John had scattered upon the bar, returned the dice to the box, and set out bottle and glasses. "A man would be a fool to shake agin luck like that," he said. "He'd prob'ly waste a middlin' good throw doin' it."

"Ain't you got that paper read yet?" asked Black John. "Here it's been better'n a week sence Red John fetched it up from Dawson, an' you been nickin' away at it ever sence."

"It's mostly about this here war that's in it, an' a man likes to keep posted. Accordin' to a piece I was readin' when you come in, it all started on account of them Spanish blow'd up one of our battleships down there in Cuby. There's a pitcher of the ship in there. The *Maine,* was the name of it. Good lookin' boat, all right. But at that, it don't look like nothin' to start a war over."

"Well, hell, you can't have a country runnin' around blowin' up another country's battleships. Boats like that runs into money."

"Wars runs into money, too," opined Cush. "An' a damn sight more money than one ship. Looks like, if the United States had sent 'em a bill fer it, they'd paid it without no war. They know'd damn well we could lick 'em."

"Yeah, but there was a lot of American sailors got blow'd up, too. You don't want to fergit that."

"Right around two hundred an' sixty of 'em, accordin' to the paper," said Cush. "But them Spanish must of know'd they'd lose more'n two hundred an' sixty soldiers in a war with Uncle Sam. What I claim, a soldier is about like a sailor, an' they'd saved theirself a hell of a lot of trouble an' money, too, if they'd of sent over two hundred an' sixty soldiers an' let us blow them up. Er else they could of replaced them sailors, an' mebbe, throw'd in a few extry fer good measure."

"Is this Cushing's Fort?" demanded a man who stood in the doorway, a pack sack dangling by one strap from his shoulder.

"Yeah," replied Cush, reaching to the back bar for another glass, "this is the place. Step up. The house is buyin' a drink."

THE MAN advanced to the bar and swung the pack to the floor between his legs. "I had a hell of a time gettin' here," he announced, filling his glass to the brim, "It's damn near three weeks sence I left the Yukon an' headed up the White River. I shoved up three wrong cricks before I come to this Halfaday. The name's Smith—John Smith."

"It might have been," said Black John, "in the early days of Halfaday, but it ain't no more. Jest reach in the name-can there at the end of the bar an' pull you out a name."

"What do you mean?" growled the other, his eyes narrowing as he regarded the big man who stood with his elbow on the bar.

"Meanin', that the name of John Smith is plumb extinct on Halfaday as fer as newcomers is concerned. There's a steadily diminishin' number of us that's got the name preempted, as you might say. I'm one of 'em—commonly know'd as Black John, on account that my whiskers is that color."

"Oh, you're the fella I heard about down on the Yukon, eh?"

"I couldn't say where I've been heard about."

"Well, you run the crick here, don't you? Held up an army er somethin' onct, didn't you?"

"Only part of one. An' as fer runnin' the crick, me an' Cush, here, tries in our feeble way to keep Halfaday moral. We don't like fer no crime to pop up on the crick."

"What d'you mean—crime?"

"Well—takin' the word in its broadest sense—like murder, all forms of larceny, claim-jumpin', an' general skullduggery."

"What's skullduggery?"

"Skullduggery is whatever hangable offense ain't included in them crimes I mentioned. Small crimes like spittin' on the floor, gittin' drunk, er blowin' in yer saucer, is overlooked. Bein' as quite a few of us up here is outlawed fer one reason er another, we don't want no police snoopin' around the crick. You see, it's either heaven er hell, er Halfaday with us—an' most of us prefers Halfaday."

"They say yer right clost up agin the line where it's handy to duck back an' forth between Canady an' Alasky in case the police does show up."

"Yeah, I don't know no other health resort that's more benefi- cially located, as a Chamber of Commerce would say. We're jest about a mile from the line—with Alasky layin' up a dry gulch with an easy grade."

"If you claim a man ain't allowed to use his own name here, what name kin he use?" asked the man sullenly.

"We ain't got no kick about a man's usin' his own name," replied Black John. "It's only the name, John Smith, that's tabooed on Halfaday. The inventive genius displayed by folks in pickin' 'em out an alias makes me wonder, sometimes, why they wasn't nabbed on the scene of their crime! As an aid to

about ninety percent of our newcomers, me an' Cush invented the name-can settin' there on the end of the bar. It consists of a lot of names we copied out of a hist'ry book that One Eyed John Smith left behind when we hung him, one time, an' we mixed up the names an' wrote 'em on slips an' put 'em in the name-can. Each prospective John Smith, when he arrives amongst us, is invited to draw hisself a name, which thereupon becomes hisn till he gits hung er is otherwise accounted fer."

"Huh," grunted the other. "An' who the hell does all this hangin' yer talkin' about?"

"The boys. What a man done before he got to Halfaday ain't none of our business—but what he does after he gits here is subject to inquiry by a miners' meetin'. You kin mebbe notice how slick an' shiny that rafter is right above where yer standin'.

Rope done that. In bad weather the boys favors inside hangin's. Mostly, though, we use trees."

REACHING INTO the can, the man withdrew a slip of paper. "Patrick Webster," he read.

"There," said Black John, "you've got a name that every Tom, Dick an' Harry won't be thinkin' up an' claimin'. Jest shove the slip in yer pocket so there won't no one else be drawin' it whilst yer amongst us. At the end of yer sojourn we'll find it, an' stick it back in the can. Now that yer all set, drink up, an' have one on me." They drank, and the stranger ordered another, tendering in payment a twenty-dollar bill. "What does a man do in a damn country like this, now he's got here?" he asked. "I don't know nothin' about gold diggin'. I jest got in on this rush to see what one was like."

"Well," grinned Black John, "they claim travel broadens a man—an' I know damn well it's apt to stretch one. While idleness, *per se,* ain't no crime on Halfaday, good honest toil on a windlass er the end of a shovel has a tendency to kind of keep his morals from runnin' hog wild on him. Gold diggin' ain't hard to learn."

"I've got plenty of money," retorted the man. "There can't no one make me work if I don't feel like it. Where does a man live up here?"

"The boys all lives on their claims. There's quite a few empty shacks along the crick that's been abandoned fer one reason er another. They're all on claims that pays better'n wages. No claim on Halfaday's been worked out. You might move into one of them. In the meanwhile, till you git a chanct to look 'em over, you kin throw yer stuff in my cabin. I've got an extry bunk in there. It's jest a short piece up the crick from here."

"I don't move in with no one," replied the man. "I want a place of my own. Much obliged to you, jest the same. Where is these empty cabins—up the crick er down?"

"Both," answered Black John. "The handiest one from here is down the crick only about a quarter of a mile. It belonged to One Eyed John, that fella I was tellin' you we hung."

"What did you hang him fer?"

"H-u-u-m, let's see—damn if I remember. Hey, Cush, what the hell was it we hung One Eyed John fer, anyhow?"

"I couldn't say," answered the somber-faced Cush. "Drink up. I'm buyin' one."

"It was ondoubtless some irregularity of some kind," said Black John. "It was away back last summer, sometime. A man can't keep all them hangin's separate."

"Yer a tough bunch up here, ain't you?" commented the man with just the hint of a sneer in his voice.

"Tough!" exclaimed Black John. "It's plain to see that someone's been lyin' to you! Fact is, we're the easy-goin'est an' moralest crick in the Yukon! I ain't sayin' but what there's them amongst us whose past might be somethin' to chaw on. But, up here, we're jest one big happy fambly. An' that reminds me, we kind of like to know which police a man's got his eye out fer—jest so we can notify him if one should show up on the crick. Now in your case I'd say offhand, that the—er, motivatin' influence that roused up yer yen fer travel occurred somewheres down in the States. Am I right; er wrong?"

FOR AN instant the man hesitated, his glance traveling swiftly from face to face. "They're layin' a bank robbery onto me that happened somewheres down in Oklahoma," he said. "But I didn't have nothin' to do with it—see?"

"Oh, shore," agreed Black John. "Me an' Cush kin see at a glance that yer jest a retired capitalist out to see the world. Fact is, anyone would know that if a fella was so damn dumb he couldn't think up no better alias than John Smith, he couldn't pull off no successful bank robbery."

"Is that so!"

"What's that?" asked Black John, as he returned the bottle to the bar after filling his glass.

"I said—about that cabin, you was tellin' me about, is it up the crick, er down?"

"Down. This side of the crick. A quarter of a mile. Better drink up an' have another."

"Not right now. I'm goin' down an' look that cabin over. Be back after a while an' git me an outfit of grub."

When the man had departed with his packsack, Old Cush glanced across the bar at Black John. "You was kind of bearin' down on him, John—about them hangin's, wasn't you? He'll think we don't do nothin' up here but hang folks."

"It'll be a healthy thought," retorted Black John. "Fact is, Cush—I don't like Pat's looks. I never seen one of them shifty-eyed liars yet that was worth a damn. Didn't have nothin' to do with it, he says. Hell!"

II

SOME THREE OR four days after the man, Webster, had moved into One Eyed John's cabin, Black John beached his canoe on a gravel bar several miles down the creek and examined some fresh moose tracks. Picking up his rifle, he was about to take the trail when a loud hail drew his gaze to a canoe that was just rounding a sharp bend, some hundred yards below. Seating himself on a rock, he filled his pipe and awaited for the canoe with its single occupant to beach beside his own. Without seeming to, Black John's gaze took in every detail of the man who stepped from the canoe and greeted him with a grin.

"Could it be," he asked, "that I'm standing face to face with Black John Smith, himself?"

"It could," replied Black John, as he removed the pipe from his mouth and spat onto the gravel.

"Just the man I was looking for! Can I have a few words with you in private?"

"I don't know how else you could have 'em, onlest we was to go on up to Cush's," Black John answered with a glance that swept the little valley of Halfaday from rim to rim.

The man's grin broadened. "They say you run things up here?"

"Well, it na'chly devolves on someone to keep a crick moral."

"I was wondering if you couldn't help me."

"We help some. Others we hinder—even to the extent of a hangin'. The law, we don't neither help nor hinder."

The grin became an audible chuckle. "Oh come now—that's pretty hard on me. There might be exceptions, mightn't there?"

"I wouldn't know of any."

"The fact is, I am the law. I'm Christopher Blue—U.S. Secret Service. We Secret Service men rarely disclose our identity—unless we know who we're dealing with." He paused and turned back his shirt on the inner side of which was pinned a silvered shield upon which appeared U.S. SECRET SERVICE and beneath the lettering the number, 407. "You see," he continued, "I'm laying all my cards on the table."

"Yeah? An' what am I s'posed to do with 'em?"

"It's like this—a couple of months ago a gang of five men rode into a town in east Oklahoma, and stuck up a bank to the tune of sixty thousand dollars. Three of 'em were just common hill billies—moonshiners and small time crooks—but the other two were old hands at the game. One of 'em was Curly Jack, a notorious Southwest desperado, and the other was Bill Crawford, an escape from Walla Walla, where he was doing life for another stick-up in which a man was killed.

"They rode into town and left the three hill billies outside to hold the horses and stand off any trouble that might start there, and Crawford and Curly went in.

"It was easy, and they crowded the packages of bills into a sack, and started for the door, with Crawford carrying the sack, when someone touched off an alarm bell, and by the time they hit the sidewalk, the citizens had opened up on 'em from windows and store doors.

"The hill billies returned the fire, and Crawford's horse went down with a bullet through his head. Just as Curly was reaching for his own saddle horn, Crawford stuck the muzzle of his gun against his back and pulled the trigger. Then he jumped into Curly's saddle, and took out after the other three who were disappearing down the street in a cloud of dust, leaving Curly there on the sidewalk with a hole in his lung you could stick your fist in. Knowing he'd been double-crossed, Curly gasped out the name of Bill Crawford before he cashed in, and the Government put me on the case.

"Posses turned out, and after about a week in the hills they rounded up the three hill billies. But they didn't get Crawford, who had double-crossed the boobs by not showing up at the hide-out where they'd agreed to meet if they got separated. Crawford's horse was found a few days after the robbery shot through the head in a bunch of timber near the railroad, so they figured he'd killed him and got away on the train.

"I didn't waste any time in the hill country. I knew that was the last place a guy like Crawford would hit for. I ran onto his trail in St. Louis, and followed it on out to 'Frisco, and from there to Seattle, then to Skagway, and on to White Horse, where I learned that a bird answering his description had inquired around a bit, and headed for Halfaday Crick. That would be nearly four weeks ago."

THE MAN paused, and Black John refilled his pipe. "Yeah," he said, "an' so what?"

"Well, what I'd like to know, has Crawford showed up on Halfaday? He's five foot-ten, and would weigh right around a hundred and seventy. Brown eyes, with a slight cast in one of 'em."

"An' if he did?"

"Why—a damn cuss that would kill one partner to make a getaway and double-cross all the rest of 'em, wouldn't be entitled to much consideration from anybody, would he?"

Black John puffed at his pipe. "Halfaday is Canadian territory," he said at length. "Have you got papers fer fetchin' him out—in case you was to find him here on the crick?"

"No, I haven't. I'd have to go clear down to Dawson for 'em, and waste a lot of time. I figured that if I could locate him, I could ease him out of the country without going clear back around by the Yukon. Someone told me there was a trail that cut back from the White River country to the coast."

"Yeah—the Dalton Trail. There's only one police post on it, at the pass—an' you could dodge that easy enough."

"Could you tell me how to strike this trail, in case I'd want to use it?" asked the man eagerly.

"Oh, shore. It ain't no trick to hit the Dalton Trail. Saves a lot of time, too—from here. All you do is go back down the crick to the White, then up the White; it's about three days' paddlin' till you come to the falls. It ain't no reg'lar falls, but a long steep rapids. You can't miss it—it's the first one you come to that you have to carry around above the mouth of Halfaday. Then you leave yer canoe, an' hit out afoot. There's two canyons on the south side of the river, right at the falls. Both of 'em are deep an' steep sided. Be sure an' take the right hand one. The left hand one runs on fer what is three, four days' walk, an' then ends in a high wall where the crick jumps mebbe two hundred foot to the bottom. A man couldn't git out of it, after he onct got in there. An' he wouldn't be no place if he did. He'd shore git bushed in them mountains. If he took that box canyon, he'd jest have to foller back down it to the mouth, an' take the other one. This right-hand one is deep an' steep, fer a couple of days, like the other, only instead of leadin' up agin a wall, it slants up to a divide, an' there you be—right on the Dalton Trail, which you can't miss from there to the coast."

"That's simple enough," replied the man. "Take the right hand canyon, you say?"

"Yeah—that's the one. But even s'pos-in' you find this here Crawford on Halfaday, you wouldn't be allowed to take him away with you. You ain't got no authority to arrest a man on Canadian territory, an' if you tried it, you'd likely be hung fer kidnapin', which is hangable under our skullduggery law."

"But hell, man—you can't hang a United States officer!"

BLACK JOHN shook his head. "I do'no," he said. "We've hung a hell of a lot of men. We could try damn hard."

"But—suppose I arrest him on United States territory? You're right close to the line up here, ain't you?"

"In such case, it wouldn't be none of our business," replied Black John. "Yeah—Halfaday's right up agin' the line. But if I was you, I'd slip back down to Dawson an' git them papers. If this here Crawford is on the crick, the chances is, he'll be smart enough not to go acrost the line."

"I guess I'll take a chance," said the man, after a few moments of silence. "I'll go up and look the ground over and see if I can spot my man. Then if I have to, I'll go back for the papers. Damn nuisance though. It'll take a couple of weeks, won't it?"

"Yeah, it'll take that long, even if you had good luck."

"Where could a man stay while he was here? Is there a boarding house of any kind on the crick?"

"No, there ain't no boardin' house on Halfaday. I've got a good cabin not far from the tradin' post an' saloon. Yer welcome to throw yer stuff in there. I've got an extry bunk."

"That's fine! I'll be glad to pay whatever you think is right."

"There'll be plenty of time to talk about the pay when we see what luck you have."

"Has anyone showed up on the crick within the past month that might answer Crawford's description, do you know?"

Black John shook his head as he knocked the dottle from the bowl of his pipe against the heel of his pac. "I wouldn't know about that," he said. "I told you a while back that, on Halfaday we don't neither hinder nor help the police."

The man grinned. "I know, but seeing that you offered to put me up, I thought maybe you'd relented in my case."

"Nope. On Halfaday there's two kinds of relentin' we don't never do. One's about helpin' the police—an' the other's about hangin' miscreants. What we better do is to go on up to my cabin, an' you lay low there till this evenin'. The boys generally collects in the saloon nights, an' then you kin slip in an' look 'em over. You kin change yer name if you kin think up one besides John Smith, an' mingle with the boys like yer some fella that's jest come onto the crick in, you might say, the nat'chel course of events. Does this here Webster know you by sight?"

"Webster?"

"Oh, er—yeah—ain't that what you said this fella's name was?"

"I said Crawford—Bill Crawford."

"Oh, shore—Crawford! The name sounds sim'lar, an' I'm a mite hard of hearin' in my left ear. Well, come on. We'll git agoin'. I had figgered on mebbe gittin' me a moose, but there ain't no hurry. I've got part of a quarter still hangin'. Git in yer canoe, an' foller me on' up."

III

ALONG TOWARD THE middle of the after-noon, Black John strolled into the barroom, where Old Cush, steel-rimmed glasses firmly astride his nose, was deep in the perusal of the newspaper spread out before him on the bar.

"Still readin' up about that damn war?" asked Black John, as Cush, without looking up from his paper, set out the bottle and glasses.

"No, I finished about that—an' it's jest like I claimed; it would of been a damn sight cheaper fer them Spanish to pay fer that boat they blow'd up, because it tells here how they lost all their own boats, besides them ones Admiral Dooley sunk over to them Phillipyne Islands."

"What with newspapers spread all over the bar, this here is gittin' to look more like a lib'ry than a saloon," opined Black John as he poured his drink. "An' besides which, it looks from here like incipient skullduggery is rife on Halfaday."

"What's 'incipient'? An' what's 'rife'?" growled Cush. "It's gittin' so you can't talk without you use words which it's doubtful if you know the meanin' of 'em yerself. Take it like if yer readin' in a Bible er a noospaper you kin skip them words you don't know when you come to 'em—but when anyone talks 'em to you, they got you cornered. An' besides, what's skullduggery got to do with a saloon lookin' like a lib'ry?"

"Nothin'," grinned Black John, "but if you really wanted to make it look like a lib'ry, you ort to git you a dictionary. It would be handy, too, fer a man of your limited vocabulary."

"What I claim, a dictionary ain't no good!" Cush retorted. "My daughter use' to have one damn near four inches thick. I'd heard 'em well spoke of, an' I tried to use it a time er two, but the way they've got 'em fixed—if you don't know how to spell a word, you can't look it up. An' when anyone is talkin' to you they don't stand around an' spell out the words."

"That's so," admitted Black John, "but you could look up the words you come acrost when yer readin'—they're already spelled out for you."

"It's a damn sight quicker to skip 'em. If a man spent all his time clawin' through a dictionary, he wouldn't never git no readin' done. What I claim, if a man wants a book, he'd better stick to the Bible. To hell with them dictionaries!

"But speakin' of readin', there's a piece here in this paper where five fellas come ridin' into some town down in Oklahoma, an' stuck up a bank fer sixty thousan', an' one of their horses got shot, an' two of 'em started fer the same horse, an' one of 'em shot the one that got to the horse first, an' jumped on the horse hisself, an' rid away after the others, leavin' this one he shot layin' there. Before he died, he told 'em the one that shot him was named Bill Crawford, an' the paper says how this here Crawford was a lifer, that had broke out of some prison, an' they're huntin' him all over hell. I hope they ketch him, too! A damn skunk that would do a trick like that had ort to be hung."

"YEAH," AGREED Black John, "he shore had. An' that reminds me—there's a fella down to my shack which he claims he's a U.S. Secret Service man. He's huntin' a man named Bill Crawford fer a sixty thousan' dollar bank job down in Kansas."

"Cripes!" exclaimed Old Cush. "You don't s'pose a damn cuss like Crawford is right here on Halfaday, do you? Say—hold on! That there Pat Webster! He said somethin' about a Oklahoma bank job, didn't he? Claimed he wasn't in on it, er somethin'?"

"He ondoubtless lied," said Black John. "Like I told you, I never did like his looks."

"But you say this here Secret Service man is down to your shack? How come you'd favor the law—an' 'specially the American law? It ain't none of our business what Webster done in Oklahoma."

"I ain't exactly favorin' the law, as such," explained Black John. "I'm puttin' this party up jest as a common citizen. I told him plain that he wouldn't be allowed to take Webster off'n Halfaday, without he had papers from the Mounted Police. He said he'd look the ground over, an' if he couldn't nab Webster on the American side, he'd go down to Dawson an' git the papers."

"How come this fella got to your cabin without showin' up here?" asked Cush.

"I run onto him down the crick. I was moose huntin' an' he hollered at me." So I took him right on up to the cabin."

"But—what with your trouble bein' over on the American side, that-a-way, if I was you, John, I'd be damn careful how I fooled around with them American police. How do you know you don't talk in yer sleep, er somethin'?"

"I prob'ly couldn't tell him nothin' he don't know a'ready. He called me by name when he first seen me. Them Secret Service men is smart as hell. You see, Cush, I couldn't hardly do no different—what with my skirts not bein' clean on that Army payroll job."

"Skirts!" cried Cush, his eyes widening as he swept the steel rimmed spectacles from nose to forehead. "That's the first time you ever told me there was any wimmin mixed up in it! You mean he's located them wimmin, an' he made a deal to turn 'em loose er somethin' if you'd help him nail Webster?"

BLACK JOHN maintained a perfectly straight face. "Well, that ain't jest exactly the thought I meant to convey," he said. "But it's clost enough fer the present. The fact is, Cush, how would you like to engage in a little secret service venture yerself? The pay should be attractive—an' you've jest showed that you've got unlimited imagination."

"No sir! Not by a damn sight! You know, John, that me an' you has made it a p'int never to have nothin' to do with helpin' or hinderin' the police. Onct in a great while we have stretched the p'int jest a mite, mebbe, in the case of Corporal Downey, where the circumstances seemed right. But that ain't no sign we should go helpin' police right an' left, every time one shows up on the crick. It wouldn't be right. The boys comes here, knowin' they'll git a square deal as long as they stay moral. That's the reputa-tion Halfaday's got—an' that's the way we've kep' it. Hell, if we begun tippin' 'em off to the police, the boys that's on the run would quit comin' here—an' then where would I be, dependin' like I do on their trade to keep me goin'? Of course, in this here partic'lar case, I ain't blamin' you—havin' them wimmin to look out fer. You couldn't hardly do no different, an' him havin' the goods on you. But it had ort to be a damn good lesson to you to leave wimmin alone. I ort to know—I've had four of 'em—an' the only good one I ever had up an' died on me."

Black John nodded. "You know I ain't never favored no wimmin on Halfaday."

"Shore, I know," replied Cush, gloomily, "but now, when these ones git turned loose, they'll prob'ly be flockin' in on you. I kin see where Halfaday ain't never goin' to be the same no more. Onct a woman gits anythin' on a man, she'll ride him till there ain't nothin' he kin do but move on. I don't know what the hell I'll do around here without you."

Black John grinned. "I ain't hangin' up no rent sign on my cabin, yet. Fact is, I'll jest slip an order to all them wimmin to stay away from Halfaday—an' they'll stay! I guess you didn't onderstand how to handle them wimmin of yourn, Cush. You've got to be masterful."

"Yeah? Well you wait an' see!"

"So you don't want in on this here secret service venture, eh?" persisted Black John. "You better think it over careful. There's liable to be good money in it."

"I won't have a damn thing to do with it, no matter how much is in it! You've got to go it alone, this time. At that, with what the paper said about that damn' cuss, I wouldn't grieve none if he was took back an' hung! Him shootin' his pardner in the back that-a-way to git his horse don't set good on a man's stummick."

"Yeah," agreed Black John, "it does look like he deserved a little bad luck, at that. I'm goin' back to the cabin. See you later!"

IV

"WELL," SAID BLACK John, as he and his guest finished washing the supper dishes that evening, "guess we might's well mosey on over to Cush's. The boys'll begin driftin' in by now. Did you say this fella yer huntin' knows you by sight, er don't he?"

"No, I don't think he does. The chances are he's never even heard of me. I wasn't working on the case he was convicted for. I don't think it was a federal job, anyhow."

"How come this here bank robbery is a Gov'ment case? I thought the local shuriffs an' police handled jobs like that."

"Well—yes—they generally do. But you see this was a national bank, so they called us in."

"Don't pay to monkey with Uncle Sam, eh?"

"You bet your life it don't! Once they put us on the trail, and we never quit till our man's either dead or behind the bars."

"Hum, if I was this here Webster, I wouldn't take no comfort in the thought."

"Why the hell do you keep calling him Webster? His name's Crawford."

"Shore—Crawford's what I meant. Fact is, I ain't no good hand at rememberin' names. I don't never fergit a face, but a name is different. Take it in a place like Halfaday, it's somehow more liable to change. You say you'd know this party if you seen him?"

"I think I would. I looked up his description."

"Come on, then, we'll be goin'. You kin ondoubtless pick him out amongst the boys. But remember what I told you—if you ain't got the papers, you won't be allowed to take him off Halfaday onless you arrest him acrost the line."

ARRIVING AT the saloon Black John sat in a stud game, leaving the other to shift for himself among the dozen or more men who stood drinking and talking at the bar. An hour later he glanced up as a man entered the room and headed for the group. He noticed that Christopher Blue was regarding the newcomer intently, and that Cush was busy serving drinks.

"Hey, Webster," he called, as the man approached the bar, "tell Cush to fetch a round of drinks over here when he gits time, will you?"

The man nodded, and Black John meticulously examined the tip of his hole card. Presently the drinks were served and glancing up he noted that Webster and Blue were drinking together at the end of the bar. Later, they left the room together, and Black John devoted his entire attention to stud.

Long after midnight he cashed in his chips. Neither Webster nor Blue had returned to the saloon, and after a few minutes of general conversation, he proceeded to his cabin to find the light burning and Christopher Blue stowing the last of his few belongings into his packsack.

"You were right," the man stated, "Crawford's too damn smart to be caught across the line. I've got to go clear down to Dawson after those papers."

"You located him, eh?" asked Black John.

The man grinned. "Sure, I did. Thanks for the tip. But I think I'd have recognized him anyway."

"Tip?"

"Why certainly! You knew I was looking right at him when you called out to him to tell Cush to bring over round of drinks."

"Oh—you mean Webster? So he's this here Crawford you been talkin' about! By God then—I bet that's how come I kep' gittin' them names mixed!"

"It must have been," chuckled the other. "Do you think I can make it back from Dawson in two weeks?"

"Well, that's accordin' to what luck you have. It would be good goin', even if there wasn't no delay about them papers. But how do you know Webster'll be here when you git back? He might git suspicious er somethin' an' pull out on you."

The man smiled. "He'll be here. He won't pull out for anywhere. He thinks he's safe here! Trust us fellows not to pull any boners. How long do you suppose we'd last if we tipped off our hand to a crook? We've got to be able to outguess any kind of a criminal we come across—that's what the Government pays us for."

"Yeah," admitted Black John, "I s'pose that's right. When you figgerin' on pullin' out fer Dawson?"

"I'll start at daylight. That's why I was getting my things all ready. I'll just flop down here on the bunk and get a couple of hours' sleep and then I'll be on my way. How much do I owe you?"

"Owe me?"

"Why, yes—for my board and lodging. Don't be afraid to make it enough—the Government pays my expenses. If we settle up now, I won't have to disturb you early in the morning."

"Yer coming back, ain't you?" replied Black John. "There'll be plenty time to talk about expenses the next time I see you. I'm sleepy now. I'm goin' to roll in. So long, if I don't see you in the mornin'."

V

NEXT MORNING, AS Black John stepped into the saloon, Old Cush looked up from his inevitable newspaper, and dropped his eyes to the place he held with a gnarled, black-rimmed forefinger; "What the hell does RECONCENTRADOS mean?" he demanded, spelling out the word laboriously. "It says here how they're collectin' 'em in them towns down in Cuby."

"Oh—yeah—Cripes, Cush, anyone would think you didn't know nothin' about a war! That there's a new kind of ammunition, they've got. It explodes, an' scatters when it hits."

"It could shore scatter all over hell with the number of letters it takes to spell it," opined Cush. "It's gittin' so a man don't have no chanct at all in a war."

"It's like I was tellin' you," said Black John as he poured himself a drink, "if you had a dictionary you could look up them words fer yerself."

"Well," said Cush somberly, "mebbe I'll have to git one, now that you'll prob'ly be leavin' the crick when them wimmin gits turned loose on you. Up to now I ain't felt the need of one, 'cause it was handier to jest ask you when I come to a word I didn't know. Things ain't goin' to be the same around here with you gone. How much to boot should a man ort to git if he traded a Bible fer a dictionary?"

"W-e-e-l," considered Black John, "you ain't puttin' it quite right. He'd prob'ly have to give boot—about half an ounce, I'd say, offhand."

"Like hell he would! Any damn fool knows a Bible is more Christian to have than a dictionary! I might trade that singin' book my wife had, though. We ain't never found no use fer that. I'd give it an' half an ounce fer a good dictionary. I'll have Red John take it down to Dawson next time he goes, an' make a trade."

"Why don't you jest buy one?" suggested Black John.

"What! An' have three books layin' around? Two's bad enough—but with three books kickin' around on the back bar, a man couldn't find no place to set the glasses! Not by a damn sight! If I git a dictionary that singin' book has got to go."

A SHADOW darkened the doorway as Webster entered the room and walked slowly to the bar.

"Have a drink!" invited Black John. "I'm about to buy one."

Old Cush set out another glass, then the three drank. After an interval Cush indicated the bottle with a jerk of his thumb. "Have one on the house," he suggested as he folded the newspaper and returned it to the back bar.

Presently Webster laid a five dollar bill on the bar. "Fill 'em up agin," he ordered. "That's the last damn cent I've got in the world. We might's well drink it up. How the hell does a man go at diggin' gold?"

"The last cent you've got!" exclaimed Black John. "I thought here a few days ago you told us you had plenty of money, an' didn't have to work."

"Yeah," retorted the man," that was true when I said it. But it ain't true no more. The facts is, men, I might's well come clean. I was mixed up in that robbery down in Oklahoma. When I hit here I had right around sixty thousan' dollars in good safe bills. Today I ain't got a cent!"

"Sixty thousan'! That's quite a haul fer one man's share. How many of you was there in it?" asked Black John.

"There was five of us. Three of us was jest some damn punks we picked up in the hills an' left outside to hold the horses, an' fog up the town in case any of the boobs got suspicious. But Curly Jack was a tough guy. Me an' him done the job. The inside part was easy—jest a scairt cashier, an' a scairter gal. We sacked the sixty thousan' in no time, but while we was goin' out one of 'em most touched off the alarm, 'cause when we hit the sidewalk a big gong was bangin' away on top of the bank, an' it seemed like everyone in town was shootin' at us. They got pore Curly, an' the three punks high-tailed it out of town, an' me after 'em with the stuff all safe in the sack.

"Well," he added, with a wink, "we got separated, an' I never did see them punks agin. I went to St. Louie an' then hit fer Seattle by way of Frisco, an' here I be. I thought I was safe here—but last night a fella shows up, an' we gits to drinkin' an' chawin' the rag, here at the bar, an' he tells me he knows of a sweet job we kin pull off an' git away with it easy. Somehow I kind of think I seen his face somewhere before, but I don't place him, an' we goes down to my cabin to talk it over. Then he pulls a gun an' a badge on me—an' it turns out that he's a damn Secret Service man! He'd be'n put on the job, on account that the bank we robbed was a national bank, an' he'd trailed me on from St. Louie clean to here."

"Well, I was in a hell of a fix, on account that I was mixed up in another bank job onct, where a feller was killed an' they railroaded me to Walla Walla fer the long stretch. Last year I crushed out—an' this guy has got all the dope on me. I tells him he ain't got no right to arrest me on Canadian territory, an' if he thinks I'm goin' onto the American side, he's a fool. He shoves the gun up agin my belly an' kind of digs it in till it hurts, an' he kind of grins an' he says how he wouldn't be half as big a fool as I'd be if I didn't take a little walk with him jest about a mile up the gulch."

"It looks like he's got me no matter which way the cat jumps, because if he pulls that trigger the gun don't make no noise up agin my belly that way, an' no one would know who done it but me, an' I'd be dead. So I starts to dicker with him. I offers him half the sixty thousan' if he'll go away an' claim he never found me, an' he pertends to do some thinkin', an' then says, 'All right, fork it over.' I've got the stuff hid in a place I found in the wall, where part of a log comes out when you pull out a peg, so I digs up the roll, an' counts him off thirty thousan'. An' then what does the crooked, double-crossin' son of a bitch do but says that, come to think it over, it's worth the hull sixty thousan' to sacrifice his honor!

"I squawks like hell, an' then he tells me that that damn Curly Jack claimed before he croaked that it was me that shot him to git his horse, an' I'd never see Leavenworth if I was took back, but I would stretch a rope instead. He even squawked when he counted the roll an' found it was short what money I'd used out of it. An' he went through my pockets an' took everything but that lousy five spot layin' there on the bar. It was fifty-nine thousan' two hundred an' twenty bucks that he took—an' he leaves me a five!"

"Well, at that," said Black John, "it was more'n you left them three punks that got away. An' he didn't shoot you in the back, like you done Curly."

"You been talkin' to this guy!" exclaimed the man accusingly.

FOR ANSWER Black John pointed to the folded newspaper. "It's in the paper, there. When we read that piece, we know'd you was this Crawford, on account you told us you was suspected of a bank robbery in Oklahoma."

Old Cush pushed the paper toward the man, who read the story, and shoved the paper back. "Well," he growled, "with only one horse left, it was him er me for it. Why in hell wouldn't I kill him?

"Tell me now—how do you go about diggin' this here gold?"

Black John cleared his throat. "Like I told you when you got here—what a man done before he come to Halfaday ain't none of our business, but after he gits here he's got to keep moral, er git hung, whichever he prefers. So if they've got a law down there in Oklahoma agin robbin' banks an' shootin' folks in the back, that's their business, an' it's up to them to punish you fer it, if they kin ketch you. Likewise, yer double-crossin' them three pals ain't none of our business. But you, yerself, admitted havin' gone down to yer cabin fer the express purpose, to wit, of plottin' a crime with this here Blue, before you know'd he was an offi-cer of the law. Now plottin' to commit a crime is, *per se,* in an' of itself a crime on Halfaday, it constitutin' skullduggery. An' when a man further complicates such skullduggery with the crime of bribin' a United States officer in the discharge of his dooty, he couldn't hardly expect to escape a speedy hangin' on Halfaday,"

"But good God, man! He had a gun borin' right into my guts—an' it was cocked! An' there was a look in his eye that meant business!"

"Um-hum," replied Black John, "an' you'll ondoubtless see the same kind of a look in our eye, when we call the miners' meetin', an' the boys hears me read that piece to 'em there in the paper. It couldn't be used as direct evidence agin you on Halfaday—but it is admissible, under our code, as character evidence. The boys sets quite a bit of store by character evidence—as some of our most interestin' hangin's could attest."

"Do you mean, that after gittin' robbed by that damn crook, you'd hang me besides? Damn him! If he hadn't throw'd my gun in the river, I'd have shot him last night when he went out with that money!"

96

BLACK JOHN nodded. "You'd of been perfectly safe in doin' that," he said. "We couldn't hang you but the onct. The boys is busy right now down to their claims, an' I've got to go out an' git me a moose. The piece I've got hangin' is kind of fly-blow'd an it's a mite high. I'll stop along up the crick an' tell the boys about the meetin,' an' tonight we'll hang you an' git it over with. We was jest sayin' the other day, we hadn't had no hangin' in damn near a fortnight. That's the way it goes, though. Seems like they come in waves. Sometimes we don't have none fer almost a month, an' then we'll pull off a batch of 'em. It's good weather now—we could hold yourn outdoors. It'll keep the boys from gittin' res'less. Well, so long ontil this evenin'. I got to git me that moose."

Stepping behind the bar, Black John picked up a rifle, and walked out through the trading room. Half an hour later, through the old brass telescope that always stood conveniently near the door, he and Old Cush watched a canoe, its single occupant paddling frantically, disappear around a far bend of the creek.

"Shootin' his pardner in the back!" said Cush. "It would served him right if we had of hung him!"

"Yeah," agreed Black John, "but under the circumstances, it wouldn't hardly of been ethical. When you come to think it over, there was somethin' to be said on his side of the case, on that bribery charge. A man of his caliber couldn't hardly be expected to stand steadfastly fer the right, with a cocked gun borin' into his guts. We're well shet of him. He ain't goin' to linger on Halfaday."

"That's right, an' if he keeps up the lick he's goin' now, he'll be overtakin' that Secret Service man—an' him without no gun."

"Mebbe."

"What time did that other fella start out?" asked Cush. "An' didn't you think it was funny he'd be goin' back so quick without out his man?"

"No," replied Black John, "he kind of slipped one over on me, I guess. You see, he told me last night he'd seen his man an' figgered he was too smart to be caught acrost the line. I'd already told him he couldn't arrest no one on Halfaday without the papers, so he said he was goin' down to Dawson an' git 'em. Then when I got up this mornin' he was gone."

"An' all that money along with him," murmured Old Cush sadly, his eyes on the far bend of the creek. "How much did Webster say it was?"

"Fifty-nine thousan' two hundred an' twenty dollars, all told. You'll remember he left Webster a five spot."

"Yeah—it's layin' there yet on the bar. When you stepped into the storeroom Webster shot out the front door without even waitin' fer his change."

"Did he put that name slip back in the can?"

"Hell—no! He didn't wait fer nothin'."

"All right, give me a pencil an' a piece of paper, an' I'll replace it. Beats hell all the trouble a chechako'll put a man to. An' while yer about it, set the dice box on the bar an' we'll shake fer that extry change. He had three an' a half comin'. He only bought the one round, an' I wouldn't want you should git balled up in yer cash."

"I'll take a chanct," said Old Cush dryly as he picked up the bill and slipped it into the till. "Here's the box. I'll shake you fer the drinks."

V

ONE MORNING, A week after the departure of Webster from Halfaday Creek, Black John, rifle in hand, stepped into the saloon to find Old Cush arranging the glasses on the back bar. "Fill me up a flask, Cush," he ordered. "I'm goin' out an' git me a moose. Been threatenin' to fer a week, but now I've got plumb down to the shank of that quarter I've had hangin'."

"Huh," grunted Cush, reaching beneath the bar for a leather covered pocket flask, "it's about time you was gittin' some fresh meat. That chunk you give the klooch yeste'day to bile up fer me stunk."

"Yeah," grinned Black John, "that's why I give it to her. My stummick ain't what it used to be. If I don't show up fer a few days, don't worry. I figger to swing over to the White, an' prospect a little in that long box canyon over there by the falls."

Old Cush paused in the act of filling the flask from a bottle and eyed the other intently. "You gone crazy er somethin'?" he asked. "You know damn well there ain't nothin' in that box canyon, an' never was. It's all hard rock, an' what little dirt there is don't go down more'n a couple of foot, at the most. It's all top-wash stuff."

"Ort to be easy to prospect then," grinned Black John, "if it don't go down no further'n that. A man wouldn't have to sink no deep shaft."

"A man would be a damn fool to even look at it. There's been a dozen tried it in there, an' they all come right down agin the rock without even strikin' a color. Even a chechako would know enough to stay out of that canyon!"

"I wonder!" said Black John, as he stowed the flask in his pocket. "If that's the case, mebbe I won't do no good over there, after all. Well—so long. I'll be seein' you."

THE STEEP, tumultuous rapid of the White River known as "The Falls" lay some fifteen miles due south of Cushing's Fort, on Halfaday. Ascending to the rim, Black John struck off at a leisurely pace through the ridge country. "Let's see," he figured half-aloud, "it would take him one day on Halfaday, an' three days up the White, then a good three days to the end of the box canyon, an' three days back down it—that's ten days, seven of which has passed. Today will make eight. That'll give me two days' leeway, in case he might of traveled a mite faster'n what I figgered. I don't mind it, though. Couple days' rest don't hurt no one now an' then. It's good fer a man to sort of lay around out in a country like this—with the hills, an' the rivers, an' the woods, an' all. Sort of warms the cockles of his heart toward God an' his fella man. I wonder if that damn cuss could of got mixed up an' took off up the wrong canyon?"

Arriving at the falls late in the afternoon, he noted that Blue's canoe lay overturned on the beach. Intensive exploration for a short distance up the box canyon satisfied him that the man had passed on up, so Black John proceeded to make himself comfortable in a cozy camp just within the canyon's mouth where no one could pass out unnoticed. Possessing the patience of an Indian, Black John sat for two days with his back to a rock, dozing, whittling, smoking. Along in the mid-forenoon of the third day, he cut a pole, tied on a line he took from his pocket, and started to fish in the pools below the falls, using a strip of pork rind for bait. It was while thus engaged that a loud hail drew his gaze to the man who, pack on his back, was just emerging from the mouth of the box canyon.

Recognition was mutual. "Well," cried Black John heartily, retrieving half a dozen small fish he had strung on a forked willow, "damn if it ain't my old friend, Chris! What the hell did you do—hit off up the wrong canyon?"

"Wrong canyon—hell! I went up the right hand canyon, just like you told me—"

"The right hand canyon!" exclaimed Black John, his eyes widening. "No wonder you didn't git nowheres. I told you the left."

"You did not! You said the right—and repeated it two or three times."

BLACK JOHN shook his head. "Well," he said, "there ain't no use fightin' about it. I still think you misonderstood me. But of course it might be such a thing as I misspoke myself. I ain't one of these guys that claims they're always right. Anyone might make a mistake that way—but I ain't apt to."

"You sure did that time," said the man, apparently somewhat mollified. "Because I'm positive you said the right hand canyon. A man would hardly make a mistake in a matter of life and death, would he?"

"Well," replied Black John, "some has. But it ain't as bad as all that—yet. You've still got grub enough to take you to the police post. If you ain't I kin spare you the difference. Set down a while now an' rest up whilst I fry us a batch of fish. You must be hungry—an' I feel like it's kind of my fault."

"No real harm done, I guess," admitted the man, as he settled the packsack from his shoulders. "But what the hell are you doing way over here?"

"Oh, jest projectin' around. I cut acrost from Halfaday afoot. But how come you're here? You told me you was go in' to hit down to Dawson an' git them papers so you could arrest that there Crawford?"

"That's what I intended to do when I left your place that morning, but on the way down Halfaday, I figured that it would be better to hit out to the coast—Skagway or some place where I could get in touch by cable directly with Ottawa, and at the same time get in touch with my own chief in Washington."

"I see," said Black John, grinning into the other's face. "You're still figgerin' on comin' back to Halfaday then?"

"Of course I am!" retorted the man, with a touch of asperity. "I've got to go back and get Crawford, haven't I?"

"Crawford! He ain't on Halfaday no more. He took out, hell atearin', about noon of the same day you left."

"Took out! Where did he go to?"

"He didn't leave no address. Didn't even wait fer his change from a five dollar bill he laid on the bar fer a round of drinks."

"What the hell got into him, I wonder?"

"I couldn't say—onlest it was fear of some kind. He looked scairt. An' the way he was paddlin' down the crick, he acted scairt, too."

For several minutes the only sound was that of the fish sizzling in the pan. "In that case," said Blue, "there wouldn't be any sense in my going back to Halfaday."

"No," agreed Black John, "quite the contrary."

"I might as well settle up with you then for that little board bill."

"Any time yer ready."

"How much is it? Let's see—there was supper that night, and the bed, and I took a bunch of those cold sinkers for breakfast. How much?"

"Altogether," said Black John, "it amounts to jest fifty-nine thousan', two hundred an' twenty dollars—not countin' this here meal I'm cookin'."

"What!" Quick as a flash, the man's hand flew to a shoulder holster that showed beneath his open coat. But it halted abruptly without grasping the gun, as his eyes focussed on the muzzle of the big black forty-five that was trained exactly upon the center of his midriff.

"Jest h'ist 'em a little higher, Chris," ordered a cold, hard voice behind the gun, "an' I'll save you the trouble of drawin' it."

AS HE spoke, Black John reached with his left hand, drew the gun from its holster, and tossed it into the river. "I'm lettin' you keep yer badge," he added with a grin. "It must of cost you a good fifty cents at some badge store."

"This is an outrage!" cried the man, his face a pasty white. "Do you realize that you're attempting to rob the United States Government?"

"Nope," replied Black John, "I don't. Even if I was, it wouldn't be the first time. But this here partic'lar transaction ain't no robbery at all—it's merely the collection of an honest debt. You told me not to be afraid to make it enough—an' I ain't. Hold on, a minute, while I git that money out of yer pack. Yeah—here it is. Wait till I count it." Very deliberately, still keeping the man covered, Black John counted the bills. "Correct to a cent," he announced, transferring them to his own pack. "An' now the fish is ready. If you stick around fer this meal, it'll be thirty-five cents more. Hell—I'm givin' you all the breaks, at that. If I was to take you back to Halfaday the boys would hang you in a minute—robbery, armed, would be the charge. If I was you, I'd hit out fer the coast."

"I'll get you for this—damn you!" cried the infuriated man. "You'll learn that you can't fool with the Government!"

"Yeah!" grinned Black John, as the other shouldered his pack, and struck off up the left hand canyon, "When you come back to do it, don't fergit to fetch along the proper papers. You might have to go down to Dawson fer 'em—er mebbe clean back to the coast!"

VI

IN THE MIDAFTERNOON four days later Black John beached his canoe, ascended the bank, stepped into Cushing's saloon, and swung his packsack to the floor in front of the bar.

Old Cush greeted him with a grin as he set out bottle and glasses. "How do you like that box canyon by now?" he asked.

"I guess there ain't nothin' there," admitted Black John as he poured his drink. "I fetched a prime quarter of moose fer you, though. It's in the canoe."

"Canoe! I thought you hit out acrost country?"

"Yeah, I did. But I come back in the canoe. It was the one that there Christopher Blue come to Halfaday in. An' by the way, before I fergit it stick this in the safe fer me, an' don't fergit to make a note of it in the book. It figgers up to fifty-nine thou-san' two hundred an' twenty dollars. It's all there. I counted it."

Old Cush's eyes seemed to fairly bulge from their sockets as the packages of bills thudded onto the bar. "The money he got off'n Webster!" he exclaimed. "But—good God, John, how come you to have it? It's be'n a couple of weeks sence he left here!"

"Yeah, I met up with him over to the box canyon. He was comin' on out while I was fishin' there in them holes below the falls."

"But what the hell was he doin' up the box canyon?"

"Jest walkin'. He claimed he'd went up to the end of it, an' back."

Old Cush shook his head somberly as he eyed the packages of bills. "You'll have the hull United State Gov'mint pilin' in on us, now," he said. "You'd ort to know'd better'n to rob a Secret Service man!"

"Rob!" exclaimed Black John, a pained expression creeping into his eyes. "Why, Cush, you'd ort to know that I wouldn't rob no one—leastwise not in the White River country. It wouldn't be ethical. An' as fer bein' a Secret Service man—Chris Blue wasn't no more one of 'em than you be. In the first place, Secret Service men don't handle nothin' but conterfeitin' an' guardin' the President. They're under the treasury department. The department of jestice handles all other cases. An' besides, when did the Secret Service start tellin' their name an' their business to everyone they met up with along a crick? An' when did they start wearin' a big tin badge in under their shirt—like a country constable?"

"But—Webster thought he was a Secret Service man, er why would he of turned over them bills to him?"

"Webster, er Crawford, rather—his eggication had ondoubt-less been neglected, er he'd of know'd about that, same as I did. The way I figger, this here Blue was mebbe a prisoner in Walla Walla, er mebbe a screw there when Crawford was doin' his time. That way he would know him by sight. An' then after readin' about this robbery in the paper, he run acrost Crawford in St. Louis, an' trailed him clean to here, an' then took him fer his roll. Secret Service—hell!"

"But what was he doin' in the box canyon?"

"Oh, that was jest some kind of a mistake. You see, when we was talkin' down the crick, that day he come, he was askin' me if there wasn't no short-cut out of the country, an' I told him about the Dalton Trail. Seems like, one of us kind of got mixed up about them canyons, er somethin'. He claimed it was me."

"Well—I'll be damned!" muttered Old Cush, as he stowed the money in the safe, and made a certain notation in his book. "Then there wasn't no Secret Service about it, eh?"

"None," grinned Black John, "except what I done, fer the good of Halfaday. That was a kind of secret service. I offered to let you in on it, Cush. You hadn't ort to turned it down. I told you the pay would be good. Half them bills would been yourn."

KIDNAPPERS
INVADE HALFADAY

I

OLD CUSH SET out bottle and glasses, and laid five dice on the bar as Black John Smith entered the doorway of the saloon and trading post known as Cushing's Fort, that ministered to the wants of the little community of outlawed men that had sprung up on Halfaday Creek, close against the Yukon-Alaska boundary.

"We'll have to shake 'em by hand this mornin', John," he said. "What with the boys boisterin' around in here las' night, the box come onsewed. I guess the thread got kind of rotten. I never seen one of them leather dice boxes give out before. I aim to fix it when I git time."

"Jest lay the dice on the back bar, an' I'll buy one," replied Black John.

"You mean—you don't trust me to handle them dice?" asked Cush, a pained expression on his face.

"Listen—you've got every damn cent I own right there in that safe, an' you know the combination, an' I wouldn't lose a wink of sleep worryin' about it, if I was to go away an' stay a year. But shakin' dice fer the drinks is somethin' else. Anyone that kin think up a way to cheat playin' fly loo ain't goin' to shake no dice with me—by hand! When you git the box sewed we'll resume our dice shakin'."

"I seen a piece in that there paper that Red John fetched up from Dawson where it tells about the boxers has uprose over in Chiny, an' all the other Gov'mints is sendin' armies in there to straighten things out. I never heered tell of no Chinee boxers. I seen a nigger go ten rounds agin' Thunderbolt McVey down to Frisco, one time—but never no Chinee."

"Oh, shore," replied Black John, "they've got boxers over there—same as any other country. They've turned out some pretty good men, too. You shorely must of heard of that Chinese heavyweight; his name was—let's see—it was Kid Whang Ho. Don't you mind the time he fought Battlin' Ker Chow fer the heavyweight champeenship of—of Borneo?"

"No."

"If you'd take a trip down to Dawson onct in a while where you could see more newspapers, you'd keep better posted. This fight come off last year in—in Hongkong, er Pekin, er some sech place. I rec'lect there was quite a stink about the decision. You see, they had a big purse up—fer them parts. It was a million yen, er mebbe it was sen—anyways it run up to damn near a box car full of them brass checks them Chinamens use fer money, an' the referee give the decision to Kid Whang Ho on a knockout, in the fifth. Battlin' Ker Chow's backers put up a squawk, clai-min' their man had got a raw deal on account that Kid Whang Ho's handlers had braided a len'th of lead pipe in his queue—"

"You started in to tell about a prize fight, an' not a pool game," interrupted Cush disgustedly.

"Shore I did. An' I'm still talkin' about one."

"Cripes! Do they lam one another with cues, over there, instead of gloves?"

BLACK JOHN eyed the other with a glance of pity. "Anyone but you would know that a Chinaman's queue is that there twist of hair that hangs down their back. Some calls it their pig tail."

"Why the hell didn't you say so, then?"

"I prefer," retorted Black John loftily, "to call a thing by its proper name, when practical—which is damn seldom, when talkin' to you, bein' as you've got some plebeian nickname fer mighty near everything that's be'n invented to date."

"What's plebeian?"

"Well—like you."

"My pa's fambly was English, an' my ma's folks come from Holland, way back," explained Cush, "But what about the lead pipe in that there Chinee's pig tail?"

"His handlers had braided it in before the fight, so it wouldn't show, an' it give their man a hell of an advantage because when he'd git in a punch to the face, er the body, he'd turn his head quick at the same time, an' that loaded queue would fly around an' ketch Battlin' Ker Chow a hell of a clout in the back of the head, where he didn't have no guard up. It didn't draw no blood, er leave no mark, on account that the hair made a paddin' fer it. A few of them wallops every round up to the fifth, they say, done the business."

Old Cush chuckled. "It was a pretty smart trick, at that. Jest lookin' at a Chinee, you wouldn't think he was smart. But I've heered you've got to watch out fer 'em in a deal. What did they do about it?"

"They took it to court. It seems that the circuit judge held that he couldn't see where a pound er two of lead pipe would overstep the bounds of good clean sportsmanship, so he upheld the referee's decision. Then, Battlin' Ker Chow's lawyers done some nosin' around an' found out where this jedge had bet a couple of ginrickyshaw loads of yen on Kid Whang Ho."

"What's a ginrickyshaw?"

"It's them two wheeled carts they've got over in Chiny to haul folks home in when they've had too many gin rickeys—'shaw' bein' the Chinee word fer 'wagon.'"

"So they turned this Kid Whang Ho loose, eh?"

"Well, he's out on bail. When his lawyers found out about the jedge havin' that money up on the fight, they appealed the case to the Supreme Court of Chiny."

"But what I can't figger," said Cush, "is why them Chinee boxers should uprise? An' if they did, what would all them other Gov'mints give a damn if they uprose, er not? It don't look like there'd be enough of 'em to cut no figger, one way er another."

"That's because you don't know yer Chiny," replied Black John. "Take a big country like that, where there ain't only two businesses a common man kin go into, an' a hell of a lot of 'em's bound to drift into boxin'—"

"But," interrupted Cush, "why would there only be two businesses?"

"It's your turn to buy a drink," reminded Black John, "an' while yer pourin' it, jest try an' think if you ever know'd a Chinaman to run anythin' but a laundry er a restaurant?"

"N-o-o, I can't say as I have."

"**SHORE YOU** ain't. An' that's because them two's the only businesses there is in Chiny, so it's the only kind they learnt to run. Course, there's a few of the high-toned ones—mandolins, they call 'em—that exports tea an' silk, but all the rest runs laundries an' restaurants, er depends on boxin' fer a livin'."

"But why should them other countries horn in on it?" persisted Cush. "It looks like they would have troubles of their own, instead of nosin' in on somethin' that happened in Chiny."

"Oh, Gover'ments likes to mess around in one another's business, that-a-way. It gives 'em a chanct to start a war. What happened over there is that the Chinee Supreme Court handed down a adverse decision in the case of Kid Whang Ho vs Battlin' Ker Chow."

"What's that?" asked Cush sourly.

"Why, they reversed the lower court, an' give the fight to Battlin' Ker Chow, on a foul. Immejitly, every damn boxer in Chiny uprose, claimin' that the Gover'ment was interferin' with their onalien rights, inasmuch as there ain't no specific statute agin' braidin' lead pipes in queues. The other Gover'ments got draw'd into the brawl on account that their diplomats all had money bet on the fight. Every last one of them consuls, an' military attachers, an' ministers, had put up real money, one way er another—"

"I didn't know a minister would bet on a prize fight," said Cush.

"These is a different kind of a minister. They ain't preachers, an' they'll bet on anythin'—an' then git their country to go to war about it, if they lose. There wouldn't be practically no wars at all, if they kep' them diplomats to home. The Gover'ments couldn't git together on no issue to fight about."

"Here comes One Armed John," said Cush, setting out another glass. "I wonder if he's found him another corpse?"

"I hope so—things is gittin' kind of dull around here."

"Yeah," agreed Cush with a dour frown, "but them ain't the times he picks to find corpses. It's always either when we're busy with somethin' else, er it's rainin', er snowin', er the mosquitoes is so bad it takes all the satisfaction out of investigatin' 'em."

ONE ARMED JOHN crossed to the bar and filled the empty glass. "There's three new fellas on the crick," he announced. "They're down in Olson's old shack."

"What they doin' down there?" asked Black John.

"They moved in. I was tryin' to snag me a mess of fish out of that deep hole there, an' they come around the bend in a canoe, an' landed on the gravel bar when they seen me. One done all the talkin'. He wants to know if this is Halfaday Crick. I tells him yes, an' then he asks if that there cabin's empty. I says it is, barrin' a table, an' a couple of bunks, an' a bench er two. He wants to know who owns it, an' I tells him a hung man does. I tells him about us hangin' Olson, an' about Stamm gittin' shot by his woman in there, an' how we figger the cabin's onlucky. He claims that's all the better, 'cause they don't like company, an' I tells him the fort's six mile up the crick, an' he says to hell with the fort, they'll find it if they want it. An' then he goes back to the others, an' they draw'd the canoe up in the bresh, an' begun packin' their stuff to the cabin."

"Went back to the others?" asked Black John. "Wasn't they all right there together?"

"No, they landed on the bar when they seen me, an' this one come over to where I was at, an' he talked kind of low, like he didn't want the rest to hear."

"H-u-m-m, what fer lookin' was they?"

"Well—two of 'em looked about like anyone else, but the other one—him that set in the middle an' didn't do no paddlin'—he was dressed up in store clo's, like a gambler, er a preacher, er someone like that."

"Have any luck fishin'?"

"No, the fish must all be up the crick. I didn't have no luck in them lower bends. I'm goin' on up an' try it there."

"Fetch me a mess," ordered Black John. "I'm gittin' tired of moose meat, an' I ain't got no time to go fishin'."

WHEN THE man had gone, the two refilled their glasses, and Old Cush made the proper entry in his day book. "What would a man in store clo's be doin' on Halfaday?" he asked.

"The matter," replied Black John, "gives food fer thought. Admittin' that most men that comes to Halfaday is fleein' from the law, we'll assume that these three is. It's a common thing fer one man to show up here claimin' his name is John Smith, an' there's been instances of two Smith brothers showin' up together. But fer three mismated ones to show up simultaneous is unprecedented."

"What's that mean?" growled Cush. "Why'n hell can't you talk so somebody would understand you?"

"It would be a joy," sighed Black John, "to converse with someone which his vocabulary consisted of more than three dozen short words."

"Short words means somethin'," retorted Cush, "an' they're quicker to say. What about them three?"

"Two might be a partnership—but three's a gang. An' we don't want no gangs on Halfaday."

"I'll say we don't!" agreed Cush. "The last gang that showed up was when they tried to rob the safe—that time we was about to hang 'em all, an' Downey made us quit. But, why would one of 'em have store clo's? An' why would they say to hell with the fort, an' not want no company? They must of know'd that most of the boys here is outlawed, er they wouldn't of come."

"If a man dresses different from the run of folks, it's a safe bet he is different. If one of a gang was different from the others, we might assume that he was the leader. But from what One Armed told us, sech don't seem to be the case—er he'd done the talkin'. You rec'lect the old sayin' 'Birds of a feather ketches the worm.' It might be that the man in the store clo's is the worm."

"What the hell you talkin' about?" snapped Cush. "Anyone would think you was crazy."

"I fergot," retorted Black John, "that reference to the classics would be practically lost on you. But mebbe you kin grasp this p'int—if them birds don't show up before supper, I'll slip down an' investigate."

II

LATE THAT EVENING, as the long twilight slipped into darkness, Black John lay in the edge of the brush that rimmed the little clearing and watched a light flicker, and then glow steadily through the window of Olson's old cabin. The door opened, and a man showed momentarily in the yellow rectangle as he emptied a pan of dishwater. Then it closed again and, slipping silently across the clearing, Black John glued his eye to a lower corner of a window. The man hung up the tin washdish that had served also as a dishpan, and turned to the two others who were seated on a rude bench beside the table. He spoke, and Black John realized with a muttered curse, that the thick log walls and air-tight windows precluded any thought of his overhearing the conversation.

It was as One Armed John had said—two of the men were dressed in flannel shirts, open at the throat, with overalls thrust into the tops of leather pacs. The third wore a brown business suit, and a blue cloth shirt, minus the collar, which had probably been discarded after becoming soiled.

The man who had spoken turned to one of the bunks, rummaged for a moment in a duffel bag, and tossed a pencil and a pad of cheap paper onto the table before the one in the store clothing, who seemed to be protesting. The third one joined in the argument. Evidently they were trying to persuade Brown Suit to write. As he turned slightly Black John saw that he was probably in his early forties, smooth-shaven, save for a week's stubble of beard, and that he seemed defiant, rather than intimidated by the threatening attitude of the others.

The argument continued for some ten minutes before the man reached for the pencil and paper and wrote, while the standing one dictated. When he had finished, the two read the document, and another argument ensued. Evidently the note was not quite to their liking, but the man refused to change it, winding up by pounding the table with his fist to emphasize his defiance.

Black John grinned. "Got plenty of guts, fer the fix he's in," he muttered to himself. "Wonder what they'll do next?"

He was not left long in doubt. Abandoning the argument, one of the two tore the sheet from the pad, pocketed it, and motioning with a jerk of his head, stepped to the door, closely followed by the other.

Instantly Black John flattened himself into the thick weeds at the base of the cabin wall, as his right hand flew to the front of his shirt and grasped the butt of a six-gun. The door opened and closed, and a voice sounded from around the corner of the cabin, not ten feet from where he lay.

"What I claim, we ought to make him put that in—beggin' the company to pay over the money. All he says is that we've got him, he's well, but we're threatenin' to knock him off if it ain't paid."

"Listen—you can't *make* a guy like him do nothin'—without you kill him, an' we don't want to do that—yet. What he's wrote is enough, along with what I told 'em in that letter of mine. They'll pay, all right. Hell—didn't we both hear that guy in the Tivoli that night say how this bird was worth a million to the company? That's what put it in our head to grab him off. They ain't goin' to balk at payin' fifty thousan' to git him back, you kin bet yer life on that. Not when they read my letter, they ain't— where I told 'em how we'd knock him on the head an' sink him in the river if we don't git it.

"You take them two letters down an' slip 'em under the office door, like I told you, an' they'll git 'em next mornin' when they open up, an' that evenin' they'll have that fifty thousan' where I told 'em—an' don't you fergit it."

"But—s'pose they don't do like you said, an' should call the police in? I'd be in a hell of a fix, then—wouldn't I?"

"They won't. I put that acrost to 'em in the letter. You read it—where I told 'em if they let the police in, they'd never see this bird agin. I told 'em how it wouldn't do 'em no good, because the guy that would pick up this package wouldn't know nothin' about where this Chase was hid, nor who had him. He was jest a go-between that couldn't tell 'em nothin'. An' I told 'em that if they done like I said, he'd be back in Dawson inside of a week."

"YEAH, IT sounds easy. If everythin' works out like you say it'll be okay, an' twenty-five thousan' apiece for a month's work. But how the hell are we goin' to git him back to Dawson? If we turn him loose on Halfaday, he'll go up to Cushing's Fort an' tell 'em what come off, an' then we'll be in a hell of a fix. You know what they claim about this here Black John Smith—he don't stand for crime of any kind on the crick. I'd rather the law caught us than him. He'd hang us shore as hell—an' the law would only jail us. We've got to hit for the outside after this job or this guy might spot us sometime. Black John might catch up to us before we could make it. They claim he's hell on the trail—an' hell on wheels when it comes to hangin' folks."

"Choke off!" growled the other. "I don't aim to run foul of this here Black John, or the law either. When you get that dough, you hustle back here an' we'll knock this guy on the head an' sink him in that deep hole where that one armed gent was fishin'. Then we'll be outside 'fore anyone starts huntin' him. They'll be waitin' in Dawson for him to show up."

"Good God!" exclaimed the other. "You don't mean murder him? Double-cross him after we've got the money?"

"The hell I don't! We've got ourselves to look out for—not him! If we knock him off, we're safe. If we don't, we never will be safe. A guy like him don't forget."

"I—I hadn't thought of that," said the other.

"There's a hell of a lot of things that I can think of that you can't. You play along with me, an' you'll be safe. Get to bed now. You'll be hittin' for Dawson at daylight. You ought to be back in two weeks."

THE DOOR opened and closed as the two reentered the cabin, and Black John got to his feet, slipped from the clearing, and struck out through the darkness on the familiar foot-trail to Cushing's Fort.

As he entered the saloon about midnight Old Cush set out a bottle and glasses. A stud game was in progress at a table across the room, but there was nobody at the bar as Black John took his accustomed place and filled his glass.

"What did you find out?" asked Cush, pouring his own drink.

"Well, it's jest like I was tellin' you, Cush—about the birds of a feather ketchin' the worm."

"Still quotin' them scriptures, eh? It looks like after a man got to your age he'd have some sense."

"There's a lot of common sense in them old sayin's—if a man ponders 'em," answered Black John. "I rec'lect another one that says how it's a long worm that's got no turnin'. Drink up, an' I'll buy one."

"Which that's the first sensible word you've spoke sence you come in," observed Cush, as he entered the drinks against Black John's tab, and refilled his glass. "An' now when you git that one throw'd into you, mebbe you'll tell me what you found out about them three fellas that One Armed was tellin' us about?"

"Oh—them fellas. Hell, they're nice enough boys—from what I seen of 'em. They'll mind their own business, an' not bother no one. Me, I'm goin' off on a little prospectin' trip. Be gone mebbe a couple of weeks—mebbe even a month."

"Prospectin' trip. Did you hear tell of a new strike er somethin'?"

"No. Jest playin' a hunch. There might not be nothin' to it."

III

EARLY THE FOLLOWING morning Black John struck out through the hills on a trail that took him to Ladue Creek. Obtaining a canoe from an Indian, he headed down the creek, well knowing that he would thus arrive in Dawson a full day ahead of the kidnapper.

After a few drinks in the Tivoli with the sourdoughs, he strolled over to the headquarters of the Northwest Mounted Police to be cordially greeted by Corporal Downey.

"Hello, John. How's things on Halfaday?"

"Everythin's fine as frog hair—far as I know. It was a little dull on the crick, so I come down fer a game of stud with the boys, an' to git a newspaper fer Old Cush, so he kin keep up with the war. A newspaper lasts him a couple of weeks. He reads every damn thing that's printed in 'em—even the advertisements. It gives him somethin' to chaw about fer the next month. How's things in the ranks of the sinful? They keepin' you busy?"

"It's been pretty quiet along the river, till a couple of weeks ago. Then the general manager of Consolidated Mines Ltd. disappeared an' we've been huntin' all over hell fer him, ever since."

"Disappeared, eh? Took about half the assets of the company along with him, I s'pose?"

"Hell no! Not that kind of a disappearance, at all. He just disappeared—dropped out of sight—vanished. It's a case of now you see him; an' now you don't see him. He disappeared right here in Dawson."

"Prob'ly got drunk an' fell in the river," hazarded Black John.

"Not a chance. He wasn't a boozefighter. He's a high grade man in every way, an' a damn fine fellow, to boot. He'd take a drink, now an' then—but that's all. His wife is damn near crazy."

"A lot of wimmin is," observed Black John. "That's mebbe why he skipped out."

"No, no! I mean, she's damn near crazy worryin' about his disappearance. She was all right before that. I sure hope we can locate him—more fer her sake, than the Consolidated's. A company can always find a new manager."

"Yeah, an' a widder kin always find a new husband, too," grinned Black John. "Remember that old sayin'—there's a sucker born every minute."

"You don't care much for the ladies, do you, John?" remarked Corporal Downey.

"Not them, nor the leprosy, neither. Even one of 'em on a crick kin raise more hell than an ice jam. So you don't figger this fella skipped out, eh?"

"What reason would he have? The Consolidated was payin' him a big salary. He was happily married to a mighty fine woman. He had plenty of friends. Why should a man like that disappear voluntarily?"

"Not only why should he? But how could he? Who seen him last? An' where?"

HE AN' Blair, the president of the Consolidated, an' some of their foremen held some kind of a meetin' in the company office that lasted till about midnight, an' when it busted up, they all stopped in the Tivoli fer a couple of drinks. Chase, that's this manager's name, he only took one drink, an' then he started fer home, leavin' the others at the bar. An' that's the last anyone ever seen of him. The next mornin' they reported the disappearance to us, an' believe me, we've been busy ever since. So far, we haven't got a damn thing to show fer it."

"What did this here labor of yours consist of?" asked Black John. "Do you figger he was murdered?"

"We did, at first. We couldn't find any motive, though. Chase didn't have any money on him, to speak of. We can't find that he had an enemy in the world. The foreman did all the hirin' an' firin', so it don't stand to reason it was a personal grudge. Considerin' all them facts, we switched over to a kidnappin' theory. But now it begins to look like a murder agin."

"Why?"

"Well, the Consolidated furnished us all the men we wanted, an' we've scoured every place a man could be hidden within fifty miles of Dawson, or so we think. Besides that, we've searched every buildin' in camp, regardless of who owns it er what it's used fer. The same goes fer Forty Mile, an' we even searched every tepee an' shack in Moosehide. It's two weeks since he disappeared, an' if he'd be'n kidnapped it looks like whoever done it would have got in touch with someone before this, to try an' collect a reward fer turnin' him loose. I'm afraid someone knocked him on the head an' throwed him in the river."

"What was his gamblin' status? Did he owe someone more'n he could pay? Er did someone owe him more'n they could?"

"He didn't gamble."

BLACK JOHN shook his head. "It don't sound reasonable anyone would knock off someone as prominent as him, without no motive, when it's a cinch there'd be a big stink raised about it. Course, if you could go clean on back through his past you might find motives enough fer half a dozen murders, an' the chances is they'd all be wimmin—him not favorin' neither whiskey nor cards. But disregardin' that an' gittin' back to kidnappin', why would they pick out a man workin' on a salary, when it's a well know'd fact that there's at least a dozen men in Dawson that rates better'n a million in dust? Besides, there's Blair, the president of the Consolidated. Why wouldn't they grab him instead of jest the manager?"

Downey grinned. "If this is a kidnappin', whoever done it knows that Chase is worth a damn sight more to the company than Blair is. Blair's a capitalist—Chase is an engineer. Blair draws down his share of the dividends that Chase makes the property earn for him an' the rest of the stockholders. They'd pay to get Chase back—an' accordin' to Blair, they stand ready to pay plenty—an' no questions asked. The company needs him, an' needs him bad.

"As fer the kidnappers grabbin' off any of the sourdoughs that have got a million in dust—who'd pay to git 'em back? They none of 'em have families. An' no company needs 'em. The other sourdoughs might—but the kidnappers would never get away with it. Them sourdoughs would be too damn tough to handle."

Black John rose from his chair and knocked the dottle from his pipe. "Guess I'll drop over to the Tivoli an' horn into a stud game. Yer reasonin' seems sound about this here bein' a kidnappin'. Leastwise, it's sounder'n to figger it fer a murder. As fer not hearin' from the kidnappers, I wouldn't worry about that, yet. They'd be damn fools to try to git in touch with the company when you've got the hills full of men huntin' 'em."

"The men have been out of the hills fer five er six days. We saw it wasn't gettin' us nowhere."

"Someone'll prob'ly be hearin' from 'em, when the stink dies down," opined Black John. "So long. I'm runnin' behind with my stud."

IV

ON THE SECOND morning thereafter, Black John again appeared in the doorway of Corporal Downey's office.

" 'Aw revaw,' as the Frenchies say. I'm on my way fer Halfaday! By God—there's a rhyme! Sometime, when I git drunk enough, I'll make me up a song, an' start it out like that."

"I'd give a dollar not to hear it," grinned Downey sourly.

"An' you'd be gittin' off cheap, at that," chuckled Black John. "Stud is more in my line. You'd ort to seen me take 'em, las' night! They kind of got me, the night before—but I more'n evened up on 'em. I took one pot off'n Old Bettles that he never will quit mournin' about. This pot had got pretty big, what with three, four of 'em raisin', an' me jest trailin' along. Bettles, he winds up with a pair of kings, an' an ace, an' a deuce showin'. I'm settin' behind a jack, an' a ten spot, an' a pair of deuces, the second one of which was the last card I ketched. Someone outs with a bet, an' Bettles h'ists, an' I h'ists him. The others drops out an' he h'ists me back, havin' him an ace in the hole to make two pair. His deuce bein' the first card he'd ketched, was exposed all the time, an' he didn't figger I'd be damn fool enough to stand them raises with a deuce in the hole. When the smoke blow'd away you'd ort to heard him cuss! It would done yer soul good! Next time you see him, jest ask him what aces up is worth in a stud game?

"What the hell you so glum about? Someone hand you a wooden nickel?"

"I'll say they did!" replied Downey. "The Consolidated heard from them kidnappers."

"Well cripes, now you got somethin' to work on!"

"That's the way I wish it was—but it ain't."

"Didn't they leave no note, nor nothin'?"

"Yeah, they left two of 'em. One from them, statin' their terms, an' givin' instructions about turnin' over the money, an' another from Chase, tellin' about him bein' all right, so fer, but he would git bumped off if the money wasn't paid. They agreed to deliver him inside a week."

"Well—that's fair enough, ain't it? All you got to do is to put a good man on the job, an' foller that money."

"Yeah—an' that's jest what we can't do," growled Downey. "Yesterday mornin', when they opened up the Consolidated office, they found them two notes on the floor, where they'd be'n shoved under the door. The kidnappers demanded fifty thousan' in old bills, er gold. It had to be delivered by one man in a canoe, er a row boat, an' left on the end of that rocky point, about a mile downriver, on the other side. The man was to make the delivery between nine an' ten in the evenin', an' he wasn't to try an' see no one, but must lay the package down, step into the boat, an' come back acrost the river.

"The note said that if the police was notified er anyone tried to follow the money in any way, it would be the last anyone would ever see of Chase. They claimed that the man that would pick up the money didn't know anything about where Chase was bein' held, er who had him—so it wouldn't do us no good, even if we followed him.

"When Blair showed Mrs. Chase the notes, they talked it over an' decided to pay the money, an' follow instructions to the letter without lettin' the police know anything about it. But Mrs. Chase knew we were workin' on the case, an' she was afraid we might pick up this bird with the money an' spill the beans, so she an' Blair come over here an' begs me to lay off the case till Chase gets back.

"I can see her angle, all right—but it puts me in a hell of a spot. With the Inspector away, an' no way to reach him, how do I know he won't call it connivin' in a crime er somethin' an' bust me? If it had been only Blair, I might of held out fer tryin' to nab 'em, but the woman was so sure that anything we'd do would cause 'em to murder Chase, that I give in, an' called the boys off. An' I ain't so sure she ain't right, at that.

"The note said he'd be returned within a week, but they begged fer three extry days, in case of a hitch of some kind, so I promised that the police would lay off till Chase returned, providin' he done so within ten days. I hate to give them damn crooks a break like that. But I'd hate to be bull headed about it, an' cause 'em to murder Chase, too."

"Yeah, it does kind of put you on the spot," agreed Black John. "I s'pose, then, they went ahead an' delivered the money?"

"Yes. They followed instructions to the letter. A Consolidated man took the package over an' left it on that point last evenin'. He was back here a little after ten."

"Did he see the fella that was to git it?"

"He didn't see anyone—no boat, no canoe, nothin'. He jest left the package on the end of the point, an' come on back acrost the river."

BLACK JOHN was silent for a moment. "Course," he said, "the main thing is to git this here Chase back. Fifty thousan' ain't nothin' to a big company like the Consolidated. I don't grieve none over their loss. They're takin' a hell of a lot out of this country. What they spend here in the way of wages an' supplies, ain't a drop in the bucket to what they take out. An' when they skin every crick right down to bed rock, they'll go hunt some other country to rape. If them crooks is smart enough to sting 'em fer fifty thousan', it's all right with me. But Chase is somethin' else agin. Now that the money's been paid, he's got a right to be turned loose. I'll keep my eyes open, an' if I run onto him—like if they had him hid on Halfaday er somethin', I'll see that he gits back safe."

"Do you suspect that he's on Halfaday?" asked Downey, eyeing the other sharply.

"I don't suspect nothin'. If he's there, I'll see that he gits back—that's all. What fer lookin' fella is he, in case I'd run onto him?"

Reaching into a drawer, Downey withdrew a photograph and tossed it onto the desk. "There's his picture. He stands five foot eight, weighs around a hundred an' sixty—blue eyes, brown hair. If you could run onto 'em an' hold those crooks for me it would be great!"

Black John laughed. "Nothin' doin'. I ain't in the crook holdin' business. Fer all of me, someone could slip up an' steal that two million dollar dredge off the company some night, an' I'd never shed a damn tear. I got Halfaday to look out fer. These Yukon River sins lay easy on my conscience."

"I don't believe they're on Halfaday," said Downey. "In the first place, if they are, they couldn't possibly return Chase to Dawson within a week. It would take at least two weeks. Then if they had him upriver, why would they want the money delivered a mile or more downriver? Besides, it's pretty well known, down here, that you don't stand for any crime on Halfaday, an' that you're pretty rough with anyone that tries to pull somethin' off. They'd be afraid up there you might consider holdin' a man fer ransom, a crime, an' hang 'em."

"Such fear would be groundless," grinned Black John. "The crime, as I see it, is in the snatchin', an' not in the holdin'. It's clearly your case, Downey. The man was grabbed off in Dawson." He stood up and retrieved his sack from the floor. "Well, so long. I've got to be gittin' back so Cush kin find out how this here Chinee war is comin'."

V

PROCEEDING TO THE river, Black John swung his pack into the canoe, stowing his rifle, and a pair of binoculars conveniently to hand, and pushed off.

"Situated the way I be," he mused, half aloud, as he paddled steadily upstream, keeping close to the bank to take advantage of slack water and eddies, "a man is kind of put to it to know what's right. Them two fellas grabbin' off Chase like that, fer to horn fifty thousan' out of a big company like the Consolidated savors of bad ethics, an' even viewed liberally, should be at least, a tort. But they've got a livin' to make, an' a man's got to think of that, too.

"The man that come down to git the money mightn't be a bad sort of a guy, but the other one—the one that figgers on double-crossin' 'em, an' knockin' Chase on the head, an' sinkin' him in the crick—he's reprehensible to a hangin' extent. On Halfaday, it's our dooty to deal stern with buzzards like him. An' yet, he ain't committed no murder till he kills Chase, an' it don't seem right to let him go ahead an' kill him, jest so we could hang him fer it. But on the other hand, there ain't no reasonable doubt that he ort to be hung. It puts me in a kind of a condiment to know jest

124

what to do. Lookin' at it from a strickly moral angle, as a preacher would say, neither one of them two should be allowed to make a profit out of a crime like kidnappin'. Nothin' discourages crime like takin' the profit out of it—an' that's the theory I'm goin' on."

Settling to the work, he bent his paddle, pausing from time to time to scan the river ahead for sight of another canoe. It was well toward evening when he picked it up, hugging the opposite shore, possibly a mile in advance. When twilight deepened into dusk, he crossed the river and camped. "Dastn't crowd him too clost on the big river," he muttered, "he might see me. After we hit the White an' Halfaday, where the bends is closter together, I kin shorten up on him. I've got to git there before they knock Chase off."

ALL THE next day and the day following, Black John paddled on, content to keep the man within range of his glass. At noon of the third day, as the preceding canoe reached the mouth of the White River, he focused the glass, and his jaw dropped in astonishment. For, instead of heading up the White, the man ahead swung nearly to the middle of the Yukon to avoid the outrushing current of the White, and, paddling furiously, he slanted again toward shore above the mouth of the smaller river.

The gape of astonishment gave place to a broad grin as Black John returned his glass to its case. "I'll be damned if he ain't goin' right on up the Yukon!" he exclaimed under his breath. "Yes, sir—double-crossin' his pardner, an' hittin' fer the outside with that fifty thousan'. By Cripes, if it ain't almost enough to make a man lose faith in human nature to see how folks carries on! Sech acts puts him in the same cattygory with the other one—they're both of 'em damn crooks! It's shore time someone stepped in an' taught 'em both a lesson in common rectitude."

Familiarity with the river allowed Black John to navigate the cross current at the mouth of the White without swinging wide and thus possibly exposing himself to the other's view. An hour later he watched through his glass as the man beached his canoe well above the mouth of the White, and when a thin plume of smoke told that he was preparing his midday meal, Black John paddled to within a hundred yards of the beached canoe, landed, and crept noiselessly through the scrub bushes, loosening a couple of buttons in the front of his shirt, as he went.

PICKING UP his teapot, the man left his fire and walked to the water's edge. When he returned a moment later, the pot of water dropped from his hand and rolled among the rocks, as he stared wide-eyed into the keen gray eyes of the huge figure that stood beside the fire.

"I'm Black John Smith," announced the figure, "from Halfaday Crick."

"Oh—er—sure—I—I've heard you spoke of," the man paused awkwardly as his glance flashed to the pack that lay near the fire. "Have you—a—et?" he asked hurriedly. "I was jest goin' to cook me up a boilin' of tea. I—I kind of spilt my water, I guess."

"It looks like a good guess," observed Black John.

"I didn't expect to—to see anyone. It kind of give me a start. I'll get some more."

"There ain't no hurry," replied Black John easily. "Where you headin'?"

"Who—me? Why—I'm headin'—that is, I'm goin' outside. I'm sick of the damn country."

"Outside, eh? That's funny. The way yer pardner talked, he was kind of expectin' you back on Halfaday."

The blood receded slowly from the man's face, leaving it pasty white. "My—my pardner," he gasped. "Halfaday! There must be some mistake. I ain't got no pardner—an' I never seen Halfaday."

"You lie natural; but not at all convincin'," replied Black John. "An' yer skippin' out with that fifty thousan' that the Consolidated paid over constitutes the crime of skullduggery, which you'll find out is hangable, when you git back to the crick."

"Good God!" cried the man, his eyes staring in terror. "I've heard how you hang men on Halfaday. I told that damn fool we better keep away from there!"

"Yer judgment was sound."

"But you wouldn't hang me fer—fer double-crossin' him, would you? Listen! I'll tell you why I was runnin' out on him—an' it's the God's truth! He figgered on knockin' Chase on the head jest as quick as I got back with the money! He never intended to turn him loose! I wouldn't be in on no murder—so I beat it!"

"Jest fleein' from temptation, eh? Well, you'll be give the chanct to put that in as a mitigatin' circumstance at the hangin'. Mebbe the boys'll believe it. You can't never tell. It would be more convincin', though, if you wasn't packin' that fifty thousan' along with you. To a casual observer the transaction savors of theft. Throw yer stuff in yer canoe. We'll cache mine. Me an' you's headin' fer Halfaday."

THE MAN'S whole body was trembling, and his words came jerkily between lips stiff with terror, "Oh, my God! Don't take me up there an' hang me! I ain't done nothin' to git hung fer!"

"Yer guilty of the crime of extortion by means of kidnappin', of the larceny of fifty thousan' dollars, of double-crossin' yer pardner, to say nothin' of such minor infringements as lyin', an' not brushin' yer teeth. We've hung dozens of men fer less."

"Listen," cried the man suddenly. "Take half of this fifty thousan'—an' fergit you ever seen me!"

"You mean—accept a bribe? Me—Black John Smith! Yer offerin' to bribe *me* to save yer own dirty neck from gittin' stretched?" Black John's voice rose to a bellow, as the thoroughly terrified man shrank back from the glare of the outraged gray eyes. "By God, yer pilin' sin upon sin till it's doubtful if one rope'll hold 'em all! Besides which, yer tryin' to make me a party to the crime of kidnappin'!"

"I didn't mean to bribe you—honest, I didn't! Take it all. Take every lousy dollar of it. Give it to the pore; give it back to the company, do whatever you want to with it—"

"That's more like it," said Black John, combing at his beard with his fingers. "It shows that possibly there's a glimmerin' of rectitude left yet in under that sin-blistered hide."

"I know I done *wrong*," cried the man, "an' I want to square it! Don't hang me, let me go. Let me git out of this damn country, which I wisht to God I'd never saw in the first place. I got a wife an' three children back home, an' there ain't no one but me to look after 'em!"

There was a softening of Black John's gray eyes. "A wife an' children, eh? An' no one to look after 'em. That puts an entirely different light on the matter. The chances is, they might miss you if we was to hang you. A man hadn't ort to let nothin' interfere with dooty—but I'm sentimental that-a-way. If I was to forego this hangin', would you promise to leave the country?"

"Sure, I'll leave it. I never want to see it agin. Here's the money—take it, an' leave me go! It's all in there—count it."

FUMBLING IN his pack, the man produced a thick package wrapped in heavy brown paper, and tossed it to Black John, who deliberately removed the wrapping and counted the bills.

"It's all here," he announced, pointing to it as he was about to rewrap it. "Look at it. Don't it make you ashamed of yerself, when you think, what you've stooped to, jest fer a bunch of dirty pieces of paper? It ort to, if it don't! Let this be a lesson to you the next time yer tempted. Remember this, my good man—honesty is the best policy. If a man heeds them old sayin's, he won't go fer wrong. Throw yer stuff in yer canoe now—an' git a-goin' before that there sentiment of mine peters out."

The man complied with alacrity, and as he shoved off and headed upriver, Black John waved to him from the bank.

"So long, an' good luck! Give my regards to yer wife an' them three children. An' treat 'em good, from now on—remember, they saved yer life!"

VI

FIVE DAYS LATER Black John drew his canoe into the brush at the big bend, just below Olson's old cabin. Cutting a slender sapling, he drew a fish line from his pocket, tied it to the end of the pole, dabbled the line in the water till it was wet, and wrapping it carelessly about the pole, sauntered into the Olson clearing, his improvised fishing outfit in his hand.

At a glance from a man seated on a chopping block, another, who had been seated in the doorway, arose and disappeared into the cabin, leaving the door open behind him.

"Fishin'?" asked the man perfunctorily, without rising from the block.

"Yeah, I thought a mess of fish would go good, when I git home. I live up the crick a piece, near the tradin' post. Been down to Dawson. By the way, I see yer pardner's quittin' you. Have a row er somethin'?"

"My pardner? What do you mean—pardner?"

"Why, that other fella that was with you that day you hit Halfaday an' was askin' One Armed John about this here cabin. Me an' One Armed was fishin' down here that day, an' I was a couple of bends down when you passed. I drawed back behind some bresh where you wouldn't see me when you went by. There was three of you—you, an' this other guy, an' another one with a suit of brown store clo's on, settin' in the middle. I jest seen Brown Suit step into the cabin. It was the other guy I seen down on the river. He claimed he was hittin' fer the outside, so I—"

"The outside!" yelled the man, leaping to his feet, and glaring into Black John's face. "Where'd you see him? What did he say? What do you mean—the outside?"

Black John frowned. "There ain't no call to git excited about it, fer as I kin see. All I said was that this here fella is hittin' fer the outside. Anyways, that's what he claimed. He seemed kind of nervous like—as though he was in a hurry. He didn't know me no more than you did. He'd camped there at the mouth of the White to cook him up a b'ilin' of tea, an' I was paddlin' up from Dawson, an' it bein' about noon, I landed. We kind of got to talkin', an' he said he was hittin' fer the outside. He thought I was jest some prospector from along the river. When I told him I was headin' fer Halfaday, was when he got in such a sweat. He told me not to tell no one that I seen him—nor where he was goin'. How could I tell 'em, when I don't even know his name? Course, you an' him bein' pardners, that's different—I thought you'd like to know. He pulled out 'fore I did, an' the last I seen of him, he was paddlin' like hell up the Yukon."

CURSING LIKE a maniac, the man leaped for the cabin. Following him, Black John paused in the doorway, and watched in well feigned surprise as he threw grub and blankets into his pack, while the man in the brown suit sat on the edge of a bunk and watched the proceeding with interest.

"What the hell ails you?" asked Black John, as the man dashed past him, pack sack in one hand, rifle in the other, and headed for the canoe that lay bottom upward on the bank of the creek.

"I'll catch that double-crossin' skunk! An' I'll fill him so full of holes he'll look like a second hand punch board! Damn him! I'll follow him clean around the world, an' I won't give him a chance to open his yap when I catch him, either!"

"It's ondoubtless somethin' important," grinned Black John, as the man shoved off. "Don't tell him I mentioned seein' him. But you'll have to hurry. It was five days ago I seen him, an' like I said—he seemed in a hell of a hurry."

As the canoe shot around a bend and disappeared from view, Black John turned to find the man in the brown suit at his side.

"Well!" he exclaimed, "damn if I hadn't fergot all about you!
It kind of looks like he had, too. What's the matter with him?
Gone crazy er somethin'?"

"Crazy man," grinned the man. "The fact is, this other fellow
is making off with fifty thousand dollars that should have been
divided between them."

"Tch, tch, tch—well, what do you know about that! You mean,
he's *stealin'* this money? An' how about you? Ain't you in on it,
too? You was in pardners with 'em, wasn't you?"

THE MAN'S grin widened. "Well—hardly. You see, they
kidnapped me, and were holding me for a fifty thousand dollar
ransom. That other chap went to Dawson to collect it."

"Kidnapped, eh? Ransom? Say—it can't be that you're this
here Chase that Corporal Downey was tellin' me about—general
manager of the Consolidated, er somethin'?"

"I'm the man. So the police have been active in the matter,
eh?"

"No—an' that's the hell of it, accordin' to Downey. They was
fer a while. They hunted all over hell fer you, an' then the Consolidated got a couple of letters, which said how if the police tried
to foller the one who got the money, they'd knock you off, an' no
one ever would know what become of you. So between yer wife
an' Blair, they managed to hold the police off till you git back,
er at least fer ten days after payment of the money. So—you're
Chase, eh? Well—I'll be damned!"

"Yes, I'm Chase. And it's all owing to you that I'm safe and
sound. I didn't trust that fellow that stayed to guard me—not
for a minute. I don't believe he ever intended to turn me loose.
If the other had returned with the money, they'd have knocked
me on the head rather than leave me alive to identify them if
they were ever caught."

"He did look a mite ontrustworthy, at that," admitted Black
John. "An' the way things turned out, the other one proved

himself thoroughly so. It looks like you was in bad company all right. It's jest as well to be shet of 'em."

"How am I to reach Dawson?" asked the man. "Can't you take me there?" As Black John hesitated, the man continued: "I haven't the least idea where I am, but I know it's a long way from the number of days we traveled. They kept me blindfolded till we hit this small river. I hate to ask a man who's just made the trip to turn right around and make it again. But, I'll make it worth your while."

"It ain't that," replied Black John. "If I take you back it won't cost you a cent. Me an' Old Cush try an' keep Halfaday moral, an' it would be extremely onethical to charge a man money fer a simple favor of that kind."

"Halfaday! Is this Halfaday Creek? And by any chance, are you Black John Smith?"

"Well, it might be called chance," grinned the other. "I prefer to think it was design."

"I've heard of you, and the rather—er, drastic methods you sometimes employ in keeping the creek free from crime."

"Yeah, we don't want no crime on Halfaday. You see, Chase, it's like this—most of us up here are outlawed, fer one reason er another, an' we don't want the police snoopin' around. My own malfeasance was the h'istin' of an Army payroll off'n a major an' three common soldiers, over on the Alasky side. I was younger then, an' more thoughtless. I kin see now that it was a crude piece of work, at best—an' if you come right down to splittin' hairs, the ethics of it is open to question. But this major had throw'd his brag about never losin' no money of all the thousan's he'd handled till someone jest nach'lly had to take him—an' it might as well of be'n me.

"The reason I'm in this quandry about takin' you to Dawson, is that it might look to some folks as if I was in on the deal. There's nothin' on me, on the Yukon side, but rememberin' that Alasky job, there might be some folks that would think that I'd stoop so low as to share the profits of a venture of this kind—when, God knows—I wouldn't share 'em with any body!"

CHASE LAUGHED. "Don't let that bother you for a minute! No one could have the slightest suspicion that you had anything to do with it—except that you rescued me from clutches of the men that were holding me. I'll attend to that. I overheard every word that passed between you and the man who was guarding me—and I can vouch for the fact that you stumbled on this affair purely by accident."

"In such case, I'll go back with you. It would be a tough trip fer you to make alone, an'—"

"I'm in no shape to attempt it," interrupted the other. "I've been under a great mental and nervous strain, believing as I did, that these men intended to murder me."

"All right. Throw yer stuff together. It wasn't jest exactly by accident, I found you, at that. I promised Downey I'd keep my eyes open, an' see that you got back safe, if you was on Halfaday. I'll be back with the canoe in a few minutes. I'm goin' to cache part of my stuff—there ain't no use in haulin' nothin' around the country you don't need on the trip."

Chase was waiting on the bank when Black John returned. "Throwing my stuff together, as you suggested," he grinned, "consisted in finding my shoes and putting them on. You see, they didn't give me time to make any extensive preparations for the trip. After we got here they hid my shoes, knowing I suppose, that I couldn't go far in a rock country like this without 'em."

"Yeah, I wouldn't want to travel fer barefoot in this country. Climb in the front there—an' we'll git goin'."

VII

CORPORAL DOWNEY LOOKED up from his desk to stare inquiringly at the unkempt, stubble-bearded figure in the rumpled brown suit that paused, smiling, in the doorway of his office. Suddenly, he leaped from his chair and crossed the room at a bound.

"Chase!" he cried. "Good God, Mr. Chase—is it really you?"

"What's left of me," grinned the man, as from behind him came the booming voice of Black John:

"I told you I'd fetch him back if he was on Halfaday!"

"Come on in," said the officer, "an' tell me about it. The ten days' truce has expired, an' I've had men out huntin' you for two days." He seated himself at his desk, and indicated a couple of chairs.

"Let's get it over with as soon is possible," said Chase. "I want to go home and let my wife know I'm safe."

"You don't look safe," grinned Black John. "She'll shore have to take yer word fer it."

The man chuckled, and beginning with his seizure in Dawson, told briefly of the long canoe trip, of his confinement in the cabin on Halfaday, and of his rescue by Black John, who happened on the cabin while fishing.

"Fishin', eh?" asked Downey, his eyes on Black John's face. "Did you catch anything?"

"No. They wasn't bitin' good that day. I didn't git none. But I might of, if I hadn't of run onto them two at the cabin."

"Can I go now?" asked Chase. "You know where to find me if you should want any further information."

"Jest a minute," replied Downey, his eyes on Black John's guileless face. "I didn't quite get the straight of this. You say John told this kidnapper that he had talked to his pardner down at the mouth of the White, an' that the man had gone on upriver, sayin' he was goin' outside?"

"Yes, that's what infuriated the fellow. He cursed and raved like a maniac as he collected his effects for pursuit."

"All right, Mr. Chase, you kin go now. I may want to question you later," said Downey, and when the man had gone, he faced Black John. For several moments he sat, his eyes on the big man's face, as he slowly drew the smooth shaft of his penholder back and forth between his fingers.

"How did you know that man on the river was a pardner of the one you found later guardin' Chase at Olson's cabin?" he asked abruptly.

"Who—me? How did I know they was pardners? Hell, Downey, I didn't know it! That is, I never seen no pardnership papers, all draw'd up, signed, sealed and delivered, as a lawyer would say. I jest guessed it."

"How could you guess a thing like that?"

"Well—by puttin' three an' two together, you might say. I seen them three on Halfaday on my way down to Dawson, an' bein' kind of mismated—Chase, lookin' different than the other two—I kind of wondered who they was, an' what they was doin' there. Them two, lookin' about of a stripe, I nach'ly figgered they was pardners. It was the third man's status that bothered me."

DOWNEY FROWNED. "Then when I told you about the kidnappin', right here in this room, you knew damn well who he was—an' never said a word about it!"

Black John shook his head. "I didn't know no sech a damn thing," he replied. "Git out that picture you showed me, an' see if it looks anythin' like Chase does now. He's a good lookin' man. The one I seen at Olson's cabin looked like a bum. As a matter of fact, Downey—what you told me did set me wonderin' if it mightn't be him. That's why I stopped there goin' back, an' pretended to be fishin'. I wanted to git a good look at him. You know damn well I don't stand fer no crime on Halfaday—an' if one was bein' perpetrated I wanted to nip it in the bud, as a poet would say—an' I done so."

"You should have told me about those three men, an' we could have gone up there an' nailed them two kidnappers as easy as fallin' off a log—an' saved the Consolidated that fifty thousan'."

"That's ondoubtless true," admitted Black John, "but you know, Downey, I ain't a man that would be runnin' down here squealin' on folks. There's been times when you've come onto the crick that I've mebbe give you some help, when I deemed the occasion demanded it—an' there'll prob'ly be other sech times. But as fer me comin' down here to headquarters out of a clear sky an' deliberately squawkin' on someone—it's jest one of them things I don't do. I ain't no policeman. An' it don't seem to irk me a damn bit that the Consolidated lost that fifty thousan'."

"Where's that fifty thousan' now?" asked Downey abruptly.

"Your guess would be as good as mine," replied Black John suavely.

"I've got my damn good guess," said the corporal.

"You an' me—both," retorted Black John. "But I couldn't prove it."

A SLOW grin twitched the corners of Corporal Downey's mouth. "Yeah," he drawled dryly. "That's my fix, too. It's too bad you let that fellow git on upriver with that fifty thousan', John. You knew that it had been paid over to him."

"Shore I know'd it. That's why I hurried so to ketch up to him. If I had, mebbe the Consolidated would of got their money back. But I didn't. I never seen hide nor hair of him. I figgered he was ahead of me all the way up to Halfaday. Then, when I come out in the clearin' at Olson's shack an' seen he hadn't got back with the money, I know'd damn well he'd never turned up the White with it—he'd double-crossed his pardner, an' kep' right on upriver. Tryin' like I do, to keep Halfaday moral, I didn't want no sech a damn cuss on the crick as this kidnapper, so I done some quick thinkin', an' told him I'd saw his pardner, an' how he was hittin' fer the outside. I figgered he'd take out after him—an' he did. I figger when he ketches him, he'll shoot him—an' he will."

Corporal Downey's grin widened. "You do a hell of a lot of quick thinkin', don't you, John?"

"Shore I do. By God, a man's got to—to keep a crick moral! An' besides, it pays. I promised you that if Chase was on Halfaday, I'd fetch him back—an' I did. 'It's a wise ox, Downey, that kin become a father.' A man's got to heed them old sayin's—an' you know damn well I always work hand in glove with the police."

BLACK JOHN BUYS
SOME BONDS

I

OLD CUSH, PROPRIETOR of Cushing's Fort, the combined trading post and saloon that served the little community of outlawed men that had sprung up on Halfaday Creek, close against the Yukon-Alaska borderline, set out a bottle, a leather dice box, and two glasses as Black John Smith entered the door and advanced to the bar.

"There was a piece in the paper you fetched up from Dawson," he began, as the other picked up the dice box, "that says where some army officer, over there in the Phillipyne Islands, took a common soldier er two along with him, an' set out fer to capture this here Aguinaldo."

"I don't know nothin' about no Aguinaldo," replied Black John, casting the dice, "but there's three fives to beat in one."

"Yeah," assented Cush, returning the dice to the box and spreading them on the bar with a flourish, "an' there's three sixes that does it. Aguinaldo, he's the nigger General that's fightin' the U.S. over there in them islands. An' there's four deuces right back at you. See what yer law of averages says about that!"

Black John cast the dice, scowled at the pair of fours that showed, and filled his glass, as Cush made the proper notation in his book. "What," he asked, "would the U.S. Army be wantin' with a General of niggers?"

"Well—hell! If they ketched their General, they could take him down an' choke him, er somethin', till he ordered the niggers to quit fightin'. Then that would end the war."

"Why would the Army want to end a war? Cripes! If it wasn't fer wars, they wouldn't have no job."

"That's so," admitted Cush, "why would they? Maybe they figger they've got him about licked, er somethin', an' want to tip him off to start another one. But anyhow, it took a lot of guts fer this fella to go off in them jungles which is full of them head-huntin' niggers—an' white man's heads figgered as blue chips among 'em—an' try to pinch off their General. I feel kind of sorry fer him."

"Sorry hell!" exclaimed Black John. "What do you want to feel sorry fer him fer? He's doin' what he wants to, ain't he? There didn't no one tell him to go, did they? It was his own idee. You kin bet that his superior officers never sent him on no sech a fool trip. An' if a man's workin' on an idee, no matter what the odds is agin him, he's happy. If you want to feel sorry, why the hell don't you feel sorry for them common soldiers he took along with him? I'll bet they ain't happy—by a damn sight!"

"The papers says where they've been gone quite a while now—an' they ain't come back. I still claim it took a lot of guts."

"I ain't deridin' his guts, none," agreed Black John. "But if a man lets his guts run away with his brains—that ain't so good neither. Their heads is prob'ly stickin' up on poles somewheres, right now."

"ONE-ARMED JOHN was in a day or so back," said Cush, changing the subject, "an' he says how them three fellas that moved into Olson's old shack, down the crick, had went."

"Yeah," said Black John. "I looked in there when I come up from Dawson, an' I seen there wasn't no one there. It's prob'ly jest as well. I never figgered they was no ornament to the crick."

"By the way, John, did you do any good on yer prospectin' trip?"

"Oh—about so-so. I done a little better'n wages. Nothin' to brag of."

"Look who's comin' up from the landin'," exclaimed Cush. "Damn if it ain't Corporal Downey! Wonder what he's doin' on Halfaday? Mebbe he's up after them three we was jest talkin' about."

"Might be, at that," agreed Black John, as he turned to greet the young officer of the Northwest Mounted Police, who was entering the door.

"Hello, Downey! Me an' Cush was jest talkin' about you! Is it, mebbe, some criminal matter that brings you amongst us? Er is this jest a neighborly call? Belly up. Cush is buyin' a drink."

"It's a kinda of a hurry-up case," replied Downey, filling the glass that Old Cush placed before him. "There was a big express train robbery down in Alberta, an' they seem to think that the robbers might of hit north. The Inspector sent me up the White, with orders to go on up the Dalton Trail as far as the detachment, an' then swing in here an' report back to Dawson."

"You got a description of the robbers?" asked Black John.

"No, all we know is that there's two of 'em, an' they might be headed north." He paused and grinned. "Any two fellows I meet on the trail headed inside are apt to get their packs searched for concealed weapons; if I should accidentally stumble onto any bonds, of course, I'd gather 'em in."

"Bonds, eh? Was there an important amount of 'em?"

"Yeah—damned important. Half a million dollars worth. They think the robbers got the wrong pouch. There was a heavy shipment of currency on the train, too. But somehow, they overlooked it an' took the bonds. It was a special shipment, to cover a deal involvin' the merger of the West Coast an' the Alaska-Pacific Steamship lines. It come through from England."

"Well, it was insured, wasn't it?"

"Yes, it was insured, all right. But that ain't the half of it—if these bonds ain't located within ninety days, the merger deal is off, an' the London Syndicate that's interested will stand to lose a couple of millions in profits. Sir Henry Billson, their representative, is sure hell-bent to get them bonds back. It's important enough so we sent out special patrols."

"But no one could cash them bonds, even if they had 'em, could they? Hell—they're all numbered, er somethin', ain't they?"

"Sure they are, but the robbers might get away with it, at that. If they hit south an' crossed into the States, there's plenty of fences that handle hot bonds. They'd have to let go of 'em at a loss on their face value—but they could get rid of 'em, all right. It's the time element in this deal that makes Sir Henry so anxious to get 'em back. Of course, whoever showed up with one of 'em would be picked up for a suspected robber."

"Yeah," agreed Black John. "When was this here event pulled off?"

"Three weeks ago—jest long enough so they could be nosin' into the Yukon country, if they hurried."

"H-u-u-m, that would be about the time I was down to Dawson, wouldn't it?"

"Yup, jest about," agreed Downey. "Has anyone showed up on Halfaday? I sure wish you'd help me out on this case, John. Practically the whole force is huntin' 'm, an' believe me, I'd like to be the one that picked 'em up. Besides, they'd ort to be caught, anyhow. They killed the express messenger, an'—it's the rope fer 'em if they're caught,"

BLACK JOHN nodded. "You might's well go on back to Dawson," he said. "There ain't no new faces on Halfaday. I give you my word, Downey, that if them bonds shows up on the crick, you'll git 'em. You'll have to take your own chances on pickin' up the robbers, though. It would probably serve 'em right to git caught, at that. I don't believe in murderin' a man fer the purpose of robbery. It don't somehow seem right."

Corporal Downey smiled a tight-lipped smile. "I'm takin' you at your word, John," he said. "Without havin' any description of the robbers, I know damn well that if they're already on Halfaday, they've had time to cache the stuff, an' I'd never find it. I know that if the bonds showed up on the crick, you'll locate 'em, an' I believe you'll deliver 'em to me. I ain't forgot that there's been times when you've turned over big sums of cash to me, that you could jest as well kept for yourself—like the money from that Boston bank robbery, an' that dust Monty had hid in the shaft, behind them dead men, that time. But there's been other times when I've sort-of had my suspicions that—" Downey paused, and the grin widened.

"Well, cripes," interrupted Black John, his keen blue eyes twinkling above the heavy black beard, "you can't expect to git all the breaks, Downey! A horse apiece is fair play, as the Good Book says. The Mounted, bein' what it is, I hold that it's bad ethics to commit practically any crime at all on this side of the line. An' you've got to remember, Downey—you can't hang a man on suspicion."

"You an' yer ethics!" grinned the corporal. "We've hung men with better ethics than yours! Drink up, I'm buyin' one, an' then I'll be movin' along."

"Yeah, mebbe you have," laughed Black John. "But you've always ketched 'em at somethin' before you done it. Here's mud in yer eye. Up here on Halfaday you'll always find us willin' to work hand in glove with the police. Ain't that so, Cush?"

"Oh, shore," agreed the somber-faced proprietor. "We aim to keep the crick moral in spite of hell."

BLACK JOHN followed Downey down to the landing. "By the way," he asked, "did you fellas grab off either one of them kidnappers before they got outside? I've kind of wondered if that last one ever ketched up with his pardner—the one that had the dough?"

"No," replied Downey, "we didn't. They'll be picked up, though, as soon as they begin to spend that money. We took the numbers of all those bills, an' they've gone out over the new telegraph wire to every police force in Canada, an' the States, too. An' not only that, the banks have got the numbers, too."

"Well, well, so they've got the wire through, at last, eh? Handy thing fer you fellas, ain't it—that telegraph?"

"You bet it is! That's how we got word of this bond robbery. Hadn't been fer the wire, we prob'ly wouldn't have heard about it yet."

"Well, so long, Downey. Don't you worry about them bonds. If them fellas hit north, the chances is they'll show up on Halfaday. Most of them damn miscreants does, fer some reason er other. We don't mind that, as long as they stay moral. But the trouble with the bulk of 'em—? there ain't no steadfastness about their morality. It's apt to be spread on kind of thin—an' when it begins to wear through, they're out of luck."

II

"IS THIS CUSHING'S Fort, on Halfaday Creek?" asked a voice from the doorway, one morning ten days after the departure of Corporal Downey.

"Both guesses is right," replied Black John, as he and Old Cush eyed the pack-laden men who advanced to the bar.

"We're glad to git here," said one of them wearily, as he wriggled from his straps and let his pack fall to the floor. "We've had a hell of a trip."

"Sech gladness might er might not be mutual," Black John retorted. "Jest reach in the name-can yonder, an' help yerselves to a couple of names."

"Name-can?" queried the other, as he too divested himself of his pack. "What the hell's a name-can?"

"It's a simple device me an' Cush here thought up for to furnish good workable names to folks that comes in here lyin' about their own. Most folks that comes bustin' in on us claims their name is John Smith, which would be all right with us, if it didn't lead to confusion."

The larger of the two men grinned. "I git you," he said, and reaching into the can withdrew a slip of paper and read off the name: "Eli Fulton."

The other man drew a slip and read, "Robert Whitney."

Black John nodded approval. "The party back of the bar is Old Cush hisself an' my name's John Smith," he announced. "I'm mostly called Black John, owin' to the fact that my whiskers turned out to be that color." He glanced toward the proprietor, who stood behind the bar, twisting an end of his long yellow mustache. "Cush, I want you should meet my old friends, Eli and Bob."

"The house is buyin' one," announced Cush, by way of acknowledging the introduction.

"I'll have some coneyack," said Whitney, eyeing the bottles on the back bar.

"You might think you will, but you won't," replied Cush evenly. "Them names is on them bottles jest to make 'em look fancy. The licker in all of 'em is drawed out of the same bar'l. It's whiskey. An' if it ain't good enough fer you, you kin go dry. Sometime some damn shorthorn is goin' to come prancin' up here demandin' beer—an' when he does, he's goin' to git a bung-starter right plumb between the eyes."

"Oh, hell—whiskey's all right with me," the man hastened to explain. "I seen that bottle with 'coneyack' on it, an' I thought I'd try a little jest fer a change."

"Changin' licker's hard on a man's guts," opined Cush, "besides bein' a damn nuisance fer a bartender. What I claim, if a man can't git along with whiskey, he'd ort to stay to home an' rig him up a sugar tit."

THE LIQUOR was downed, and, ordering another round, Fulton turned to Black John. "So you're Black John Smith, eh? We heard about you an' Cushing's Fort down on the Yukon. Some fellers was tellin' us how you boys was all outlaws up here—an' how the police don't never dare to stick their nose on

Halfaday Crick. We was headin' fer the Klondike, till we run onto these fellers at Selkirk. An' when they told us about this crick, we decided to come on up here. We thought it might suit us better than down around Dawson."

"Well, it might, at that," agreed Black John, ordering a round of drinks. "It's true that most of us here on Halfaday is outlawed, fer one reason er another, but it ain't true that the police don't dare show up here. The fella you was talkin' with must of been a chechako, er he'd knowed damn well that the Mounted would dare to go anywhere they wanted to, an' it would be jest too damn bad fer anyone that tried to stop 'em. The facts is, the police don't bother us none up here—not because they don't dare to, but because there ain't any reason they should. Me an' Cush, here, we try to keep the crick moral—an' all the rest of the boys backs us up in it, by votin' a hangin' onto anyone that would commit any crime on the crick that would fetch in the police. Keep a crick free of crime, an' the police will let it alone."

"That's good common sense," approved the man. "But what do you fellers do up here?"

"We work," replied Black John. "There ain't nothin' like good honest toil to keep a man out of mischeef. Cush, here, he runs the saloon an' tradin' post—an' all the rest of us works on our claims."

"You mean, dig fer gold?"

"Yeah—that's about the only enterprise that's flourished, so far, on the crick."

"We don't know nothin' about gold diggin'," protested Whitney, calling for a round of drinks.

"It ain't no complicated business to learn," said Black John. "You stake out a claim, an' then you dig. You sink a shaft, an' throw the gravel onto a dump, and then sluice out the dump. We kin show you about riggin' up a windlass, an' a sluice."

BLACK JOHN noted that the man was beginning to show the effects of his liquor, and he ordered another round. As Whitney refilled his glass, he scowled. "I didn't come up here to dig in the ground like a damn badger," he said. "From what we heard about the gold camps, a man could have a hell of a good time, an' clean up good money at poker, an' roulette, an' faro—provided he had a stake to start with."

Black John nodded. "Yeah, I guess some of 'em's doin' it down around Dawson. But Halfaday ain't that kind of a camp."

"I don't notice you breakin' yer back none with no shovel," retorted the man.

Black John took no offence. "I took a day off," he explained. "I got up this mornin' with a bellyache, an' I figgered a little licker would do it good."

"Accordin' to what we heard from them fellers down on the Yukon, there's plenty of money on Halfaday—gold an' paper money, too. They claim that every onct in so often you go down to Dawson with a hull damn boatload of gold an' trade it in fer bills. They said you had plenty—an' Cush, too. They claimed that jest about everyone on the crick was well fixed."

Black John, himself, was obviously beginning to feel his liquor, so that Old Cush eyed him quizzically as he thumped the bar with his fist, and bellowed for another round. "Oh, shore!" he boasted. "Take us per capita, an' we're a damn rich crick! I've got plenty of dust an' bills, too! Plenty—an' more than a plenty fer all my needs an' requirements. But I'm a fly in my ointment, as the Good Book says—meanin' that I'm all bogged down in my own wealth. What good does it do a man to have a lot of gold, an' a lot of bills? No good whatever! Not a damn bit of good—if they ain't earnin' him nothin'. Gold an' bills cached away in holes in the rocks, an' in iron safes ain't producin' a man nothin'! They don't draw no interest. That's the trouble with Halfaday, gents— a man's got to keep toilin' away, no matter how much money he's got, er he ain't earnin' nothin'. Take it now in cities an' places like that, if a man's got money, he don't never have to work. No sir— he kin set back an' take life easy, an' let his money work fer him. He kin buy store buildin's an' houses, an' rent 'em out to folks.

He kin put his money in a bank an' let it draw interest, er he kin buy stock in some company, an' drag down dividends, er he could buy bonds, an' live like a king on the interest of 'em. But here on Halfaday, we're cut off from all them advantages. I feel sorry fer us, gents. Yes, sir, much as we'd like to have you settle amongst us, I can't see no future in it fer you. You'd jest have to go on diggin' out dust, that you ain't got no use fer when you git it dug." He appealed to Cush, who stood eyeing him with a disapproving frown. "Am I right, my dear friend—er am I wrong?"

"Yer soused," growled Cush, "an' talkin' like a damn fool."

"Oh, I don't know," interrupted Fulton, ordering a round of drinks. "There's a hell of a lot of good common sense in what he says. If a man's got money he's out of luck if he can't set it to workin' fer him. Money ain't no good layin' around idle. Like he says, if he could invest it in good stock, er bonds—'specially bonds. They're safer, an' they don't fluctuate, like stocks does. Good sound bonds is damn good property."

"You said it, ol' pal!" agreed Black John, throwing an arm about the man's shoulder. "Don't pay no 'tenshun to Cush. I know a smart man when I she one. Yer smart, 'cause yer smart enough to know I'm smart, an' that makes two of us. It's onearned incre-ments that's the bane of—of—of the financial strucher of—of civilization—you know that, 'cause yer smart—an' I know it—but, Cush—he don't even know what we're talkin' about. He's good fella—Cush is—but he ain't smart—an' he never will be. Fill 'em up again, Cush! An' listen around a while, an' mebbe you'll git smart, too. Thish man's right—if I could buy some bonds, I'd be happy."

THE MEANING look that passed between the two strangers at Black John's statement was not lost on Old Cush, whose frown deepened at Fulton's next words:

"Fact is," he said, casually, "we've got a few gilt-edged bonds with us that we might part with fer ready cash."

Black John regarded the man owlishly: "Wha's a difference if a bond's got gilt edges? It's wha's on the flat side of a bond that counts—not wha's on the edges of it. You think I'm a sucker, eh? Think you kin sell me some bonds because it's got fancy edges, eh?"

Fulton laughed good naturedly, and ordered a round of drinks. "You don't quite git me," he explained. "What I meant—gilt-edged—was jest a way us bond salesmen has of sayin' a bond is A Number One. Anything that's an awful good buy, we say it's gilt-edged; Like a deck of cards—the gilt-edged ones is the best cards; they cost the most, an' they're worth more."

"Yeah," agreed Black John cagily. "But there's jest as-many aces in a cheap deck. Like I was tellin' you—it's what's on the flat of 'em that counts, not the edges."

"You're right," agreed the man, "an' our bonds have got the goods on the flat of 'em—you kin bet on that. Hell—you don't suppose we'd try to unload no phony bonds on anyone, do you? Not with the laws what they be, we wouldn't. The Gover'ment checks up on all bonds before they'll let 'em be offered fer sale. Hell's fire, a man could go to jail fer tryin' to unload phony bonds!"

"They ort to, too," acquiesced Black John solemnly. "It would be one of the worst forms of skullduggery—an' on Halfaday it would be hangable. So you two is bond salesmen, eh? Funny place fer bond salesmen to come. I'd think they'd stick around cities, where there's more folks to sell bonds to."

"THAT'S WHERE yer wrong," replied the man. "The cities is all full of bond salesmen. The competition's fierce. Me an' my pardner, here, we figgered this way—here's them gold camps, we says, up north, where they've got plenty of gold and nowheres to invest it—jest like you was sayin' yerself. We figgers that if we was to take a bunch of bonds up there, we could sell 'em easy, 'cause there wouldn't be no competition, an' plenty of gold an' money jest itchin' to be invested in good solid securities, where it would be workin' fer a man, an' not layin' around idle—jest like you was tellin' us."

"That's right," agreed Black John. "Men like us is smart 'nough to see them things, an' grab the bull by the horns before the horse is stole, as the Good Book says. But how come you showed up on Halfaday? Dawson's a bigger camp. There's lots of dust in Dawson."

"We're goin' on to Dawson," replied the man. "We jest stopped in here 'cause we heard, from them fellas at Selkirk, that you boys had a lot of dust an' bills on hand, an' we figgered to give you a chanct to invest it, if you wanted to. We figgered we'd be doin' you boys a favor, besides doin' some business fer ourselves, to boot."

"Tha's right," agreed Black John. "What's bonds worth, a dozen? I might buy some."

"They ain't sold by the dozen," grinned the man. "Each bond is sold separate—accordin' to what it's worth. Like—a thousan', er five thousan', er ten thousan'. Each one has got the amount printed onto it, an' what company issued it, an' what's backin' it, in the way of property—an' all that stuff. It's all printed right on the bond where you kin read it yourself before you buy it. There ain't no chanct fer a fake."

Black John seemed to lose interest. "I guess you boys better go on down to Dawson," he said. "I wouldn't care to piffle around buyin' bonds one to a time. An' read each one out before I bought it. Hell, if I want to read, we've got books on Halfaday—Cush, here, has got a Bible, an' I've got a law book damn near a foot thick. You prob'l ain't got enough bonds to int'rest me, nohow. If you had a job lot I could pick up reasonable, I might talk to you."

Fulton smiled. "We've got half a million dollars' worth," he said. "Would that interest you any?"

"Half a million dollars!" exclaimed Black John. "Cripes— them bonds runs up into figgers! Trot 'em out—let's look 'em over."

AS THE two men stooped to open their packs, Old Cush, by means of frantic head-shaking, and frowning grimaces, sought to dissuade the huge man from dealing with the strangers. But his efforts were futile, and presently the bar was decorated with an assortment of official looking documents in green, and yellow, and brown.

"Look a there, Cush!" exclaimed Black John, indicating the array with a wave of his hand. "Ain't them the purtyest layout of bonds you ever seen? Cripes—anyone could tell, jest by lookin' at 'em that there ain't nothin' phony about them bonds. They're the real article. You better git in on this, Cush. I'm goin' to take a bunch of them yeller ones. They look important as hell!"

"I wouldn't have nothin' to do with 'em," growled Cush. "An' if you've got any sense, you won't either."

"There you go," exclaimed the big man impatiently. "Always tryin' to obstruct civilization! If I was as gloomy minded as what you be, I'd of strangled myself at birth, an' saved a whole lifetime of misery! Why, jest lookin' at all that there wealth spread out on the bar makes me feel happy. Fill 'em up again—an' then open up the shafe, Cush! I'm a-goin' to make an investment."

Old Cush's lips straightened into a firm white line beneath his yellow mustache, as he reached beneath the bar and picked up the bung-starter, which he balanced in his hand with a certain devoted regard, as he eyed Black John through narrowed lids.

"I ain't openin' no safe—an' you ain't buyin' no bonds," he announced in a flat, cold tone. "Not with no dust er money you've got in that safe, you ain't. Yer licker's went back on you today, John. Yer drunker'n a fool, right now. It ain't none of my business how drunk you git, but when it comes to blowin' all yer money into a lot of junk like that, I'm agin it. An' if you go makin' a move to open the safe, yerself, I'll knock you cold as a wedge with this bung-starter—an' when you come to, you'll thank me."

BLACK JOHN'S brows drew into a frown as he eyed the determined figure that stood behind the bar. Surprise was mingled with wholesome respect, as his eyes dropped from the other's face to the weapon that he fondled most caressingly. Long years of professional practise had made Old Cush a past master in the technique of the bung-starter, and Black John had seen too many demonstrations of his skill on the skulls of obstreperous customers, to ask for any of it on his own account. He sought, by means of soft words, to win the other over.

"Aw, lishen, Cus', I ain' drunk. I know damn well I ain'! Cripes—I couldn't talk buishness—businish, if I was drunk, could I? Course I couldn't. C'm on—open up the shafe, like a good fella, and lemme have some money. You wouldn' she all them good bonds go to waste, would you? They'd look as important as hell in the shafe, along with the dust an' bills."

"They ain't goin' to look important in this safe," replied Cush obstinately, "an' you ain't goin' to git no money out of it, neither."

The big man switched to bluff and bluster. "Why, you damn ol' badger! It's my money I want out of that safe—not yourn. An' I'm entitled to it, too. Open up, now—er damn if I don't climb the bar an' git it!"

"You'll sleep a while before you do," replied Cush dryly, waggling the bungstarter a bit as he rolled back his sleeve suggestively.

Black John assumed an air of outraged dignity. Ignoring Cush, he turned to the others. "It's pitiful, gents," he said, "how, in the hour of need, a man's friends goes back on 'em. Look at him—my pal—standin' there with a bung-starter ready to brain me, jest 'cause I want to draw a little of my own money out of his shafe! But, gents, to hell wish him! Yesher—to hell wish him an' his shafe, too! I got some spare change to buy bonds wish. Got it right over to my cabin. You wait right here, gents, an' I'll go git it. Firs' though, we'll have a li'l drink all 'roun'. Cush shays I'm drunk—hell, I'll shtart in an' show 'm how to git drunk! An' I'll buy all yer damn bonds, to boot. I know a businish man when I she one—an' I'm him. I c'n tell it jest by lookin' in the glash. Ain' I a bushiness man?"

"Sure you are!" exclaimed Fulton, turning to Cush. "Fill 'em up, barkeep. I'm buyin' this one. He's all right—let him alone."

"I don't give a damn how drunk he gits," said Cush, "an' I guess he won't buy no hell of a lot of bonds with what cash he's got in his cabin. Let him blow it, if he wants to—but he don't get a damn cent out of the safe."

"Don' need no money out of yer damn shafe!" retorted Black John, swallowing his liquor. "Got plenty over to my cabin. You wait an' she!"

CROSSING THE floor unsteadily, Black John disappeared to return a few minutes later with a bulky package done up in brown paper. Setting the package on the bar, he undid the wrapping, and three pairs of eyes widened in surprise as Old Cush and the two strangers gazed at the neat packets of bills, held together with rubber bands.

"There she ish, gents—jes' a li'l loosh change I keep on me in case I might wan' it. Fifty thousan', in good paper money! Fifty thousan' dollars, gents—bring on yer damn bonds!"

Eagerly the two strangers began sorting over their bonds, and presently Fulton handed Black John several of them. "There you be," he said. "Fifty thousand dollars worth, an' no charge fer accrued interest."

"Fer what?" asked Black John, fumbling the bonds over as he examined them.

"Accrued interest, they call it. You see, them bonds has already earnt some interest sence they was issued, an' it belongs to the one that owns 'em. But we ain't chargin' you fer that. We're sellin' 'em at face value—you keep the interest."

"Shore, thash all right," said Black John, "but all of 'em only adds up to fifty thousan'."

"Well—that's what you claimed you've got there in bills. Fifty thousan' in bonds, fer fifty thousan' in bills—that's fair enough, ain't it—with us throwin' in the interest?"

Black John shook his head. "Nope—that ain't the way I do businesh. Them bills ish real money. Bonds ain' money—they're jes' bonds. I gotta make a profit. Man would be a damn fool to give fifty thousan' in money fer fifty thousan' in bonds."

"Tell you what we'll do—we'll throw in an extry ten thousan'. There's a bargain fer you! Sixty thousan' in A Number One, gilt-edged bonds fer only a lousy fifty thousan' in cash."

"You talk kind of big, don't you? Lousy fifty thousan'! By God, fifty thousan' dollars in cash money ain' lousy—no matter how you look at it. It's important money, an' you'd think so, too, if you'd toiled fer it, like I did!"

"I didn't mean it that way—it was jest a way of speakin', to show you what kind of a bargain you was gittin'."

"Yeah, tha's what I think, too—lousy bargain! Tha's right. Come on agin with them bonds, if you want to do businesh with me!"

"What do you mean?"

"Mean? I mean keep shovin' them bonds over, till I git my money's worth. What you think I mean?"

FULTON FROWNED. "What kind of a bargain do you expect? We offered to throw in an extry ten thousan'."

"Yeah—an' you ain' started to throw in. Come on—keep 'em comin'."

"Tell you what we'll do—seein' you've got the ready cash handy. We'll sell 'em to you at seventy-five cents on the dollar. There's a bargain for you—seventy-five thousan' in bonds fer fifty thousan' in cash!"

"That's a li'l better—but not nowheres near good enough," replied Black John, shaking his head. "Yer willin'ness to part with 'em cheap, kind of warns me that there's somethin' shady about 'em. The bonds theirselves looks genuine—but yer title to 'em is ondoubtless open to suspicion. They might even be the product of some crime."

"Listen," said Fulton, scowling, "I'll give it to you straight. We ain't reg'lar bond salesmen, like I told you. We got holt of this stuff on a deal that was a little shady. The bonds is good as gold. We figgered we could git rid of 'em fer ready cash up here in the gold country, an' like I told you, we was headin' fer Dawson. But when we heard about here, we come on up, figgerin' that some of you would know how to git rid of 'em, an' we could, mebbe, git a better price than we could in Dawson. Tell you what I'll do—an' it's the best I kin do on 'em. Give me fifty cents on the dollar an' take 'em. At that price mebbe yer friend, here, would go in with you—two hundred an' fifty thousan' fer a half a million in bonds. You double yer money—not to say nothin' about the interest."

"I wouldn't have 'em at no price," said Cush. "Buyin' hot bonds ain't in my line—never was an' never will be."

Black John listened to Cush's dictum with drunken gravity. "Cush is right," he announced. "We might find ourshelf in a hell of a lot of trouble. Guesh I don' wan' none of 'em neither." Deliberately he began to arrange the packets of bills on the brown paper, preparatory to doing them up. "Damn shite better to have fifty thousan' in good honest bills than half a million in bonds that might git you in jail. Better take 'em on down to Dawson, boys, an' peddle 'em down there."

BOTH STRANGERS were eyeing the money avidly as Black John drew the paper around it.

"Hold on!" Fulton cried. "It's a damn hold-up—but I'll tell you what we'll do! We need the cash, bad. Fifty thousan' is nothin' but chicken feed, side of half a million in bonds—but it's a stake. If the play is runnin' like we hear tell of in Dawson, we kin hit there with fifty thousan' an' clean up a million with the cards. Shove us the money an' take the bonds—all of 'em! Half a million fer fifty thousan'! Ten cents on the dollar is all they're costin' you. You'll make four hundred and fifty thousan' profit—besides the interest. It's jest like you stole 'em!"

"We-e-e-l," hesitated Black John, "at that prishe mebbe a man might take a chanct."

"Course you kin take a chanct—only it's a sure thing fer you. We're the ones that's takin' the chanct—we've got to git our money out of the cards. If it worn't that we figger we kin git it back, we wouldn't let than bonds go at no discount whatsoever. Here's the bonds—all of 'em."

"All right," agreed Black John. "It's a deal. There's yer money—count it, while I figger up these bonds. Then we'll all know we ain't be'n short-changed."

A quarter of an hour later, bonds and bills having been checked to the satisfaction of all concerned, the two men took their departure.

"Sho long!" called Black John from the doorway, as the two shoved off in the canoe. "You boys be careful you don' take no wooden nickels!"

Returning to the bar he stood contemplating the pile of bonds while Old Cush scowled in silent disapproval. "By God," he exclaimed suddenly, "I know'd there was somethin' wrong! Them birds fergot to put them slips back in the name-can! What was them names they draw'd out, Cush? I'll write out some new slips."

OLD CUSH snorted his disgust. "Somethin' wrong—a couple of strips of paper out of a can! Sometimes, John, you kin be the damndest fool I ever seen. Most gen'lly when you git soused you've got some sense left in yer head—damn little, sometimes, but some—but this time—fifty thousan' dollars in cold cash fer a lot of bonds that's so sizzlin' hot that they're sendin' out special patrols of the Mounted fer 'em! Ain't you got no sense, at all? Take it from me—yer goin' to come out of this drunk with a hell of a headache!"

White teeth showed through the black beard, and suddenly Old Cush was aware that the drunken stare had disappeared from the blue eyes that twinkled into his own. "What do you mean—cold cash?" he asked. "By God, when them boys begin shovin' out that cash in Dawson, they're goin' to find out it's a damn sight hotter'n them bonds ever thought of bein'!"

"You mean to tell me you ain't drunk—an' ain't be'n all along?" demanded Cush.

"I don't rec'lect of tellin' you I ain't drunk," grinned the other. "Where'n hell did you git the idee that I was? Cripes—I ain't had more'n a dozen er fifteen drinks. What would I be drunk fer?"

"Well, you talked an' acted drunk as hell."

"Oh, shore—I done that fer to give them birds a chanct to unload them bonds onto me. It was jest a little play actin', Cush. You know I always wanted to be an actor. Sometimes we'll go to work and stage a real drayma."

"Like hell we will! We've had enough of yer damn draymas, as it is! If anything had went wrong with them other ones you pulled off, I'd of been in a hell of a fix! What you goin' to do with them damn bonds, now you've got 'em?"

"Don't you rec'lect that I promised Corporal Downey, I'd git 'em fer him, if they show'd up on Halfaday?"

"Yeah—but it looks like you went in kind of deep, jest to do Downey a favor. When all's said an' done, John—fifty thousan' dollars is fifty thousan' dollars."

"Oh, hell," replied Black John, "what's little amounts like them, amongst friends?"

OLD CUSH eyed the other narrowly. "Where'd you git all that money, John? An' what d'you mean about it bein' hot?"

"It's what you might call the emolument of virtue—havin' to do with them three fellas that One Armed John told us was in Olson's shack, down the crick. I mistrusted they was malefactors of some kind, so I took that there prospectin' trip. In the course of my peregrinations—"

"What in hell's them? Can't you talk no English, at all?"

"As I was sayin'," continued Black John, ignoring the interruption, "whilst I was on that trip, I was instrumental in the prevention of a crime, as a reward fer which meritorious act I took over that money. An' it wasn't till Downey came up here the other day huntin' fer these bonds that I realized, from somethin' he told me, that them partic'lar bills was ondesirable property to have. An' them fellas will be findin' it out, too, jest about the time they begin shuckin' it out around Dawson. Guess I'll jest drop down an' watch the fun. Besides, I've got to fetch Corporal Downey them bonds. You know, Cush, up here we've got to work hand in glove with the police."

III

"HELLO, JOHN—BACK AGIN already?" Curley, the genial bartender of the Tivoli Saloon in Dawson, greeted the huge man who faced him across the bar, as he set out a bottle and two glasses. "You folks can't be very busy up on Halfaday, the way yer runnin' back an' forth."

"Oh, we're busy, all right," replied Black John as he filled his glass. "But, cripes, you can't expect a man to spend his whole life in toil. Time a man cranks a windlass, an' shovels gravel eighteen, twenty hours a day, over a period of years, he's entitled to a little vacation, now an' then."

"Yeah," grinned Curley, "but they tell me there's a hell of a lot of windlasses you never cranked—an' a hell of a lot of gravel you never shovelled."

"Shut up, an' have another," laughed Black John, laying a bill on the bar. Picking up the bill, Curley glanced at its number, and dropping it into the till, laid the change on the bar.

"What the hell's the matter?" queried Black John. "Think it's counterfeit, or somethin'?"

"No, it ain't that it might be queer. But ever sence Chase was kidnapped, an' the Consolidated paid out that fifty thousan' to git him back, we're s'posed to look at the numbers on all bills.

We've got a list of 'em a yard long there in the till. When we take in a bill that might be one of 'em, we check it with the list. This here bill you give me was only five numbers long, so it couldn't of been on the list. It's a cinch that some time or other, some-wheres, them bills is bound to show up—an' the police is hopin' it'll be here. The kidnappin' bein' in their territory, they'd like to grab off the ones that done it. You was the one that found Chase an' fetched him back—where do you think they're at?"

"Well," replied Black John, "that would be hard to say. Of course, they might have hit fer the outside. But then ag'in, they might jest be layin' low till the stink blow'd away. I don't claim to be no authority on them criminal matters, but off hand I'd say that them bills would begin showin' up most any time, now."

"How long you goin' to be here?"

"Oh, not more'n a night er so. I jest run down fer a couple of sessions of stud."

Curley grinned. "Old Bettles says you're the world's worst stud player. He claims you stayed through four or five stiff raises with a pair of deuces, back to back, an' him with one deuce showin' all along—and then you ketched the case deuce fer yer last card, an' beat him out of a hell of a big pot."

"Yeah, that's the way of it," chuckled the big man. "Trou-ble with most folks, they ain't got no faith in deuces jest 'cause they're little. Guess I'll set down by the table, yonder, an' read the paper till the boys drifts in."

BLACK JOHN, taking the Ladue Creek shortcut, had timed his arrival in Dawson to correspond as closely as possible to that of Fulton and Whitney, who would reach the big camp by way of the White River and the Yukon.

Thus, it was that, some two hours after he seated himself, he watched with interest through a small hole punched in the newspaper that concealed his face, as the two men entered, strode to the bar, lowered their packs to the floor, and demanded refreshment. He saw Curley set out the bottle and glasses, and saw Fulton lay a bill on the bar, in payment. He saw Curley pick up the bill, glance at it, and turn toward the till. Then, as the men filled their glasses, he noted that the bartender laid the bill on the back bar, counted out some change, which he placed on the bar before Fulton, then, with a casual air, turned his back upon the two, removed a long slip of paper from the till, and once more consulted the number on the bill.

A grin twitched the corners of Black John's lips as he watched Curley beckon to Joe, the porter, whisper a few words into his ear, and then turn toward the two customers with a genial invitation to have one on the house—as Joe slipped unobtrusively out the back door.

It was evident, during the next half-hour, that the two strangers found themselves amid congenial surroundings. The house matched their purchases, drink for drink, and roars of laughter greeted the pithy but unprintable stories that bandied back and forth across the bar.

Then Black John drew the newspaper a bit closer for better concealment, as Corporal Downey stepped into the room and, crossing to the bar, paused behind the two. Receiving an almost imperceptible nod from Curley, the young officer laid a hand lightly upon the shoulder of each.

"I want to have a little talk with you men down to headquarters," he said.

The two turned swiftly. "What the hell!" exclaimed Whitney.

"There's some mistake here," blustered Fulton, truculently.

"Maybe," replied Downey. "I don't claim to be the man that never makes 'em. If there is, you fellows have got nothin' to fear. Until we find out, though, you're both under arrest for the kidnappin' of Frederick Chase, an' possession of the ransom money."

"Kidnappin'!" scoffed Fulton, with a laugh that Black John interpreted as one of vast relief. "Yer crazy as hell! Where was this kidnappin' pulled off—an' when?"

"Oh, a couple of months ago—right here in Dawson."

"That lets us out. We never seen Dawson till today!"

"Maybe," admitted Downey. "Come along with me, an' we'll find out."

"Sure we'll go," agreed Fulton with alacrity. "Why the hell wouldn't we? We ain't got nothin' to fear. Come on, cop— let's get it over with."

IV

AN HOUR LATER, Black John rose from the table, yawned, stretched prodigiously, and stepped to the bar. "I'm buyin' one," he announced, as Curley turned from the back bar to face him.

"Hell's fire, John—you been here all the time? I'd plumb fergot you. Where the hell was you at?"

"Oh, I set down over there to the table to read the paper, but I might have got kind of sleepy, an' took a little snooze."

"An' you didn't see what come off?"

"What come off? There couldn't be no hell of a lot come off, er I'd of woke up. I ain't no sound sleeper. It don't pay to be."

"There wasn't no excitement. It all comes off nice and quiet. Downey slipped in here an' pinched them kidnappers!"

"Well," grinned Black John, "you wouldn't expect him to let 'em run around loose, would you? That's what police is paid fer— to pinch miscreants like them."

"Yes, sir—two guys come in an' ordered the drinks, an' one of 'em lays a bill on the bar, an' I checks the number of it with that list, an' damn if it wasn't one of 'em! So I slips Joe the word to go fetch Downey, an' he come, an' pinched 'em both."

"Good work," approved Black John. "It looks like you both done yer dooty."

"You bet! Damn cusses like them had ort to git pinched. Chances is, if the Consolidated hadn't paid that money, like they told 'em to, they'd of knocked Chase off. What'll they git fer it, John? What's the law on kidnappin'?"

"A term of years," answered the other. "I can't say off hand, jest how long. But it'll give 'em plenty of time to think things over."

"Damn if you wasn't right—about them bills bein' about due to show up. How the hell could you tell?"

"Oh, jest common sense—an' mebbe some slight insight into the workin's of the criminal mind. Cripes, anyone could of doped that out."

"Yeah?" retorted Curley, a vast respect showing in his eyes. "Well, no wonder there ain't no crime on Halfaday! Gosh, John—you'd ort to be in the police!"

"No, no! I wouldn't make a good policeman. Hell, a policeman's got to be smart." Passing around the end of the bar, Black John retrieved his light pack and slung a strap to his shoulder. "Guess I'll jest percolate around a while. If the boys drops in tell 'em I'll be back. Tell Bettles he better be practisin' up on his stud."

BLACK JOHN, as was his privilege, opened the door of Corporal Downey's office at detachment headquarters of the Mounted and stepped into the room, to find the young officer, his desk top covered with bills, and a long strip of typewritten numbers in his hand.

"Hello, Downey!" he greeted. "Cripes it must be pay day!"

"Yeah," grinned the officer, "an' I draw'd my salary fer the next twenty-five years in advance, eh? Do you know what this stuff is?"

"I might hazard a guess that it's money."

"It's money, all right! It's the money the Consolidated paid over to the kidnappers to get Chase back."

"Well, well! So you got it back, eh? Good work, Downey! Did you git the kidnappers along with it? I run acrost 'em, you remember, when they had Chase up on Halfaday. I wouldn't have no compunctions about helpin' identify sech damn scoundrels as them, because, by fetchin' Chase up there, they might have jeopardized the morals of our crick."

"I don't think you could identify these two that had the money," replied Downey. "I had Chase in here a few minutes ago, and he said he'd never seen these men. He definitely stated that they were not the ones who held him prisoner. Kidnap, gangs work like that. The ones that do the snatchin' an' holdin' ain't the ones that handles the money. They work it that way so that in case they're picked up passin' the stuff, the victim can't identify 'em."

"Ain't they smart?" grinned Black John. "Why, if they'd put all them brains into honest pursuits, they'd prob'ly do well."

"They're smart, all right," replied Downey, "but they ain't quite smart enough. They overlooked the fact that possession of this money is a criminal offense of itself, and to any reasonable jury the fact that they had it would link them up with the kidnappin'. Here's how I've doped it out. You remember, you told me that you followed the man who had this money up the Yukon, but failed to overtake him?"

"Shore, I remember that."

"Well, he went on up past the mouth of the White, where these two were prob'ly waitin' for him. Then they took over the money. An' the chances are they knocked off this bird an' the other one—the two that done the snatchin'—because these two I've got had every damn cent of the fifty thousan'."

"Tch, tch, tch! Don't it beat hell how some folks carries on? It's a wonder to me that them damn crooks trusts one another out of their sight!"

"I'm mighty glad I picked these birds up, John—as much for your sake, as for the Consolidated's."

"My sake? Cripes, Downey—I'd of got along; if you'd never ketched 'em."

"YEAH," GRINNED Downey, "but if I hadn't picked up these fellows with that money, I'd have always held a sneakin' suspicion that you had it. You see, I was never quite satisfied that you didn't lie to me when you said you never overtook that bird goin' upriver. I figured you had overtook him, an' made him fork over the bills. Of course, I never could have proved it—but jest the same I'd have always thought it. I'm damn glad that this clears you of even that suspicion."

"Well, so'm I, Downey—if that's the way you felt about it. Cripes, I never had no idee you'd think I'd lie to you! How about givin' me the chanct to look these birds over, anyway? You see, they might of been hidin' out on Halfaday, too—an' I never connected 'em with the crime. Strangers comes and goes, an' a man wouldn't know who was mixed up in it, if they kep' away from them others."

"That's so," agreed Downey. "Wait till I call Constable Peters to watch this stuff, an' we'll step into the cell room."

"I s'pose they denied they know'd anythin' about the kidnappin', eh?"

"Sure they did. However, when I questioned them about the possession of the money, they were mighty vague, an' wound up by claimin' they found it in a cache."

WHEN PETERS appeared, Black John followed Corporal Downey into the cell room, where the two prisoners sat in adjoining iron barred cages. Both stood up and paled perceptibly at the sight of Black John.

"There they are," said Downey. "Have you ever seen 'em before?"

According the men scarcely a glance, Black John swung his light pack to the floor in the little passageway before the cells, and turned suddenly upon the officer. "By gosh, Downey!" he cried suddenly, "here I be, foolin' around like this, an' plumb fergot what I come clean down from Halfaday to fetch you." Fumbling in his pack, he drew forth a sizable packet, which he extended toward the officer. "Here's them bonds you was inquirin' about up to Cush's that day. Half a million dollars' worth of 'em; they're, all there—count 'em."

"You mean," cried Downey, eagerly seizing the packet, and cutting the cord that bound it, "you located those bonds? The ones that were stolen in that express robbery?"

"I wouldn't be surprised an' them's the ones," replied Black John. "They're bonds—an' the amount of 'em checks with what you claimed was stole. An' by the way, Downey, didn't you claim there was a murder connected with that robbery?"

"Sure there was. A damn dirty murder, too. They never gave the poor devil of a messenger a chance. They'll sure swing for that job, when we lay hands on 'em!"

There was a movement in one of the cells, and Downey looked up from his scrutiny of the bonds to encounter the pale face of Fulton.

"Hey, Corp'rl," said the man huskily; "we want to come clean on that kidnappin' job. We was in on it, all right We lied to you, but we been talkin' it over—an' we decided to plead guilty."

"All right," said the officer, "I'll take yer statements, later."

HE TURNED to give Black John a rousing thump on the back with the flat of his hand. "By gosh, John—you don't know how glad I am to get hold of these securities! But how about the men that had 'em. Did you bring them down?"

"Nope," replied Black John, "I didn't. You know damn well, Downey, that I never had nothin' to do with arrestin' anyone—er even squealin' on 'em. It ain't ethical, an' I wouldn't have nothin' to do with it. If you think them men's on Halfaday, an' you kin locate 'em—go to it. You won't be neither helped nor hindered when you git there. I promised you I'd try an' locate them bonds if they showed up on the crick—an' I done so."

"You sure did, John—an' I thank you for it. But my thanks don't stack up very big beside what you've got comin'. It jest goes to show that it pays to be honest. Sir Henry Billson has posted a reward of a hundred thousan' dollars in cash fer the return of those bonds before October first—the date when the merger deal expires. An' it all goes to you."

"Well, well," grinned Black John. "That change'll shore come handy."

"Oh—yes—how about these two fellows—did you ever see 'em before?"

Black John eyed the two white-faced men deliberately, and subjected them to long and careful scrutiny. "No," he said, shaking his head in a slow negative. "No—I can't say that I ever laid eyes on either one of 'em—an' I've got a good mem'ry fer faces, too."

"Come on, then," said Downey, turning to lead the way back to the office. "I want to wire Vancouver about these bonds."

As he was about to follow the officer, Black John turned a solemn face toward the two men in the cells. "There's an old sayin', my men," he boomed sententiously, "that honesty is the best policy. If you two had learnt to live moral, you wouldn't be where yer at now. Jest remember that—when they turn you loose twenty, thirty years hence. It'll do you good."

THE FORTY-NINER

"KNOW ANYONE NAME of Smith around yere?" Black John Smith turned from the bar where he and Old Cush had been heatedly discussing the relative merits of John L. Sullivan and James J. Corbett, and regarded the stranger who stood just within the doorway. He was an old man, tall and angular, with a droop to his powerful shoulders that bespoke many years of toil. A goatee, neatly trimmed to a point, matched in whiteness the mustache whose ends curved slightly upward against a pair of weather-beaten cheeks. A thin nose, hooked like a hawk's beak, showed prominently beneath a pair of gray eyes that twinkled like twin points of steel from under their bushy white brows.

"The name," admitted Black John, with a smile that exposed white teeth behind his jet black beard, "has a sort of familiar sound. Would the party's front name be John?"

"No, answered the stranger gravely. "It's Al—the one I'm huntin'. He's my son. Mine's Catteraugus."

"J'ine up," invited Cush. "The house is buyin' one."

When midway of the floor, without halting his advance to the bar, and with scarcely a perceptible turning of the head, the man's lips ejected a short brown jet that, with the accuracy of a well-placed bullet, landed squarely in the center of a spittoon that stood near the end of the bar.

"Would you mind," asked Black John respectfully, "rehearsin' that name of yourn again? I don't rightly believe I ketched it."

"Catteraugus Smith," replied the man, ranging himself beside the other at the bar where Old Cush had already set out bottle and glasses.

"There's lots of Smiths on Halfaday," said Black John. "But Catteraugus, now! I don't rec'lect no Al, neither."

"My pappy was a York State man. He fit in the war, an' when it was over he married an' settled down in the Tennessee mountains. He named me fo' the place he come from. I went to Californy back in fo'ty-nine, an' when I come back I boughten mo' land, an' married my woman, an' then they found coal on the land, an' I don't farm no mo'."

"There's a few assorted Smiths on the crick, like Hank, an' Bert, an' Tom, an' Jim, but mostly us Smiths runs to John fer a front name—er did, till me an' Cush invented the name-can."

"The name-can?" queried the other, his brow furrowing.

"Yeah. There it sets on the end of the bar. You see, layin' up here next to the bdund'ry, like we do, Halfaday is a kind of a Mecca, you might say, fer some of the boys that's wanted, here an' there, fer one thing an' another. We've had 'em from as clost as Dawson, an' as fer away as Massachusetts. I'm an Alasky wanted, myself—h'isted an army payroll off'n a major an' three common soldiers over to Fort Gibbon, a few years back. Most of the boys arrives here with the mistaken notion that their name is John Smith, it bein' a good old fambly name, an' the first one they could think up. But the habit had a tendency to cause confusion that would of bordered on actual chaos if we hadn't thought of the name-can, which is a simple device an' as near fool-proof as any invention kin be, consistin' merely of copyin' the names out of a hist'ry book which One Eyed John Smith left behind when we hung him one time, onto slips of paper an' puttin' the slips in that molasses can that sets there on the bar! Now when anyone reaches here with the information that his name is John Smith, we invite him to dip in the can an', help hisself to a more distinctful name. He don't need to fear no consequences, 'cause most of the folks whose names we borrowed is ondoubtless dead, but to make sure—we mixed up the front an' hind names on the slips till their own mother wouldn't know em.

"It looks like a good idee," opined Catteraugus, "An' now, if you ge'men will allow me, I'll buy a li'l drink."

"You won't be interfered with," grinned the other, "an' I might add that my name's John Smith—Black John, by way of warnin' unobservant folks that that's the color of my whiskers. Lyme Cushing is the party's name behind the bar."

"I'M RIGHT proud to meet up with y'all. I reckon if most of the folks yere is—er—outlawed, like you might say, a man might kind of suffer from murder, er robbery, er some such orneriness."

"Not in a thousan' years! Halfaday is the moralest damn crick in the Yukon. We don't want the police snoopin' around here, so we don't permit nothin' bein' pulled off that would fetch 'em in.

Murder, an' all forms of larceny, claim-jumpin' an' general skull-duggery is promptly dealt with by miners' meetin'—"

"Miners' meetin', eh!" exclaimed the" oldster, his keen eye lighting with interest. "Now yer talkin'! We used to hold 'em out in Californy, back in fo'ty-nine. Hung a sight of folks, too—cache robbers an' sich varmints. One good miners' meetin'll make more Christians than fo'ty camp meetin's."

"Shore as hell!" agreed Black John, heartily. "An' they stay Christian, too. There's damn little indoosement to backsliding to see some feller you know'd hangin' there on the end of a rope. Yer a right-thinkin' man, Catteraugus. I'm buyin' a drink. An' now, if a man might ask, howcome yer huntin' yer son up here on Halfaday? Seems like it lays quite a ways back from Tennessee."

"Yes suh. That's right. But us Smiths is what you might say, loose-footed folks. My pappy's gran'pappy, he immigrated out to York State when that part of it wasn't nothin' but Indians an' trees. An' then pappy's pappy he went off to sea, an' he must of sunk somewheres, 'cause he ain't never come back yet. An' then pappy he went an' fit in the war. An' me, I hit out fer Californy when the talk run to gold out there. So I figgered Al would go a long ways, onct he got started—'specially with the shuriff after him like he was. Bein' as Al had often heer'd me talkin' about them gold days, I figgered he'd prob'ly hit out fo' this yere Klondike country we be'n hearin' about."

"You say the sheriff's after him?" asked Black John casually.

"No. I said he *was*. They've got a new shuriff now. I don't rightly know what he's doin' about it. I come away, after shootin' the other one. He had Al cornered in a coal-bank; an' I aimed to give the boy a chanct. It's all on account of them damn Deet-ses. He's a good boy, Al is—kind of prankful, that's all." The old man's eyes took on a far-away reminiscent expression, as his long, strong fingers toyed with his liquor glass. "I rec'lect the time he beat up the schoolmaster. He wasn't only fifteen, an' the schoolmaster was a Deets man, an' he didn't like Al, nohow. One evenin' he kep' him after school fo' the purpose of floggin' him fo' some prank, an' Al watched his chanct an' laid him a crack side of the head with a stove chunk, an' then he beat him up till there wasn't hardly anyone thought he'd live—but he did. He quit the mountains, though—an' Al he quit school. Them Deetses is upity folks. They're Dimmecrats, an' between 'em they run a store, an' a tan-yard, an' a grist-mill, an' a stavemill, an' they tried to make trouble fo' Al on account of the schoolmaster. But Al he laid clost till it blow'd over—helpin' me around the still an' such like. Then one night, jest to show them Deetses they wasn't so much, he slipped down an' robbed old Clay Deets's sto'. I told him he might git in trouble that-a-way, but like I said, Al he's young an' pranky. Old Clay, he set the shuriff on him, an' one day he ketched Al wearin' a suit of clo's he tuk out of the sto' that night, an' he tuk Al to town an' stuck him in the jail house. But nothin' come of it. I went down to the trial an' set there where the jury could git a good look at me, an' they decided there wasn't no evidence, an' turned Al loose—which' is jist as well they did, as it would of turned out.

NOT LONG after that they found where a big vein of coal run under our land, an' we give up stillin' on account of the coal royalties the Company was payin' us. I reckon we got mo' money comin' in now than all them damn Deetses—an' they got to work fo' theirn, an' we don't.

"It run along an' this spring young Valandingham Deets give out that he was goin' to run fo' the legislator, come fall, in place of old man Fannin. When Al heered about it he 'lowed there wasn't no mo' reason a Deets should be in the legislate than a Smith. So he set up to run agin Val Deets on the Republican idee that a damn Dimmycrat ain't got no business to be 'lected, nohow. The campaign run along into the fo' part of the summer, with Val Deets makin' speeches all through the mountains—an' Al puttin' out a heap of money buyin' up votes. Val, he'd be'n off to some school somewheres—Knoxville, er mebbe Chattenoogy—an' he began belittlin', an' makin' light of Al in his speeches. When

Al found out about it, he loaded up the old rifle an' laid in the laurels. In a few nights he got his chanct an' ketched Val right plumb through the heart. It was as pretty a shot as a man would want to see, from where Al laid—an' the light he had. The bullet went in Val's back right in under the shoulder blade.

"Well, the shuriff was up fer 'lection, too—an' he figgered he better do somethin', what with all the Deetses pesterin' him about it, though God knows, Val wasn't no loss to no one but a Deets. So Al, he tuk to the mountains, 'lowin' to lay low a few weeks till it blow'd over. But like I said, the shuriff stuck his nose in an' cornered Al in an old coal bank. Knowin' Al like I did, I realized he done it more as a prank than anythin' else—an' besides, it looked like Val was linin' up more votes than he was on account of the lies he was tellin' around. So I shot the shuriff an' told Al mebbe he better give up the idee of runnin' fer office till some other fall, an' kind of git out of the country fer a spell. He done so, an' I slipped over home an' give my woman a power of attorney to draw the royalties, an' I come away, too—till after 'lection when things quiets down in the mountains."

"H-u-u-m," said Black John. "An' what makes you think this heer prankful son of yourn is on Halfaday? You mentioned the Klondike. That's down around Dawson. It's more'n likely he's down there."

"No, Al ain't there. I be'n down to Dawson. Looked fo' him all amongst them camps, an' asked everyone I thought looked like he might know. When I mentioned to one man about the shuriff bedevilin' Al like he done, he says how if there's a shuriff after him, he's more'n likely hit fo' Halfaday Crick, as that's where most of 'em hits fo' when folks like police, an' marshals, an' shuriffs is on their trail. So I come here. Al, he's a good boy an' me, knowin' the temptations there is around minin' camps, I figgered I could mebbe kind of steer him straight. I wouldn't want he should git into no trouble."

"YEAH," AGREED Black John. "It would be a pity if he should git into trouble. Take boys that-a-way, I guess they're kind of hard to raise right. I never tried it myself—but my folks did, an' it seems like they didn't meet with no more than middlin' success. I couldn't say if Al is amongst us. If he is, he's ondoubtless livin' under some alias he draw'd out of the name-can. It don't look like there'd be much future fer a boy like Al on Halfaday, so why don't you jest hole up with me, an' stick around a spell an' kind of look the boys over? Everyone on the crick gits in here to Cush's about onct in so often."

"Well now, I sure take that kind of you. I don't like to put no one to any trouble—"

"No trouble, at all, Catteraugus," interrupted Black John. "Me an' Cush'll do all we kin to help you locate yer son. From what you've told us it looks like mebbe he'd kind of be better off fer a guidin' hand. Jest throw yer stuff in my cabin yonder, an' come on back so we kin be gittin', on with our drinkin'."

II

WHEN THE MAN had disappeared with his pack, Old Cush eyed Black John with twinkling eyes. "If this here Al's on Halfaday, I shore hope his pa locates him. Prankful—an' him beatin' that teacher damn near to death with a stove, chunk, an' robbin' a store, an' bushwhackin' that feller from behind!"

"Yeah," grinned Black John, "them mountaineers is hardy folks, Cush. Even their light-heartedest pranks is liable to run into felonies. If Al's on the crick I'd shore like to know which one of the name-canners he is."

"It's comfortin' that his pa'll be here to pick him out. Like you said, they all come in the saloon every onct in so often."

"Yeah," agreed Black John, "an' election bein' over by this time back there in Tennessee, mebbe they'll be pullin' out fer home."

"I hope they will. It would be hell if a damn cuss like Al should settle down amongst us permanent."

"Yeah. Well, permanent as fer as he would be concerned, prob'ly wouldn't be no hell of a while on the calendar. Not if he pulled none of his pranks, it wouldn't. But if old Catteraugus stayed, too, he'd prob'ly exert a restrainin' influence, as a preacher would say."

"It don't look like he done a hell of a lot of restrainin' back there where they come from," argued Cush. "He even bragged about what a good shot this here Al made when he plugged that feller through the back. An' then him shootin' that shuriff an' all—"

"Well hell," interrupted Black John, "you can't blame a man fer takin' a little pride in his own son—an' you couldn't expect him to stand around an' see him git shot, neither. It looks like there's a prudish streak in you, Cush. I kind of like old Catteraugus. He didn't exactly condone these here felonious acts of Al's—he's jest tryin' to laugh 'em off an' make light of 'em. Here he comes, now. Fine lookin' old codger, ain't he?"

"Humph," grunted Cush. "What with them eyes, an' that eagle's beak he's got fer a nose—no wonder that jury decided there wasn't no evidence agin' Al, that time—an' him ketched with the clo's on him that he stole out of that store! Here comes One Armed John, too. He gits up an' down the crick considerable. Mebbe he could figger out which one of the name-canners would be Al."

"He might," admitted Black John, and turned to the two who had just entered the door. "Catteraugus, meet One Armed John Smith. John, that there's Catteraugus Smith, which he's come to Halfaday huntin' his son, Al."

"I don't know no Al Smith," said One Armed John, ranging himself at the bar between Black John and Catteraugus, as Old Cush set out the bottle and glasses. "But I jest come down from up the crick, an' yesterday that there Bert Smith shot Santa Houston. You know, they're them two kind of youngish chechakos that come to Halfaday a month er so ago."

"Shot him, eh?" observed Black John, returning his empty glass to the bar. "Did he make a thorough job of it?"

"I'll say he did. Houston's deadern hell. Bert, he claimed it was self-defense. But Houston's shot in the back."

"H-u-u-m," said Black John. "The case would bear lookin' into. We'll go on up an' investigate, an' if the circumstances warrants, we'll fetch this here Bert Smith down an' call a miners' meetin'."

"That's right," seconded Catteraugus. "That's the way we used to deal with killin's back in fo'ty-nine. Yes, suh—an' if it was murder, the killer was hung to the nearest tree jest as quick as the vote was took on it. There ain't nothin' like miners' meetin' to put the fear of God in the heart of a murderer."

"You bet!" agreed Black John. "There ain't no question but what they have a beneficial effect on a murderer, er a thief, er any other kind of a skulldug." He turned to One Armed John: "Where did this probable murder come off?"

"Well, Houston's layin' on his claim, near the crick an' right clost to his tent. His rifle's leanin' agin a guy rope, an' Bert Smith claims he was reachin' fer it when he plugged him. He might of be'n at that, but somehow it looks kind of like a set-up. Bert's claim lays right next to Houston's. Herman Miller an' that there Benjamin Cleveland, they've got claims down this way from Houston's, an' they didn't know nothin' about the killin' till I stopped in an' told 'em. They said Bert an' Houston had had several quarrels lately over a canoe."

BLACK JOHN turned to Old Cush. "You're the coroner, Cush. The case calls fer an inquest, an' if the circumstances p'ints to a crime, it's your dooty to order the suspect fetched down here an' tried by miners' meetin'. Me an' One Armed an' Catteraugus will constitute the jury, in such cases made an' provided."

Old Cush frowned. "It'll take half a day," he objected, "an' I'd have to lock up the saloon, an' besides—them fellers is checha-kos an' ain't be'n there long enough to of took out any dust to speak of. We prob'ly won't find enough on this here Houston to pay my fee, let alone what I'll lose by lockin' up fer half a day."

"There'll be the two estates to pick from," retorted Black John. "It looks like their combined assets had ort to reimburse you fer whatever loss you sustain."

"Two estates?"

"Why, shore. There ain't a-chanct in a thousan' that we won't be hangin' Bert Smith. That'll make his effects available as well as Houston's."

"That's so," admitted Cush. "Well, let's be gittin' along so's we kin git back before dark. I wouldn't want to miss the night trade."

III

THE FOUR ARRIVED at the adjoining claims of the two chechakos to find the killer explaining to Miller and Cleveland the reason for his act, and the manner of its accomplishment.

The steely gaze of the eagle-beaked old mountaineer dwelt for a single instant on the corpse, and swept in a blaze of fury to the killer whose eyes seemed fairly popping out of his head as he stared into the face whose every hair of goatee, mustache, and beetling eyebrows seemed aquiver with hate. The oldster's gaze never left the man's face as he pointed a long forefinger at the dead man.

"Damn you!" he cried, in a shrill falsetto. "You've killed my boy. My boy, Al! As good a boy as ever walked in shoe leather. I ort to kill you where you stand. But I know minin' camp law, an' I aim to abide by it. Miners' meetin'll 'tend to yo' case—an' all I ask is fo' the boys to let me haul on the rope!"

"He had it comin'," muttered the man sullenly. "He—"

"Shet up!" ordered Black John. "You'll be give a chanct to tell your side of it in miners' meetin', that is, providin' the coroner's jury arrives at the conclusion that this here corpse is dead." He turned to Cushing. "Call the inquest, Cush, an' we'll set on him."

Old Cush wangled the corner from a plug of tobacco, returned the plug to his pocket, and nested his quid firmly against his cheek. "Inquest's called," he announced. "All them present, except the one that killed him, is app'inted on the jury. Look the corpse over careful an' if you believe him dead, it's yer dooty to pronounce him such, an' determine if possible what he died of. An' in case you was to conclude that such demise was brought about by someone else, it's yer further dooty to order such other person, if any, to be took down to the saloon an' tried fer the murder by a miners' meetin'."

Gathering close about the body, the jury accorded it a perfunctory examination and, acting as spokesman, Black John reported to Cush: "This here corpse, to wit, formerly alias Santa Houston—

"Hold on," interrupted Catteraugus. "His name ain't Santy Houston. It's Al Smith, an' I'd ort to know, 'cause he's my own son. An' not only that, but he's wearin' that same coat I was tellin' you about him stealin' out of old Clay Deets's store that time. It was a good coat onct, an' now look at it—what with bullet holes, an' blood an' all! That Santy Houston name he must of draw'd out of that can."

"All right," replied Black John. "We'll begin over. This here corpse, havin' be'n dooly identified as onct belongin' to one Al Smith of Tennessee, a man of good character—"

"Well," interrupted Catteraugus, "I wouldn't hardly go so fer as to say that, Al had his faults—if he was my own son."

A MAN of good character, barrin' certain faults," continued Black John, "is hereby pronounced dead; such death bein' the direct an' continuous result of a bullet fired from a rifle held in the hands of one, to wit, alias Bert Smith, with malice aforethought an' homicidal intent, to boot. Said rifle bullet ketchin' said Al Smith in the back in under his left shoulder blade an' goin' on through him, thereby causin' his death. Therefore the Jury recommends an' orders that the said alias Bert Smith be hereby forcibly seized an' fetched down to Cush's saloon an' tried by a dooly called miners' meetin' an' hung fer such murder. The prisoner is hereby remanded to the custody of me an' Catteraugus Smith fer delivery to the saloon."

"Inquest's adjourned, an' jury dismissed," announced Old Cush, "an' I now app'int the rest of the jury to skuttle around an' collect whatever they kin find of property an' effects that formerly belonged to the deceased an' the prisoner."

"How about the funeral?" asked Catteraugus.

"The which?" asked Black John, eyeing the oldster with a quizzical frown. "Oh—you mean fer the corpse?"

"Yes, suh—certainly. Don't you bury the dead up yere?"

"Shore, we bury 'em all right—but the facts is, we ain't what you might say long on funerals on Halfaday. In fact, I don't believe we ever had what you could rightly call a bang-up funeral. Mostly there ain't no regrets connected with a demise up here, except such as is occasioned by the bother we're put to in diggin' the grave. Of course, when one of the more notorious of us dies er gits hung er somethin', we bury him in the graveyard down to the fort, an' burn his name er his alias into a slab. But even in such cases, we don't hold no reg'lar funerals."

"I'd kind of like fo' Al to be buried in a reg'lar grave yard," said the oldster wistfully.

"Well, bein' as this is the first time any relative of a deceased has be'n present, I'm inclined to agree with you. I'll app'int Miller an' Cleveland to fetch the corpse down. They kin load it in the canoe yonder. We always keep a few graves dug ahead down to the fort—in case of emergency. Al kin have one of them. Come on, let's git goin'."

Catteraugus picked up the rifle that leaned against the guy rope of the tent—the rifle for which Bert Smith said the victim had been reaching—and nested its barrel in the crook of his left arm as the forefinger of his right hand caressed the trigger.

"Walk on ahead!" he commanded the prisoner. "An' remember—I'm jest a-hopin' you'll break fo' the bresh!"

IV

WORD PASSED UP and down the creek, and by the following midforenoon, Cushing's saloon was crowded with men. For miners' meetin' was a serious affair on Halfaday, attendance being compulsory upon all who had been notified.

Promptly at ten o'clock Black John thumped the bar with his fist. "Miners' meetin' called to order fer the purpose of tryin' one, to wit, alias Bert Smith, fer feloniously, an' with malice aforethought murderin' one Al Smith, a chechako, formerly know'd on Halfaday as Santa Houston—that bein' the name he draw'd out of the can. The *corpus delicti*, havin' be'n declared dead by a dooly app'inted coroner's jury, an' buried this mornin' by request of its pa, won't need to be produced fer evidence, the coroner's jury bein' able to testify that a rifle bullet fired by the defendant, went in his back an' come out his chest, killin' him in transit, as a lawyer would say.

"I'll app'int myself chairman of this meetin', an' warn you-that it's yer dooty to listen-to all the evidence, whether you believe it er not, an' to give the prisoner all the breaks you think he's got comin'. We'll start out with One Armed John—him bein' the first one, outside of the prisoner, to see the corpse."

One Armed John told of coming upon the corpse on his way down the creek, and that, upon inquiry, the prisoner, who was on the adjoining claim, told him that he had shot the man on the previous afternoon, in self-defense, as he was reaching for his rifle. The witness further testified that he saw a rifle leaning against the guy-rope of deceased's tent in such a position that the dead man might well have been reaching for it when he was shot. Also, the witness pointed out, it may well have been placed there after the shooting. He was followed on the stand by the two chechakos, Cleveland and Miller, who told of hearing several violent quarrels between the prisoner and the deceased relative to the ownership of a canoe. Old Cush followed with a brief summary of the findings of the coroner's jury.

WHEN HE had finished Black John addressed the assembly. "You've heard the testimony agin the defendant who will now be give the chanct to offer any excuse he kin think up fer murderin' the deceased." He turned to the prisoner who had sat through the testimony in surly silence. "Stand up here in front of the bar. Do you solemnly swear to tell the truth, er any part of it, s'el'p'e God?"

"Yes," answered the man sullenly.

"What's yer name?"

"Albert Smith."

"Did you shoot the deceased, to wit, one alias Santa Houston, later identified as Al Smith, through the back a couple of days ago on his claim?"

"Yes."

Black John glowered at the man. "You'd better talk faster'n that if you don't want to git hung. I'm givin' you fair warnin' that so many men has be'n hung from that rafter under which yer standin' that this room wouldn't hold even their ghosts. Besides which, Pot Gutted John there is already tyin' the noose. Believe me, if I was in your shoes I'd have a string of mitigatin' an' extenuatin' circumstances thought up that would take from now till supper time to tell 'em. Go ahead now, an' the glibber you talk the less liable you are to git hung—provided yer believed; which ain't likely."

"Well," began the man, eyeing the assembly with sullen defiance, "it all started over the canoe. We bought it in partnership to fetch our stuff up to the claims with. Then we agreed to flip a coin fer it. He done the flippin'' an' I called tails. Heads come up, an' I says, 'horse on me,' an' he says, 'one flip is as good as a hundred. The canoe's mine,' he says. I claimed that flippin' was always the best two out of three, but he wouldn't give in, an' fer a couple of days we had it back an' forth, callin' each other what names we could lay our tongue to, an' cussin' one another out. Then, day before yesterday evenin' he went to the crick an' started to drag the canoe out onto his claim. I warned him not to lay a hand on it, but; he reached out fer it, an' when he seen that I'd throw'd down on him with my rifle, he turned an' reached fer his own gun, which he'd set it close by the tent guy, where you seen it when you-all come up there. So I let him have it—an' that's all there is to it."

"H-u-u-m," said Black John, allowing his glance to travel over the faces of the assembled miners, "there's an interestin' an' intricate p'int involved in this here case that has got to be give due consideration. You men has got to deliberate, pro an' con, on whether, in coin-flippin', the first throw wins, er as this here defendant contends, it takes two out of three throws to win. We all know that in shakin' dice, the custom of the country calls fer the best two out of three shakes. But coin-flippin' is inherently different, an' you've got to remember that a neck depends on your decision. Inasmuch as dust takes the place of coins in this country, coin-flippin' is seldom if ever resorted to, but an' at the same time we've got to admit that it is a reasonable an' dependable method of decidin' an argument. We don't want to make no mistake in our decision of this p'int, which it is the crux of this whole hangin', if any. We'd feel kind of cheap if we was to decide that the deceased was correct in his contention that one flip wins; an' then later we was to find out that in coin-flippin' communities, the rule called fer two out of three. An' layin' aside our own embarrassment over the matter, we must remember that it makes even more difference than that to the prisoner. I'm jest callin' attention to this p'int, so you'll give it due thought.

"But there's another p'int that should be brought up which, while it don't pertain to the actual killin', prob'ly shows a depraved attitude of mind, an' a gross disregard of what might be called the ettycut of murder. You men know as well as I do that in murder, as well as anything else, the right-thinkin' man will observe certain obvious niceties—I refer to the defendant leavin' his corpse lay where it was at durin' one night an' the parts of two days, entirely disregardful of the fact that if a police should of happened along instead of One Armed John, it would have made it mean fer all of us. It would of meant an investigation, besides givin' Halfaday the reputation of bein' a crick which is strewn with corpses. An' as you all know, such reputation might have a tendency to keep the better element away. An' I'm warnin' you men right here an' now that in order to prevent corpse-leavin' becomin' prevalent on Halfaday, I'm hereby an' from now on incloodin' it in the skullduggery law." He turned abruptly upon the prisoner. "Why didn't you either bury yer corpse er report his demise so proper steps could be took in its disposal?"

THE MAN shrugged. "I don't know. I didn't give a damn. It was him or me—an' I beat him to it."

"Well, men," began Black John, after a moment of silence, "you've all heard the evidence, pro an' con, an' it's yer dooty to render a verdick in conformity therewith."

"Jest a minute," interrupted a voice, and all eyes turned to Catteraugus, who was rising slowly to his feet. The picture of sorrow and dejection, he had occupied a chair during the proceedings, drawn close beside a card table upon which he had rested his elbows with his face buried in his hands. The powerful shoulders drooped, and the man regarded Black John with lackluster eyes from which all the fire had died. "I'm jest wonderin', suh, if an old man who cain't help but feel an interest in this yere case, would be allowed to say a few words?"

"Shore, Catteraugus," assented Black John, "jest go right ahead. But I warn the boys that, out of fairness to the prisoner who's in a hell of a fix as it is, onless what you've got to say is evidence bearin' direckly on the case, they've got a right to disregard it."

"Well, ge'men, it is; an' it ain't," began the oldster, his eyes roving slowly over the faces of the crowd. "As y'all know, that was yere to the funeral this mornin', the deceased was my son, Al. It's mighty hard fo' a man to lose his only boy. An' yeste'day when I seen him layin' there dead, the devil riz up within me an' demanded vengeance. But, ge'men, that was yeste'day. Sence then, I've had time to study the whole thing out. I reflected that place in the Good Book where it says, 'Vengeance is mine, saith the Lord.' An' in studyin' back over Al's past, I seen where there was times when, mebbe, he hadn't done jest the right thing. It ain't easy fo' a man to speak ill of his boy—an' him dead. But I reflected certain acts an' doin's of Al's that might be regarded as oversteppin' the bounds of mere prankishness. An' the mo' I studied it, the mo' I got to thinkin' that mebbe there might be somethin' in this yere prisoner's defense—an' sence I heard what he had to say, I'm convinced that there is. In the first place, ge'men, knowin' Al like I do, an' his ability with a rifle, I know that if Al's rifle stood where we seen it standin' agin' that guy rope, an' him reachin' fo' it, like the prisoner says; then if he hadn't shot jest when he did, it would be Al we was tryin' fo' murder instead of him. Al would of plugged him shore. He wouldn't never of missed at that range.

"An' in the second place, ge'men, in jestice an' fairness to the prisoner, I've got to admit that he's right in contendin' that in coin-flippin', it's the best two out of three that wins—the same as in dice-shakin'. Ge'men, I come from a coin-flippin' country, an' I know the rules an' the customs an' so did Al. Now I ain't claimin' nor admittin' that Al would steal a canoe—but I do claim that he know'd he was cheatin' when he didn't flip that coin ag'in. Al know'd it. An' the prisoner here, know'd it. Therefore, ge'men, under the circumstances, even though Al's my own son, if we was to hang this man fo' what he done, I wouldn't never rest easy in my mind about it, 'cause I know Al was in the wrong, an' I know he'd shot the defendant, if he'd got holt of his rifle. That's all, ge'men. I'm thankful to y'all fo' hearin' me out."

AS THE man resumed his seat Black John combed at his beard with his fingers. "You've heard what Catteraugus had to say, an' it's up to you to vote. All in favor of hangin' the said defendant, to wit, Bert Smith, er alias Bert Smith fer the murder of said Al Smith, signify by sayin' 'Aye.'"

Silence followed the words, as men glanced uneasily into each other's faces.

"Contrary—'No.'"

A scattering of "nos" responded, but it was evident from the volume that most of the occupants of the room had refrained from voting.

Black John turned to the prisoner. "You've heard the vote, an' I might add that yer damn lucky to git off without a hangin', which as anyone kin see at a' glance, you ondoubtless deserve. You kin lay yer acquittal to old Catteraugus, there—an' nothin' else. But an' however—you ain't plumb out of the woods, yet. Corpse-leavin' havin' be'n brought under the head of skull-duggery, as you ondoubtless took notice of—an' you, bein' a corpse-leaver by yer own admission, yer thereupon guilty of skullduggery, which is a hangable offense on Halfaday. But bein' as the corpse got eventually buried without no more inconvenience than a funeral, an' bein' as the offense was brought under the skullduggery act, *ex post facto*, as a lawyer would say, I deem that a hangin' in this case might be a mite drastic. Nevertheless, we don't aim to allow no habitual corpse-leaver to remain on Halfaday, so I propose that you be give till four o'clock this afternoon to git to hell off the crick." He paused and swept the assembly with a glance. "All in favor of the verdick as I jest outlined it, signify by sayin' 'Aye.'"

A thundering chorus of "Ayes" filled the room, and without a word the prisoner turned and made his way hastily to the door, through a lane opened to give him passage.

DRINKS WERE had, and the crowd gradually dispersed, leaving Black John and Old Cush alone in the barroom. Old Cush glanced at the clock.

"Four o'clock," he announced. "I s'pose by this time that there Bert Smith has left the crick."

"Yeah," agreed Black John, "it's more'n likely."

"That was a fine speech old Catteraugus made," opined Cush. "You've got to hand it to him fer bein' fair an' square—what with Al bein' his own son, an' all."

"Yeah. It was a good speech. A man might say it was a masterful one."

"That's right. Hadn't be'n fer him comin' out that-a-way, the prisoner'd of be'n convicted. I kin always tell how the vote's goin' by jest watchin' the boys' faces."

"Yeah. It was Catteraugus saved him, all right. You've got to hand it to them old forty-niners."

"I s'pose he's down there in your shack now, a sorrowin', all by hisself. Go on down an' fetch him up, John. We'll slip a few drinks into him, an' kind of cheer him up."

"I don't expect he's down there," said Black John.

"Well, where else would he be? I ain't seen him sence the meetin'."

"No—an' that ain't all. I've got a hunch we won't be seein' him no more."

"Why—why?"

"Well, he done what he come here to do—he found his boy. An' the election bein' over an' all—back there in the mountains—I reckon he's on his way to Tennessee, right now."

V

THREE MONTHS LATER, as Black John entered the saloon one morning, Old Cush tossed a letter onto the bar.

"Red John fetched up the mail from Dawson," he said. "An' this was in it. It's fer you, an' it's from somewheres in Tennessee. I wonder if it would be from Catteraugus?"

"I wouldn't wonder," said Black John, slitting the envelope with his knife. "Yup—that's who it's from. Here's what he says:

Dear John:

I take my pen in hand to let you know I went huntin' this mornin' an' got two turkey. Likewise, the Republicans won the election like I figgered they would, an' the new shuriff ain't bothered me none about shootin' the other one that had Al cornered, that time. He was a damn Dimmycrat, anyhow. Speakin' of Al reminds me that I kind of put one over on you boys up to Halfaday. When me, an' you, an' Cush an' One Armed John went up to investigate that killin', I seen at onct that, what with the dead man bein' shot in the back, an' all—the one that done it wouldn't stand no show in miners' meetin'. So I claimed he was my son, Al—instead' of which Al was the one that done the killin'. He'd pulled another one of them pranks that was always gittin' him in trouble, one, way an' another. Al's right name is Albert—down yere he's know'd as Al, whilst up there on Halfaday they used the hind end of his name an' called him Bert. I seen how I had a bare chanct to git Al off if I could make a speech fer the prisoner, with the boys all believin' that the murdered man was my own son. I had consid'ble to do with miners' meetin's in Califorchy, back in forty-nine, savin' not only myself a couple of times, but also some others, by quick thinkin' an' fast talkin'. Mind, I ain't upholdin' Al's murders—but blood's thicker'n water, as the sayin' goes. It was kind of up to me to save the boy from gittin' hung, if I could. I don't know who the other one was—the one Al shot—so if you want to, you kin take down that slab with Al's name burnt into it. If you was here, I'd buy a drink. Hopin' you feel the same I remain y'rs truly,

Catteraugus Smith

"Well—I'll be damned!" exclaimed Old Cush. "Think of that old cuss puttin' it over on us that-a-way!"

A slow grin widened behind Black John's beard. "He didn't put nothin' over on me," he said. "I know'd it all the time."

"You know'd it! An' you let him git away with it!"

"Shore, Cush. Why not? I kind of liked old Catteraugus. He was a game old sport—tryin' to make the most of a son like Al, which he was prob'ly as nocount an' worthless an' crooked a scoundrel as ever walked in shoe leather. Catteraugus know'd it, too—but he never let on. An' when the time come, he saved him. An' I let him do it. Hell Cush, you can't hang a man right in front of his own pa! No matter how ornery he is, you can't. But you notice, I took damn good care Al didn't stay on Halfaday."

"That's right. But how'd you know this here Bert was his son?"

Black John's grin widened. "I seen the look that passed between 'em when we got up to them claims. Old Catteraugus give this Bert a mighty meanin' wink—an' Bert, his eyes was fairly, poppin' out of his head at sight of the old man. You see, he didn't know he was within three thousan' miles of Halfaday. Then I kind of sized 'em up together—same hooked nose, same shaped ears, same colored eyes. Only their eyes was different— there was humor in Catteraugus's eyes. Bert had the hard, cold eyes of a killer."

"That's right," agreed Old Cush. "I took notice of them eyes of Bert's. They was about as friendly as a snake's. Say—there's somethin' else wrote on t'other side of that last page. I kin see it from here. Turn it over an' read it."

"That's right," agreed Black John, turning over the sheet. "P.S. it says. *'Speakin' of Al, I fer got to say he was killed a couple of weeks back. One of them damn Deetses laid in the laurels an' shot him in the back when he was passin' by. I was huntin' Deetses when I got them two turkey, this mornin'. Better luck next time—an' hope your the same.*

" 'Catteraugus.' "

187

TROUBLE ON
HALFADAY

I

"WHAT I CLAIM," observed old Cush, proprietor of the trading post and saloon that ministered to the wants of the little community of outlawed men that had sprung up on Halfaday Creek near the Alaska-Yukon border, as he collected the dice from the bar and placed them in the leather box preparatory to shaking them, "what in hell is the United States goin' to do with them islands way over there when they git 'em?"

"Well," replied Black John Smith, eyeing the other's hand for evidence of manipulation as he rolled out the cubes, "islands is a good thing fer a country to have. You only got one more shake fer to beat them four fours of mine."

"Accordin' to the piece I was readin' in that paper Red John fetched up from Dawson, these here Pillipyne Islands is half ways around the world—way over by Chiny, er somewheres like that. An' there's about a thousan' of 'em all full of niggers. What would a country want with a thousan' islands full of niggers? That's a horse on me."

"Yeah, an' added to the other horse you jest lost, it's a game on you. Set out the bottle. Them islands might be a damn handy thing to have, sometime."

"What fer?" demanded Cush, as he reached to the back bar for bottle and glasses.

"Well, same as any other island—to git on 'em like in case of shipwreck, er somethin'."

"Hell, they wouldn't have to own 'em to git on 'em! An' who'd want to git on 'em, anyhow? Accordin' to that piece, them niggers runs around huntin' one another's heads to cut off—an' if they git a white man's head, it's so much the better. I'd ruther drown."

"It would be shif'less to drown, if a man didn't have to," opined Black John, filling his glass. "Here comes One Armed John," he added, glancing through the doorway.

"Yeah," agreed Cush, peering through his steel rimmed spectacles, "an' by the way he's walkin' he's got somethin' on his mind."

"Which is givin' his head all the best of it," grinned the other. "At that, though—he does look a little more purposeful than a man jest stoppin' in fer a drink."

"Prob'ly run onto another corpse, somewheres. He'd ort to of been born a buzzard."

The one armed man entered and approached the bar as old Cush slid a glass toward him. "There's a woman," he announced, "comin' up the crick."

"A woman!" exclaimed Cush. "Dead—er alive?"

"A dead woman," grinned Black John, "might be comin' down a crick, Cush, but not up one." He turned to One Armed John. "Is she alone?"

"Yeah, there ain't no one with her."

"You shore kin think up the damndest things to find!" growled Cush, eyeing the man sourly. "It might better of been a corpse! Leastwise, a corpse has got through with his hell-raisin' when you find him—but a woman!"

"Yeah," agreed Black John, "takin' 'em by an' large, as the Good Book says, they're a detriment to any crick."

"It don't make no difference if they're large er small," grumbled Cush. "A little woman kin raise jest as much hell as a big one. Take my first wife, she wouldn't go no more'n a hundred pound—stripped. But she—"

"I didn't know you ever had but the one wife, Cush!" interrupted Black John.

"Yeah? Well, by God, I do!"

"What did you do—git a divorce?"

"Not from her, I didn't. She wasn't worth one. I jest up an' walked out on her. The second one walked out on me. It was the third one I got the deevorce from. Seems like I never had no luck with wimmin till I got me my fourth one. She was more religious than what I be—but you can't blame her fer that. It's the way she was rose—her folks was religious. What I claim, if a man can't git but one good one out of four tries, he better quit marryin' 'em altogether."

"Oh, I don't know," grinned Black John, "the law of averages would—"

"To hell with yer law of averages!" scoffed Old Cush. "Here, a few days ago, you claimed that the law of averages says I couldn't beat four sixes in a thousan' shakes, an' I up an' beat 'em in one!"

"That ain't what I said, at all. I claimed, accordin' to the law of averages, you couldn't beat four sixes in *one shake* more'n once in a thousan' times."

"Yeah, you'd try to squinch out of it, someway! I s'pose you think I'd ort to go ahead an' marry a thousan' wimmin!"

"King Solomon did," chuckled Black John, "an' he got his name in the Bible.

"Yeah—an' he's welcome to all the publicity he got! God knows, he earnt it! Damn if I'd marry another woman, big er little, if I could git my name in the *Police Gazette!*"

"WHERE AT is this woman?" asked Black John, as the one armed one returned his empty glass to the bar.

"She was down to the flat rapids. I was fishin' down there, an' I helped pack her stuff around, an' drug her canoe up through the rapids fer her. Then I come on a-foot."

"What would she be wantin' on Halfaday?"

"She claimed she was huntin' her brother. Said his name was McCoy—Julius McCoy. Wanted to know if I know'd him. I told her there wasn't no McCoys on Halfaday, as fer as I know'd. But she kep' on a-comin'."

"I wonder," mused Black John, "which one of us John Smiths he is? Er, mebbe he's a name-canner. Did she say when this here brother got misplaced?"

"No. She didn't say no more about him."

"She done damn well to git up that fer alone."

"She said she hired a Siwash to fetch her up here. But at the mouth of Halfaday he quit an' wouldn't come no further."

"Prob'ly one of 'em that trades here, an' knows we don't want no wimmin on the crick. What fer lookin' is she?"

"She's damn good lookin'. I'll bet she ain't a day over twenty—er mebbe twenty-two, er twenty-three. She kin handle a canoe an' a pack, too. With the water low as it is, we had to pack most of her stuff around the rapids."

"Why in hell couldn't she stay where she belongs?" growled Black John testily. "Chances is, with the boys all busy, she'll git here without no one else seein' her. You keep yer mouth shet about a woman bein' on the crick till me an' Cush kin figger out what to do."

"Mebbe," ventured Cush, twisting at the end of his long yellow mustache, "if she minds her own business it won't be so bad."

"That," replied Black John dryly, "is what I'm afraid of. Generally speakin', a good lookin' young woman's business in the Yukon ain't nothin' to write home about. But there's exceptions to all rules. The hell of it is that no matter which way the cat jumps it means trouble. If she's on the level, we've got to look after her till she finds this brother—er don't find him. An' with some of the characters that's loose on this crick, that's goin' to be a sizable chore. If she ain't, we'll run her off the crick—an' God knows, that'll be a chore. If a man wants to let hisself in fer all kinds of hell, jest let him try to make a woman go somewheres she don't want to!"

"You're tellin' me?" asked Old Cush wearily. "I hope this here brother of hern ain't hard to find."

II

AFTER ANOTHER DRINK or two, One Armed John returned to his fishing, and Black John refilled his glass from the bottle that stood before him on the bar, a trivial incident that did not escape the notice of Old Cush, who replenished his own glass and made proper entry in his day book.

"These two is on you," he observed, as he shoved the steel rimmed spectacles to his forehead and leaned his elbows on the bar. "Now, what I claim about them niggers—if they'd kill 'em all off, an'—"

"To hell with a lot of niggers half ways around the world!" interrupted Black John. "We've got troubles of our own right here on Halfaday. How do you figger is the quickest way fer this here young woman to find her brother, if any? Of course, he might be jest an excuse fer her to come up here."

"Well—with the spring sluicin' goin' good, the boys congregates in here pretty thick of nights. She might jest stick around an' look 'em over. She could fetch a chair an' set over agin the wall some-wheres an'—an' knit, er somethin'."

"Knit!" exclaimed Black John in disgust. "Cripes sake, Cush! No right thinkin' young woman could tend to her knittin' with the kind of talk that goes on around here when the boys gits to drinkin'. An' besides, they wouldn't understand why a good lookin' young woman would be hangin' around a saloon knittin'. They'd be slippin' over to her with propositions that would be embarrassin' as hell! An' if she ain't a right thinkin' woman, she wouldn't git no knittin' done, nohow."

"Well, what would she be doin' if not knittin'?" asked Cush. "She prob'ly wouldn't care to set in no game. She might read— but there ain't no books on the crick except that there Bible of my last wife's, an' the law book you as good as stole off'n that crooked lawyer. It would look kind of funny if a young woman was to set around a saloon nights readin' a Bible er a law book."

"That's jest what I'm tellin' you—she can't set around here. It wouldn't look right, no matter what she was doin'. We might rig up a seat under the peep slot, an' let her set in the store room."

"Shore we kin!" agreed Cush. "You do have an idee onct in a while! We kin roll up a pork bar'l fer her to set on, an' if her brother shows up she kin spot him through the peek slot, an' there won't no one know there's sech a party as her on the crick."

"It looks like the only way. We can't let her go prowlin' around amongst the claims alone, an' we couldn't very well go with her or send no one. Of course, this way will take time. But inside ten days er two weeks everyone on the crick will show up. Meanwhile, where's she goin' to stay?"

OLD CUSH'S keen eyes twinkled in his somber face. "Well, John, you've gen'ally told a stranger to throw his stuff in your cabin till he got located. Claimed it give you a good chanct to look 'em over an' git a line on 'em. You could prob'ly find out if she was wrong thinkin' er right thinkin'."

"Not by a damn sight! You've got two, three empty rooms upstairs. I won't have no woman in my cabin—her nor no other one! Shut up! Here she comes! One Armed shore had both eyes open when he claimed she was good lookin'!"

A moment later the young woman stood poised uncertainly in the doorway as her glance swept the room, lingered upon the back bar, with its array of bottles and glasses, and shifted to the faces of the two men.

"Come on in, miss," invited Black John, removing his hat. "Step right up here to the bar. The house is buyin' a drink."

"Isn't this Cushing's Fort?" asked the girl, little wrinkles of perplexity gathering between her eyes.

"It shore is, mam. That's Old Cush, hisself, back of the bar. My name's Smith, to all intents an' purposes, an' Black John, by way of identification."

"But—I thought Cushing's Fort was a trading post!"

"That's right. Tradin' post an' saloon combined. Tradin' room's in through that other door. We generally hang out in the saloon, here. It's more cheerful like."

The girl advanced slowly into the room, as Old Cush set out a fresh glass and placed the bottle beside it. "No, thank you," she said. "I don't drink. I—I'm up here hunting my brother. Do either of you gentlemen happen to know him? His name is Julius McCoy."

Stepping to a card table, Black John withdrew a chair and placed it facing the bar. "Set down, mam," he invited, "an' make yerself to home while we talk it over. I don't recall no one, off

194

hand, by the name of McCoy. But we might be able to locate him fer you. There's quite a few men along the crick, an' some of 'em might of been named McCoy, back where they come from. You see, mam, here on Halfaday there's quite a lot of us is outlawed, fer one thing an' another—an' our names, mebbe, ain't jest what they used to be. Have you tried the police down along the big river? They're pretty lucky in huntin' up missin' persons."

The girl colored and dropped her eyes to her lap where her fingers worked nervously, twisting and untwisting a handkerchief. "No," she replied, "I didn't ask the police. I—I—didn't dare to. You see, Julius is—is wanted by the police."

"Lots of folks is," comforted Black John. "Was it a Yukon job?"

"What?"

"I mean, was this crime, er peccadillo, er act, whatever it was that the police wants him fer—was it committed in the Yukon, er elsewhere?"

"It was in Minnesota—an express robbery on the railroad, not far out of St. Paul. The express agent was killed, and the police sent Julius's description all over. I was afraid maybe the Canadian police had it, too. I don't believe Julius had anything to do with the robbery. But if he did, I don't believe he killed the man. Julius wasn't bad at heart. He was a little wild, but he wasn't a murderer."

"Jest a might prankful, mebbe—was this here express venture of his successful, financially speakin'?"

"Why—yes. That is, the two men who did it got away with two packages, one contained fifty thousand dollars in twenty dollar bills, and the other held about seventy thousand dollars in bonds, or stocks, or some kind of securities. But the men made a mistake in taking that package, because the securities were non-negotiable, some way—they could never realize anything on them. The express people said that the men were evidently after another package of money that contained fifty thousand dollars in ten dollar bills. But they got the package of securities, instead. The fact that the securities were non-negotiable was kept out of the newspapers in hope that the men would try to cash them someplace."

"H-u-u-m, kind of looks like an inside job. How did the robbers know that them bills was goin' to be on that train?"

"The police figured that all out. That's how they implicated Julius. But, it's just a police theory, that's all! Mother and dad think so—and so do I. We know Julius isn't a murderer!"

"Shore not, mam. It don't stand to reason he would be," agreed Black John gently. "How come the police to be so dumb as to think he done it?"

THE GIRL'S eyes flashed a grateful look into the bearded face. "I hate to bother you with my troubles," she said. "But I must find Julius! It's a question of dad and mother and me losing everything we have in the world, if I don't find him. I know he'll help us if he can, when he hears what terrible trouble we're in. Of course—if it should turn out that—that he did have anything to do with that robbery, we wouldn't touch a cent of the money. But I'd know the money if I saw it. It was in new bills, numbered consecutively, and I have the numbers. You see, neither those bills nor the securities have ever turned up. So, you see, I must find him. Oh, if you could only help me! It means so much— and I've come so far—and met with nothing but discouragement! And if I don't get back with the money before the first of September, it will be too late!"

Black John noted that the dark eyes were very near to shedding the tears she was fighting back so bravely. "Now you listen to me, miss," he said, clearing his throat roughly. "There ain't a chanct in the world that if this here brother of yourn is on Halfaday, me an' Cush won't locate him. It ain't only June—an' you've got plenty of time till September. S'pose you jest go ahead an' tell us all you know about this case—so we'll have somethin' to go on."

THE GIRL drew a deep breath of relief. "I will tell you," she said, "because I believe you will try to help me. I've never been able to talk about it before, except with mother and dad—and we've gone all over it till we just talk in circles. The police asked thousands of questions at first, but they've let us alone since they became convinced that we know nothing about it.

"Julius is eight years older than I am, and when he finished high school in Minneapolis, dad wanted him to go to the university—but he wouldn't. He said he didn't want to be a doctor, or a lawyer, and that he was tired of school. He said that he could make a fortune with a billiard parlor and bowling alley right there in Minneapolis.

"We live on a farm ten miles out from the city, and Julius hated farming. Dad managed to keep him there till he was twenty-one, and then he finally persuaded dad to back him. Dad put in what money he had, mortgaged the farm for twenty thousand more, and set Julius up in the best billiard parlor and bowling alley in the city.

"But in less than two years Julius had lost it. It seems that he'd got to gambling heavily, and the police kept arresting him for running what they called a 'hand-book'—it had something to do with gambling, or horse races, or something. Anyway, they put him out of business, and for a while he just hung around town, as far as we could learn. Dad tried repeatedly to see him, but Julius kept out of his way, and he never came near the farm. He was ashamed, I guess. But, he needn't have been. Dad only wanted him to quit the city, and begin all over on the farm.

"Then, the robbery occurred and the police blamed it onto Julius—at least, part of it. When they investigated the case they found out that Julius was a friend of the express messenger. He was a man who had frequented Julius's billiard parlor, and was in the habit of playing his hand-book. They also found out that a clerk in the Metropole Bank, a man named Avery, was another friend of Julius's, and that he, too, used to play this hand-book.

"Just before he died, the express messenger told the police that it was Julius who shot him. He said that for several weeks before the robbery, Julius had been getting on his car in St. Paul, and riding to Minneapolis with him. He admitted that it was against the rules, but said that he knew Julius well, and that one night Julius stepped up to him in the depot and told him he had been playing cards, and had missed the owl car for Minneapolis, and asked to ride over with him. The man consented, and after that Julius got into the habit of riding back with him every time it was his run. He said that Julius used to give him tips on the races, and he didn't see the harm in letting him ride.

"He said that the night of the robbery, when the train was about half way between St. Paul and Minneapolis, Julius pulled a gun on him and ordered him to stand back from the open safe. He jumped at Julius, and Julius fired. The bullet penetrated his chest, and he fell.

"Then, he said, Julius grabbed up the two packages out of the safe, pulled the signal cord, and when the train slowed down, he jumped off. The messenger said he crawled to the door and saw Julius get into a buggy that had evidently been waiting for him, and the driver whipped up the horse, and they disappeared in the darkness before the train came to a full stop. The messenger told this to the police while they were taking him to the hospital. He died the next day.

"This money had been shipped to the Metropole Bank, and this bank clerk knew about it. He didn't show up for work next day, and he hasn't been seen since. Neither has Julius. The police found an abandoned horse and buggy in St. Paul next day, and the livery stable man in Minneapolis, who owned it, identified the bank clerk's picture as the man who had hired the rig the evening before. The police also claimed to have checked the messenger's story that Julius had ridden with him from St. Paul nearly every trip for a month before the robbery. And that's all they've got against him! We think—dad, and mother, and I— that it was just a frame-up. The police had been hounding Julius about the hand-book, and so when the messenger told that story, they saw a good chance to put him out of the way."

THE GIRL paused, and Black John nodded thoughtfully.

"Yeah," he agreed, "that would be a good chanct all right."

"Of course, it would! That messenger probably implicated Julius to save some friend of his. Julius has refused to have a picture taken since he was a little boy. How could the police say he was the man who rode with the messenger? Besides that, he hated St. Paul. Why would he go over there? Why would anybody go there when they could stay in Minneapolis? There were plenty of places he could have gambled in Minneapolis, if he had wanted to gamble. It doesn't stand to reason!"

"That's right, mam," agreed Black John. "It couldn't hardly have been him, could it?"

"Of course not! Oh—you're the only sensible person I have talked to—except dad and mother! Our friends never mention anything about it—but, we know they believe Julius is guilty—and I hate them for it! They should know that he isn't a murderer!"

"Shore, they should. You say Julius disappeared the night of the robbery an' ain't been seen sense?"

"Yes. The newspapers were full of it next morning, and we think that when Julius read the expressman's dying statement, he got scared and disappeared, knowing as he did, how the police were always hounding him."

"It's more'n likely he would," agreed Black John. "How long ago was this here job pulled off? An' what makes you think he might be on Halfaday?"

"The robbery was a year ago this month. Last fall, at the State Fair, dad overheard two men talking at the race track. One of them said: 'I kind of miss Jule McCoy here at the races.' The other said, 'Yes, he always made the best book, all right. But he sure pulled a boner on that express job.' 'Oh, I don't know,' the other answered, 'fifty thousand ain't so bad between him and that bank clerk. Of course, if he hadn't snatched the wrong package they'd have got fifty thousand more. I wonder where he skipped to?' The other man leaned closer: 'Klondike,' he said, in a low voice. 'I got the tip from a guy in Seattle.'

"Dad wanted to question the man further, but they both looked kind of tough and sporty, and from what they said, he knew they believed Julius guilty so he wouldn't speak to them."

"Klondike, eh? Well, it sounds reasonable, at that. The way the chechakos was pourin' in last summer, it would have been his best bet. But this ain't the Klondike, sister. It's likely yer brother's hangin' out somewheres around Dawson."

THE GIRL shook her head. "No, he isn't around Dawson. I was there for nearly a month. I caught the first boat down from White Horse. I made inquiries from nearly everybody I saw, and watched the men who went into the saloons and restaurants. A waitress introduced me to an old man named Bettles. She said he knew more people than anyone else in the Yukon, and he might be able to help me. He's a nice old man—a perfect dear, even if his breath did always smell of whisky. He advised me to go to the police, and I told him why I couldn't. Then he said that maybe Julius was up here on Halfaday. He said that was where most of the men went that were wanted by the police. When I asked him how to get here, he told me not to try, but to wait till you came down to Dawson. He said that you could help me find Julius, if he was on Halfaday, and that you would be showing up in Dawson pretty soon—that you always came down every spring to exchange gold for bills, and to—to have a—a—" The girl was stammering in confusion.

"Go right ahead, miss," encouraged Black John. "He said I come down there fer what?"

"He said—a spree."

White teeth flashed behind the black beard as the big man's lips widened in a grin. "Why—the dog-gone old scamp! Defamin' my reputation that-a-way! How come you didn't wait in Dawson, like he said?"

"Oh, I just couldn't wait! I got to thinking that something might happen to delay you. And, anyway, if Julius was here, I'd have to come up and see him. You see, I've got to get back with the money by the first of September, or we'll lose the farm. So I found an Indian who agreed to guide me here. But he wouldn't come beyond the mouth of the creek. I didn't care, though. I'm used to camping and canoeing."

"You mean you'll lose the farm on account of the plaster yer dad slapped on it fer to finance this Julius?"

"No—the mortgage. I don't know about any plaster."

"Jest a nickname," grinned the man. "So, they're goin' to foreclose on him, eh? What's the matter? Ain't he kep' up the interest?"

"Yes, he has. But, you see, he had borrowed the money from the Metropole Bank, and the president told dad that his board of directors ordered the loan to be called. He said that under the circumstances they didn't care to carry it. Dad went to the other banks, but they all declined the loan, although the farm is worth sixty thousand, if it's worth a cent."

"H-u-u-m, kind of goin' into the hold-up game theirselves, eh? Well, sister, we'll have to see what we kin do about it."

"We shore will, mom," seconded old Cush. "Come on back to the kitchen an' I'll make you acquainted with the klooch, an' whilst she's cookin' you up a mess of vittles, we'll pack yer stuff up to yer room, an' cache yer canoe."

"My room!" exclaimed the girl, a hint of uneasiness in the glance she flashed from face to face.

INTERPRETING THE glance, Black John smiled reassuringly. "Yeah, sister, yer room. You see, it's like this—a good lookin' young woman is liable to be a disturbin' element on a crick where there ain't no other white wimmin, an' we figger that it'll be jest as well if there don't no one but me, an' Cush, an' One Armed John know yer here till we kin locate this here brother of yourn.

"When One Armed reported you had showed up on the crick huntin' yer brother, we figgered that the quickest an' best way to locate him was fer you to stay right here, instead of wanderin' up an' down the crick. We'll rig you up a seat in the store room so you kin look the boys over when they collect in here of nights. There's a peek slot runs along under the bottom edge of that shelft there with the stuffed owl on it that don't show up from this side—but it gives anyone lookin' through it a good view of the whole saloon. There ain't a spot in this room, except behind the bar, where a man can't be saw an' shot at from that slot. It's an invention that no one knows about except me an' Cush. We rigged it up—jest in case.

"The boys congregates in here of nights, an' we figger that inside a week er ten days everyone on the crick would show up. We'll fix up a signal, an' when you see yer brother I'll slip into the store room an' you kin p'int him out to me, an' then I'll ease him out fer a pow-wow without no one else bein' the wiser.

"In the meantime, you'll have to do most of yer sleepin' daytimes, so you kin look the boys over nights. An' I'm warnin' you that you'll prob'ly ketch you an earful of pretty rough talk. The boys won't know there's a woman listenin', an' some of their conversation might be a little—er—raw."

"An', about this here room, mom," added Cush. "It's upstairs, right next to the klooch's. The door locks with a heavy bar on the inside, an' the winder is nailed shet."

III

AS BLACK JOHN had said, with the spring sluicing well along and plenty of dust in their pokes, the men of Halfaday congregated nightly at Cushing's for whisky, and poker, and stud.

When a week had passed, during which the girl had kept her regular nightly vigil at the peep slot, and Black John had mingled freely with the revellers, he sought her out in the kitchen where she was eating supper with the Indian woman.

"If he don't show up tonight, miss," he said, "I'm goin' to take a little prowl up the crick. Most of the boys has showed up, one night er another, but there's half a dozen, er more, that ain't. It might be that they won't show up fer quite a while, an' there's no use wastin' yer time. If you could give me some idea about what yer brother looks like, I might be able to locate him, seein' it's narrowed down to them few."

"Well, he's rather tall—just about six feet—and quite slender. His eyes are about the color of mine, and he has dark hair that is inclined to curl. He's smooth shaven—"

"The smooth shaven part don't mean nothin'," grinned the man. "Whiskers grows easy—on Halfaday. If he don't drift in tonight, I'll hit out in the mornin', an' if he's on the crick, I'll locate him. Oh, yes—this here bank clerk—you don't happen to know what he looks like, do you?"

"I never saw him. They printed his picture in the newspapers. He looked to be about twenty-five, or thirty, blond, and heavy-set, with a wide, round face. But you can't tell much by a newspaper picture."

"That's right," smiled Black John, "A newspaper cut is the most unkindest cut of all, as the Good Book says. Well—so long. I'll be seein' you later."

THE FOLLOWING morning at daylight, he struck out, rifle in hand, and a light stampeding pack on his back. On and on up the creek he went, pausing now and again to chat with men who toiled at sluices or shafts.

"Accordin' to her description," he mused, "this here bank clerk would be the one that draw'd the name of Nathan Arnold out of the can, an' her brother would be Benedick Hale. I kind of had a sneakin' suspicion that he was the one, when she told about him bein' a gambler. Hale's a gambler, all right—an' a damn crooked one, to boot. When we ketch onto his racket, me an' Cush figger to hang him higher'n hell fer skullduggery. Beats hell how a fine young woman like her could have such a brother as him. An' her believin' he ain't guilty of that robbery! Well—if he comes through with that money fer the old man, an' interest throw'd in, we'll jest run him off'n the crick instead of hangin' him. It'll show that he's got some good in him, anyhow."

With the floor of the narrow valley deep in the shadow of the western hills, Black John reached a claim where a tall, dark eyed young man was cleaning the last few grains of dust from the riffles of a sluice. The man greeted him with a grin that disclosed white, even teeth, behind a dark stubble of beard.

"Hello, Smith!" he greeted. "Didn't know you ever got as far as this from Cush's. I'm just about to call it a day. Better hole up with me for the night."

"All right, McCoy—mebbe I will. I come up to have a little talk with you, anyhow."

"McCoy!" exclaimed the man, eyeing the other sharply. "What do you mean—McCoy? The name is Hale. You saw me draw it out of the can!"

"Yeah," grinned Black John, "so I did. But us old timers— sometimes we disregards them name-can names, an' gits right down to cases."

"But where did you get that 'McCoy'?"

"Yer sister. She told me that. She's up here huntin' you."

"My sister!" cried the man, his eyes widening in a look of mingled terror and wrath. "You mean—Rose—here, on Halfaday?"

"Yeah, she's down to Cush's. Been here better'n a week. We figgered you'd be showin' up down to the fort one of these nights. But when you didn't, I come on up to see you."

"DAMN HER!" cried the man, in a fury. "What's she trying to do—get me hanged? How could she have followed me here? She's blabbed her way clear from Minneapolis, and I'll have all the police in the Yukon on my tail! Wait till I see her—and I'll bet, by God, she'll never follow me again!"

"She ain't blabbed to no police, McCoy," replied Black John. "The fact is, neither she, ner yer ma, ner yer pa believes you had anythin' to do with that express job."

"Yeah. The dumb eggs! What the hell do they think I lammed out for?"

"They thought you got scairt when you read in the papers that the police suspected you."

"How in hell did she find out where I am?"

"Yer dad overheard a couple of race track touts talkin' at the State Fair. One of 'em told the other that some Seattle guy tipped him off that you'd hit fer the Klondike."

"Well—what was that to her? If I'd wanted the whole damn family up here, I'd have brought 'em along!"

"It's quite a bit to her, McCoy—an' to the old folks, too. You see, when the old man set you up in that pool business in Minneapolis, he stuck in all the ready cash he had, an' slapped a twenty thousan' dollar plaster on the farm. He got the money from the Metropole Bank—an' they've called the loan. He's got to raise the money by the first of September, er the bank'll take over the farm."

"The Metropole ain't the only bank in Minneapolis. Let him get it at some other bank and pay off the Metropole."

"He's tried that, an' they all turned him down. The fact is, that you've blackened the name of McCoy, in them parts, till there won't no one loan him no money."

"Sure! They'd blame all their troubles on me! If the old man's let the farm run down till he can't borrow any money on it, that's my fault, I suppose! To hell with 'em."

"It would be kind of doin' the square thing, wouldn't it, if you'd fork over the money the old man put into that billiard room?"

"What! Twenty-eight thousand dollars! You mean—me— fork over twenty-eight thousand? Don't make me laugh! If the old man made a bad investment, why should I pay it off for him? I agreed to pay him back out of the profits—and there weren't any profits. It wasn't my fault the business didn't pay!"

"It looks like you'd want to help out all you could," replied Black John mildly. "When all's said an' done—they're yer own folks."

"To hell with that stuff! A man's got to look out for himself in this world! The old man made his bed—let him lie in it! He was always pestering me to stay on the farm. What the hell does he think I am—a plow hand?"

"Prob'ly not, by now," replied Black John. "But—you been doin' pretty well here on Halfaday—what with yer claim, an' yer winnin's at cards."

"Pretty well—hell! I haven't made chicken feed! About three hundred ounces of dust to show for a lot of hard work—and maybe six or eight thousand on the stud game!"

"That's ten, twelve thousan'," figured Black John, "besides your half of the fifty thousan' you an' the bank clerk lifted off'n the express car. Looks like you could pay the old man off, an' have money to spare."

THE MAN threw back his head and laughed uproariously. "Oh, Jeez! That's a good one! Erring son comes to rescue and pays off the mortgage on the farm! Make damn good newspaper headlines, wouldn't it? And someone would probably write a song about it, too. Not me, bo. I'll keep what I've got right in the old leather. And my share of that express job was a damned sight more than half of those new bills, too. I pulled a fast one on Avery. He'd put me wise that there were two packages of currency for the bank in that safe, but he forgot to mention the securities—so I grabbed off the first two packages I came to with the Metropole's name on 'em. Avery was waiting with a rig when I jumped off the train, and we drove to a jungle I knew over in Hamline. We traded clothing with a couple of hobos and told them to drive the rig to St. Paul and leave it. We opened the packages among some lumber piles, and when Avery saw those securities, he cussed me out for getting the wrong package. They totalled up to seventy thousand, and when I lamped those brand new bills in the other package—all numbered consecutively, I suggested that he keep the bills for his share and I'd take the securities. He took me up on the proposition. You see, I knew the police would have those numbers as soon as the bank opened in the morning, and I wasn't taking any chances of getting picked up shoving them.

"I'd made a killing with the cards earlier in the evening and had a nice roll on me. I could afford to wait and get rid of the securities later, and make a clean twenty thousand on the deal, and not risk passing any new bills, either.

"We climbed a freight about daylight, and rode a side door pullman to Grand Forks, where I bought us an outfit of farmer clothing, and two tickets to Seattle. When we got there I paid the boat fare to Skagway, so Avery wouldn't be leaving a trail of new bills for the cops to follow.

"I figure to hole up here for a year or so till the heat is off, and then hit out for Chicago or New York, where a man can get a run for his money. The police will forget that express job by that time—what the hell's one express agent, more or less, anyhow? But, first, I've got to get rid of that damned Rose! If she finds out I'm here, after coming this far, she'll snivvle all over the creek, and pester me till she drives me nuts. Why the hell can't they leave a man alone?"

"I guess wimmin's like that," said Black John evenly. "I don't know much about 'em. From what she told me, I thought mebbe you'd kind of like to pay yer dad back that money. But after listenin' to your side of it—I kin see your p'int of view."

"Sure you can! And you could do me a big favor if you'd go back to Cush's and tell her I'm not on the creek. Then she'll go back where she belongs—or move on somewhere else. If she hangs around here shooting off her mouth, she's liable to have the police up here hunting me—and that's the last thing you fellows want."

"Yeah," agreed Black John, "we don't want no police snoopin' around on Halfaday. I've helped put lots of folks like you where the police wouldn't bother 'em."

"Fine! And—you'll do the same for me?"

"I shore will. There ain't no one I ever seen that I'd ruther do it fer. It'll be a pleasure fer me—an' fer Cush, too—when he hears the circumstances. But while you was talkin' I was doin' some thinkin'. If I go back an' tell her I couldn't find you, she might suspect I was lyin', an' come on up the crick, herself. Er she'd move on to some other camp, an' keep inquirin' till the police would git holt of it—an' believe me, if they did, they'd be up here after you in no time. The Mounted don't fool around like them city police. It would be a lot better all around, if I was to tell her that yer dead—that I found yer body in yer camp, way to hell an' gone up some feeder. I could tell her that you'd been dead quite a while, from the shape yer in—so she wouldn't be askin' to see the body. What you better do, is set down there an' write out a notice statin' that you didn't have nothin' to do with that robbery, an' that the thirty thousan' that's done up in the old shirt in yer bunk is clean money that you traded dust fer—"

"But—I'm not going to kick in with any thirty thousand!"

BLACK JOHN grinned. "Shore not—there won't be no thirty thousan' in no old shirt. I'll tell her there wasn't no sech package nowheres around there. But you write it out in yer own handwritin', which she'll ondoubtless recognize, an' state that the money is to pay back yer old man what you owe him, with a couple of thousan' throw'd in fer interest. You want to say that yer took turrible sick, an' you believe yer goin' to die, an' you want whoever finds you to ship this here money to yer dad—an' then set down his name an' address. That way, she'll think you intended to do the right thing, an' she'll believe someone found the body an' stole the money—she might even think I stole it—

but she can't do nothin' about it. She'll go back home then, an' show that notice around, an' even the police back there'll believe it, an' scratch you off the books. I wisht you had somethin' to go along with the notice—somethin' she knows you owned—"

"My watch!" interrupted the man. "This watch, here! It's just the thing! See—it's got my name on the inside of the case! 'Julius McCoy', it says, 'with love from father and mother, Christmas, 18—.' She'll recognize that watch. I'll get right to work on that note. By God, Smith—you've got a head on you!"

"Yeah? Well, a man's got to have—what with some of the folks he runs up against."

A few minutes later McCoy read the note aloud. Black John approved, and thrust it into his pocket together with the watch.

"Guess I won't be stoppin' over night," he said. "I ett a while back, an' I've got a good moon fer travellin'. The quicker I git that woman off'n the crick, the better I'll like it."

"Maybe that would be best," agreed McCoy. "When she's gone, come on back and tell me about it. You'll sure be welcome!"

"Yeah, I'll be back," replied Black John. "An' by the way—that there fast one you put over on yer pardner—it wasn't so damn fast, at that. It's too bad you couldn't locate him. Bein' a bank clerk, he know'd damn well that them securities you got wasn't worth the paper they was printed on—they're non-negotiable. Wherever he is, he's laughin' up his sleeve about what's goin' to happen to you when you try to cash in on 'em."

"Non-negotiable!" cried the man, in a voice that choked with rage, as a murderous gleam flickered in his dark eyes. "How do you know they are?"

"Yer sister told me. The police kep' it out of the papers, hopin' that whoever had 'em might try to cash 'em, instead of destroyin' 'em. Them new bills the other lad got will be easy to pass after they're dirtied up a little, an' shoved out one at a time. Well—so long. I'll be gittin' back."

IV

EARLY THE FOLLOWING morning Black John stepped into the saloon where old Cush and One Armed John were having an eye-opener. As the proprietor slid out another glass, Black John turned to the one armed man.

"Throw that drink into you an' go fetch Red John an' Long Nosed John over here. Tell 'em to fetch along their stampedin' packs. I want they should take this here Miss McCoy down to Selkirk where she kin ketch the steamboat fer the outside. Tell 'em I say there ain't no two ways about it. They're about the only ones on the crick I'd trust fer the job. An' tell 'em to hurry."

When One Armed John had departed, Old Cush eyed Black John as he laid his rifle on the bar, swung his pack to the floor, and poured his liquor.

"The young woman said you'd gone to find her brother. Did you have any luck?"

"Yeah, I found him. He turned out to be that there Benedick Hale, jest as I figgered he would when she described him."

"What! That damn crooked card sharp that we figgered on hangin' fer skullduggery as soon as we could ketch onto his tricks?"

"Yeah, that's him. But there might be worse fellas than Ben—when you come to know him better. I don't know who they'd be—but there might. Fact is, Cush, I'll bet you the drinks we don't hang him fer skullduggery. An' by the way, jest count me out thirty thousan' in big bills an charge 'em to me. It's too damn much money fer the girl to be packin' in dust. It's fer her pa—that there money she was tellin' about her brother borrowin' fer to git his pool room goin'."

"You mean," asked Cush, peering intently at the other through his steel rimmed spectacles, "that yer advancin' thirty thousan' out of yer own pocket on the say-so of a damn ornery skunk like him?"

"Yeah, shore—it's on his say-so. I didn't talk to no one else about it. I told Ben the old man needed the money."

"What did he say?"

"He said the debt was twenty-eight thousan', an' he wrote out a nice letter fer his sister, claimin' he never had nothin' to do with that robbery, an' how he wanted the old man should have back every cent he'd borrowed, an' a couple of thousan' along with it fer interest. He said how it's good clean money—an' not the result of no robbery."

"Clean money!" snorted old Cush. "That rat never handled no clean money in his life, outside of what he got off'n his old man! Knockin' off that expressman, which he claimed to be his friend! An' cheatin' in card games to boot! You must be crazy, trustin' a damn scoundrel like him! I wouldn't trust him no further'n I could reach him with a bung-starter!"

"You wouldn't want in on the venture, then?" grinned Black John.

"Not by a damn sight! I wouldn't have nothin' to do with him, except it would be to help hang him!"

"Well—count out them bills, an' I'll step back an' have the klooch call the girl. The sooner we git this over, the better."

Half an hour later Rose McCoy stepped into the barroom and advanced eagerly to Black John. "Oh, did you find him?" she cried. "Did you find Julius? Where is he? Did he come back with you? I'm just dying to see him!"

THE BIG man regarded her gravely, a kindly expression in his gray eyes. "I've got bad news for you, mam. Some good; an' some bad. This here brother of yourn, Julius McCoy, that you folks back home all loved, is dead. He's been dead a long time. Here's a letter I got off'n the corpse of Julius McCoy. You better read it."

The girl's face had gone dead white at the words, but her eyes were dry, and the fingers that took the paper from Black John's hand did not tremble. In silence she read the note. Then the tears came in torrents as she buried her face in her arms upon the bar and sobbed. In a few moments she got hold of herself and raised a tear-stained face to the two men.

"He didn't do it!" she faltered. "I knew it. We all knew Julius didn't kill that man. He had nothing to do with the robbery."

Black John nodded solemnly. "Yes, mam. It looks like yer faith in him was justified. That'll be a comfort to yer ma an' yer pa, won't it?"

"Oh—it's the grandest news in the world! The uncertainty—the worry, was killing them! Of course, they'll grieve over Julius's death—but to know, at last, that he was innocent! That will take away all the bitterness."

"Yes, mam. An' the financial worry will be gone, too. I've got the thirty thousan'. It was done up in an old shirt, along with the letter, there—an' this watch."

Sight of the watch brought fresh tears. She hardly glanced at the thick packet of bills that Black John had deposited on the bar. "I'll keep this, always," she said. "He got it for Christmas years ago."

"Would you count the money, mam? I counted it—but I want you should know it's all there."

"Oh—the money. I'd forgotten all about the money. Thirty thousand dollars, you say? Why—that's two thousand more than dad advanced him!"

"Yes, mam," said Black John, as he watched her count the bills. "Like he said in the letter—the two thousan' is fer interest."

"Oh, if Julius could only have lived to go back with me and see how happy he'd made us all! I hope he knew that we believed in him."

"He'd know that, mam. He'd know that folks like you would stay loyal, no matter what happened."

"Did—did—you bring the body back? Can—I see him?"

Black John shook his head. "No, mam. I couldn't do that. It's way back from here. An' you see, mam—yer brother has been dead fer quite a while. You—you wouldn't recognize him. Me an' Cush will go back later an' see that he gits a decent burial."

Tears flowed gently as the girl turned streaming eyes to the kindly eyes of gray. "Oh—how can I ever thank you? You—and Mr. Cushing, too? You two gentlemen have been just wonderful!"

"There ain't no need to thank us, mam. We ain't done nothin' that anyone else wouldn't do." He paused and white teeth showed as the bearded lips smiled. "An' as fer us bein' gentlemen—that's twict you've made that mistake. Cush there, he runs a saloon, an' eats his vittles with his knife. An' me—I'm an outlaw."

"An outlaw!" exclaimed the girl, smiling through her tears, "Nobody could ever make me believe you're an outlaw! Why— if you were an outlaw, you could have kept that thirty thousand dollars—and I'd never have known the difference! You could have told me you couldn't find Julius."

"Yeah, I s'pose I could, at that. But you've got to remember, miss—there's a difference in outlaws—same as anyone else."

"But, a gentleman is a gentleman—no matter what his business is, or how he eats his meals. And I'll always believe that you are two of the finest gentlemen I ever hope to know!"

V

WHEN THE GIRL'S canoe, with Red John and Long Nosed John paddling bow and stern, was a mere speck in the distance, Old Cush turned to the bar and set out bottle and glasses.

"About them niggers, over there in the Phillipynes—what the hell would they want to cut off one another's head fer?"

"Why—like the Injuns used to scalp folks, I s'pose. Jest to have 'em fer souv'neers. Mebbe, the one that's got the most is the best man, er somethin'."

213

"A head would be a hell of a thing to have layin' around. By the way, John—did you knock off this here Benedick Hale?"

"Cripes, no! You know damn well, Cush, that I don't go 'round murderin' folks! It ain't ethical."

"Well—you claimed he was dead, an'—"

"Hale ain't dead—an' what's more—I never claimed he was."

"Why you did, too! I stud right here an' heard you tell her! An' you give her that letter, an' told her he'd been dead fer a long time, an' that me an' you would bury him!"

"We'll bury him, all right," replied Black John grimly. "But you didn't listen very good. I told her that her brother—the brother her an' the old folks loved—was dead, an' had been dead fer quite a while. An' that's the God's truth. This damn skunk that calls hisself Benedick Hale ain't no more the brother she thought she had than the devil hisself is! Near's I kin figger, that brother—the real McCoy—died damn soon after he left the farm."

"An' you dug down in yer own pocket to pay her them thirty thousan' dollars!" exclaimed Old Cush, a look of vast admiration in his eyes. "An' you got that damn cuss to write out that letter so as to make her an' the old folks happy. By God, John, I've changed my mind. I'll take half of that, myself. I'm jest as big a fool as you be!"

"All right," grinned the other. "You're in. There'll be profit enough fer two."

"Profit! You don't expect to git that money back off'n that damn Hale, do you?"

"Shore I do. Why not? It was him borrowed that money to start a pool room—not me. An' he's the one that's got to pay it back."

"Yeah—but how the hell you goin' to collect it? He'll claim he ain't got no money."

"He owned up that he'd took out about three hundred ounces. That, an' what he win off'n the boys would run right around ten twelve thousan'. An' there's them fifty thousan' in new bills they got off 'n the express car."

"He wouldn't have only half of them bills," objected Cush. "He'd have to divide up with that there bank clerk the girl told about."

"Well—even if he only had half, the venture would show a modest profit. But I figger we'll find the whole damn shipment in his estate."

"Estate! You jest got through tellin' me he ain't dead!"

"He will be, by the time the miners' meetin' gits through, with him."

"Miners' meetin'! Here a while back you was offerin' to bet we wouldn't never hang him! You gone screwy, er what?"

"I told you you didn't listen good. I offered to bet we'd never hang him fer skullduggery. I figger, though—as soon as you an' me go up an' fetch him down here, we'll be hangin' him fer murder."

"Murder? Who'd he kill?"

BY THIS time he's ondoubtless killed Avery, the bank clerk—which he's the one we call Nathan Arnold. That is, onless Arnold seen him comin' an' got him first. In such case, we'll hang Arnold. It'll amount to the same thing. We don't give a damn whose estate pays the bill. I looked it up in my law book. They was co-pardners in the express venture, an' as such, either one is liable fer the debts of the other. If they'd incorporated fer the job, it would of be'n different."

"But why would he kill him?"

"Because, Arnold double-crossed Hale in the matter of dividin' up that loot—when Hale thought he was double-crossin' Arnold. Hale claimed he'd put over a fast one on Arnold by takin' them securities an' leavin' Arnold have the new bills. But when I told him the securities wasn't no good, that they was non-negotiable, an' that bein' a bank clerk, Arnold would know that—if I ever seen murder shine out of a man's eyes, it shore shone out of his! You see, I figgered when I told him about it, that we'd be killin' two birds with one stone, as the Good Book says."

"We prob'ly won't never find where the stuff's cached," said Cush, lugubriously.

"Oh, shore we will. I know where both their caches is. You see, when I found out Hale was robbin' the boys at cards, I know'd it wouldn't be long till we was hangin' him. So, in case we'd want to do it on short notice, I slipped up an' located his cache. Then whilst I was there, I located Arnold's too—jest in case. Looks like he'd ort to have around three hundred ounces, too, that is, if he was as diligent as Hale, which seems likely.

"Take it all in all, Cush, the profit won't be so bad. At that, though, we better burn them securities. They're like them heads you was talkin' about—a hell of a thing to be layin' around."

"Yeah, we better," agreed Cush. "That won't be injurin' no one. It looks like everything worked out fine. You've shore got a good head on you, John. We jest about double our money. Old man McCoy gits his money back with damn good interest. An' the hull fambly is happy on account of Julius's name bein' cleared. Nobody loses but the bank er the express company, an' at that, the chances is the shipment was insured. An' besides, them two damn crooks gits what's comin' to 'em!"

"Oh, shore—it all worked out good," agreed Black John heartily. "An' it jest goes to prove what I always claimed—if a man can't git along without double-crossin' his pardner, crime don't pay!"

"Yeah," seconded Cush, "an' on Halfaday, it don't pay nohow."

A LETTER FROM
HALFADAY CREEK

YOU CAN FIND *Short Stories* lying around most any old camp—cow, gold, logging or what not. We were a bit surprised, however, not to say gratified, to learn that it had penetrated as far as Halfaday Creek on the Alaska-Yukon boundary. Perhaps if James B. Hendryx had known that Black John and all the other Johns were in the habit of reading his stories, he would have been a bit more careful about what he said. Anyway, Black John Smith—the "Black" referring to his beard and not to his character, we hasten to mention—wrote us the following letter:

Halfaday Crick, Y.T.

"Whoever runs Short Stories Magazine
"Garden City, N.Y.
  "Dear Sir:
  "This here is to let you know that we like yer magazine, which we git it frequent. We think them stories by Tuttle an' Mulford about what come off in the cattle country is fine. But the things this here Hendryx sets down about what come off up here on Halfaday in stampede days is plumb libelous, on account that folks readin' 'em might git to thinkin' that some of them sons of ——* (Note: word deleted for obscenity.) that we hung in miners' meetin' didn't git no square deal.
  "The facts is that every last one of 'em got all the breaks he had comin' to him, on account that none of 'em was ever hauled up before miners' meetin' ontil me an' Old Cush know'd damn well they needed a hangin'. Such being the case, anyone kin see that disregardless of any evidence either produced er omitted durin' the trial, the hangin's

was all proper an' reg'lar. Hendryx claims we was all outlaws up here. Well—we was. But we was a damn sight moraler, an' more ethical than any other crick in the Yukon, at that. Besides which, he must of be'n here hisself on account he sets down things that come off that no one could know about onlest he was here. What I claim—if he wasn't on the run hisself, what was he doin' on Halfaday?

"Me an' Cush has put away several gallon, by the glass, whilst rackin' our brain to figger which one of us John Smiths he might of be'n. But we ain't had no luck, it bein' quite a while back, an' most of them old-timers bein' gone—one way an' another. He wasn't no name-canner, on account he has set down a lot of stuff that come off before me an' Cush invented the name-can.

"Next time you see him you tell him that if he ever gits up this way ag'in we'd be pleased to have him drop in to Cush's an' kind of talk over old times—but tell him if he comes, to come a-smokin', on account of some of the things he set down reflects on my personal character, which I claim to be jest as ethical as the next man. That army payroll job I done, which Hendryx is always harpin' on, only netted me thirty-nine thousan' seven hundred an' twenty dollars—an' not forty thousan', like he tries to make out—an' the loss fell equal on a good many million taxpayers, which spreads it out mighty thin—'special' when you see the way congress is flingin' away the taxpayers' money now days by the millions an' billions. Looked at right, that payroll job was more of a sportin' proposition than a crime, anyways—the odds bein' agin me, an' that major havin' made his brag like he done. I jest bet with myself that he could be took—an' I won.

"A few years back I quit Halfaday an' went back to the States an' opened up a nice quiet little speak in Chicago. But what with the different gangs tellin' me I had to handle their beer, er else—an' the politicians sendin' their ward men around to see me—an' the enforce-ment guys callin' in fer their cut, it took me jest nine months to go broke. The trouble is with them damn city crooks—they ain't got no ethics. I learnt my lesson, an' come back to Halfaday to git Cush to help me figger out how a enforcement officer could buy him a Pack-ard automobile, an' build him a sixty-thousan' dollar house to live in out of what he could save on a salary of eighteen hundred a year, when he only helt the job fer twenty-six months? Mebbe you folks knows the answer. Cush claims it can't be done—but I seen it—an' besides, where did that thirty-nine thousan' seven hundred an' twenty dollar honorarium go that I h'isted off'n the army?

"Yrs truly,

"*John Smith*

(know'd locally as Black John on account of that bein' the color of my whiskers.)

"P.S.

"From what is printed in the paper, now an' then, it looks like this here John Dillinger, by dint of hard labor, an' close application to dooty, has built him up quite a nice little bankin' business. The bankin' business always looked too confinin' to me—but it don't seem to bother John none.

"Seein' as his jobs is all pulled, what you might say, open an' above board, the boys claims he'd be welcome on Halfaday whenever he gits to feelin' that the odds is agin him. But that don't go fer no congressmen, nor politicians, nor enforcement officers, which if one of 'em would show up on the crick, we'd call a miners' meetin' as quick as we could git a quarum, an' try him fer skullduggery.

"*J.S.*"

www.ingramcontent.com/pod-product-compliance
Lightning Source LLC
Chambersburg PA
CBHW030541030726
47495CB00004B/1079